MOONSTROKE

MOONSTROKE

Blaine C. Readler

MOONSTROKE

Copyright © 2016 by Blaine C. Readler

This is a work of fiction. Names, characters, places and incidents are either the product of the author's wild imagination or are used fictitiously. Any resemblance to actual events, locales, organizations, or persons, living, dead, or one foot in the grave, although inevitable and in a weird way complimentary to the author, since it shows he is not so insulated from reality that the products of his imagination are totally alien to the average mind, is nevertheless entirely coincidental and beyond the intent of either the author or the publisher.

Visit us at: http://www.readler.com

E-mail: blaine@readler.com

ISBN: 978-0-9834973-8-7

Printed in the United States of America

To Robert "Red" DeVecca, who expanded the boundaries of my teen imagination beyond the merely real.

ACKNOWLEDGEMENTS

This book would be only barely readable without the steady guiding hand of my editor, Jennifer Silva Redmond. Thank you, Jennifer.

www.jennyredbug.com

A grateful nod to Michael Ilacqua for the cover design:

http://cyber-theorist.com

Check out his new book:

http://thephantomparadigm.com

When in the Course of human events, it becomes necessary for one people to dissolve the political bands which have connected them with another, and to assume among the powers of the earth, the separate and equal station to which the Laws of Nature and of Nature's God entitle them, a decent respect to the opinions of mankind requires that they should declare the causes which impel them to the separation.

—Introduction to the United States Declaration of Independence

Chapter 1

"He's dead," Van said.

He looked up from where he knelt next to the prone sixteen-year-old. His friend Burl stood over them, blinking a reluctant agreement through his transparent faceplate. Van couldn't feel for a pulse through the skin-tight pressure suit, but the utter stillness, the absolute lack of motion in the boy's chest, was compelling.

"Randy's gone?" Tyna's voice said in Van's earpiece. His feet caught vibrations every two seconds as she ran in long, slow-motion strides across the harvester platform. A moment later her slim form knelt beside him, and she placed a dirty, suited hand on the fallen boy's torso, an act of honor and respect. "Crimps," she said quietly.

Van stood up and flicked his finger across the top of his face shield, bringing down the menu, then flicked this way and that until he'd opened the command window. He tapped the virtual button that would alert their boss, Dirk Meyer. "Ops Head—you there?"

"Here, Van. What's up?"

"It's Randy. He's … gone."

Silence, broken by a short, raucous burst of static. Van's suit had been doing that more often lately. He'd been putting off trading it for another—the devil you know. After a few seconds of silence, Meyer replied. "Okay. Bring him in."

"To confirm—we should interrupt the shift?"

Both Burl and Tyna glanced at Van. This was an obvious poke

at Meyer, but the Ops Head Manager refused to take the bait, and simply repeated, "Bring him in."

Van and Burl lifted Randy's twenty-three pounds—lunar weight—and, with a nod, they side-hopped to the edge of the platform, and leapt the fifteen feet down to the Moon's surface. Nobody had invented side-hopping—an efficient way to carry loads in Moon gravity—the technique of continuous, coordinated sideways jumps had naturally evolved early on with their parents.

Tyna ran ahead of them, and the rest of the shift crew stood watching at the platform's edge as Van and Burl hopped the quarter mile of well-trodden dust to the base entrance. She had the air-lock door open, and all of them squeezed in with Randy's body. They waited while the lock genie made sure the outer door was properly sealed before allowing air back into the small space. The hissing subsided, and Van unzipped his helmet as the inner door slid open. He remembered a time—he was maybe ten—when the lock genie would announce that the pressure was equalized, and safe. Nobody knew if her speaker had failed, or if she'd simply decided in her algorithmic logic that it was a waste of her AI cycles. An air-lock genie's voice was an incidental convenience. There were at least a dozen other failures with true quality of life consequences waiting for attention.

Meyer was waiting for them. Balding and dour, he wore the standard blue jumpsuit reserved for Managers, faded and limp after nineteen years, but still proclaiming authority. Van, Burl, and Tyna removed their oxy-packs, and placed them on the charging station. Then they peeled away their pressure suits, and lifted their own clothes off wall hooks—burnt sienna jumpsuits inherited from their parents, and equally weary with age.

Van looked at the Operations Head a moment. "Hope you're happy, Meyer," he said, hanging his pressure suit on the hook. Their boss was called Ops Head only when they were working on-shift outside.

"That's not my fault," Meyer said calmly, gesturing at Randy lying on the floor, as though the dead sixteen-year-old was a spill needing to be mopped up.

"The facts say otherwise," Van retorted, not nearly as calm. Burl and Tyna fussed unnecessarily with their pressure suits as they hung them, not looking at Meyer or Van.

"Okay," Meyer said with exaggerated patience, "let's look at the facts. One, it was going to happen sooner or later, we all know that. And, two, it was Randy's choice."

It was true that they'd known that Randy had a problem with his heart. The med-genie had been tracking his decline, and Randy had stopped checking in at the unit months ago, not wanting to know the specifics of the final countdown. His parents had been saving their earnings to send him to Earth for an operation before the Blast. He'd been just two years old then.

"He hardly had a choice." Van said. "You effectively forced him out on the platform. There was plenty inside to keep him busy."

Meyer's mouth tightened. "How many times have we been through this? The company policy is clear."

"Your interpretation of the policy."

"What interpretation? To quote, 'Any hourly worker who is not actively contributing to the harvest will not be allowed to interfere, or in any way impede, the activities of those that are. Additionally, non-harvest personnel will receive only the negotiated fixed hourly rate, and will not be entitled to harvest percentage.' How can that be more clear?"

"That's not what I mean," Van said. "I understand that. But you're the one who sets the rent and meal rates. You know damn well that without the harvest percentage, Randy would have had to move back to the kids' dorms and live on soy and hydro sludge."

Meyer held up his palms. "Like I said, it was his choice. And watch your language. A union steward title doesn't give you free reign with Management."

Van knew what he meant—even the hourly workers union head isn't equal to anyone in Management. "It's easy for you to say that he had a choice—"

He stopped when Meyer pointed a thick finger in his face. "One more word, Van, and I'll request two points from the CTO."

Two more points would push Van into a misdemeanor, which meant denial of archive privilege for two months. It was possible that Zeedo—the hourly's name for the CTO—would deny Meyer the punishment points, but Van wasn't about to risk it. Definitely not now with Randy as a reminder.

Van turned away from Meyer and gestured for Tyna and Burl to help him lift Randy. "Come on, we'd better get him down to the Lab." Looking back, he said, "Does Zeedo know?"

Meyer eyed him levelly. "The CTO knows." He carefully pronounced each letter, rebuking their casual slurring of the title for the leader of the entire Moon base.

It was easier for just Van and Burl to carry the dead youth along the narrow corridors, so Tyna followed behind. "I'm nervous," she said.

"For Randy?" Van asked. Tyna had just turned eighteen, a year younger than Van, the oldest of the nexgens. That's what Management called the "next generation." Van didn't remember Tyna's parents, but he'd seen photos, and she was an even mix of her European and Japanese heritage.

"Yeah, sure," she said. "I mean, he's the first one."

"All of our parents were archived."

"Of course, but that was twelve years ago. Randy's the first of the nexgens."

"True." He grinned. "What if there's no room?"

She couldn't see his grin. "What are you *saying?*" she asked.

"I'm joking," he laughed. "Of course there's room. Zeedo said there's storage for all forty-two Moon base living souls."

"Ah, but is there room for forty-two *dead* souls?"

"Ho, ho. You know what I mean."

"Wasn't Randy on misdemeanor?" Burl asked, changing the subject abruptly. Van and the seventeen-year-old were friends even though there were plenty of nexgens closer in age. He liked Burl—his sarcasm could be wearing, but was more than made up for by dry humor. He was bright, maybe the top of the pile of all thirty-seven nexgens.

"He was," Van said. "But one of his points expired a couple of weeks ago."

"Why did he cut it so close?" Tyna asked. "All five points were his own fault. He knew he was coming to the end."

"Points are always one's own fault," Burl said, quoting Meyer. "He obviously suffered from self-loathing."

"And cows can fly," Van replied. He'd seen pictures of cows, and knew the implication of the saying he'd inherited from his parents.

"Do you think so?" Tyna asked. "About the self-loathing?"

"He's kidding on both counts," Van said, looking down at the body they carried. "I think Randy was just frustrated at his situation. He was lashing out at the universe, at fate. It was reckless and stupid, but maybe understandable."

"Define fate," Burl said.

"Oh, no. You're not going to get me wrapped up in that one. How about karma?"

"Earth drivel," Burl said, using the nexgen's tag for useless references to a disconnected history. His friend had been slapping the label at him a lot lately.

They came to the door leading into the area of the base collectively called the Lab, even though only a small portion was actually laboratory space. Four-fifths of the base, a labyrinth of caves carved from the crater's wall by the early robots, was devoted to the commercial operation of extracting platinum, but the base included the kids' dormitories (now empty of nexgens), the adult apartments (now full of nexgens), the maintenance shops, cafeteria, gym, and theater—all operated by nexgens. The three scientists and Meyer had been the only adults inside at the time of the Blast. They, along with Meyer, now lived behind this closed door, the section devoted to R&D. The door genie didn't open for nexgens.

"One moment," the genie said, as Van and Burl lay Randy carefully down.

Zeedo's voice came over the speaker, "Be right there."

Van tapped his fingers nervously on his thigh. He was always uneasy talking to Zeedo. His real name was Arthur Cummings, and he'd been one of the leading scientists on Earth. At least, that's what Meyer said.

"What will they do with him ... after?" Tyna said.

Van glanced at her. Where Burl was smart and sarcastic, Tyna was smart, serious, and strong. Van couldn't remember seeing her so distraught. "Policy says that his body will be recycled," Van said, then paused. Saying out loud what he'd known all his life came as a minor jolt. The last death, before Randy, had been their parents, and the nexgens were all too young to remember the details. If any of them had asked questions at the time, they'd probably been given a vague and innocuous answer, which would have faded with time.

She shook her head with determination. "I'm not going inside."

"I doubt Zeedo's going to let any of us inside."

The door suddenly hissed open, and Arthur Cummings stood looking at them. The scientist's cropped salt-and-pepper beard was now ninety-five percent salt. The Moon-raised nexgens were tall, but Zeedo was even taller. He must have seemed a lanky giant back on Earth.

Zeedo looked down at the dead teenager. He stared a long time, as though lost in reverie. He looked up at each of them in turn, ending with Van. "I'm sorry we couldn't do anything for him," he said.

Van's thigh tapping sped up. It wasn't usual for Zeedo to speak with so much familiarity, almost as if he'd forgotten he was a Manager—the Moon base leader, in fact.

"On Earth," he went on, his face hardening, "Randy could have been saved." He shook his head. "I'm sorry," he said again.

He wasn't apologizing for an inability to help Randy, it seemed, so much as bemoaning the fact that he—all of them—were marooned on the planetoid.

"He's not really gone, sir," Tyna reminded.

Zeedo looked at her in surprise. "Dirk—" He caught himself. "Ops Head didn't tell you?"

Tyna's brow furrowed. "What?"

Zeedo's mouth tightened. "He called ahead. He recommended a point for Randy."

Tyna hissed, "That bastard! Whatever he said, he's exaggerating!"

Van gripped her shoulder, but Zeedo held up his hand. "It's okay. We'll let that one go. Randy forgot to charge his oxy-pack and used Troy's instead, according to Ops Head."

"He's lying!" Tyna exclaimed, kneeling to inspect the pack still attached to the boy's back. She froze, staring.

"It's true, isn't it?" Zeedo asked softly.

Tyna stood up. Her stubborn silence was the answer.

"He didn't use much of Troy's oxy," Burl pointed out. "Troy can have the oxy from Randy's station." He said this deadpan.

They glanced at him, but nobody responded. They knew he was

joking. Each nexgen had to pay for the oxygen he drew from the charge stations, but it was a trivial expense next to the meal tickets.

"Sir," Tyna said, with forced politeness, "can't you let this one go?" Her attempt to stay unemotional broke down. "For God's sake!" she cried. "He'll be dead forever!"

Zeedo looked at them, one by one, and then nodded. "This time only." His gaze landed on Van. "We'll allow leniency because Randy's the first. But no more. Everybody has to keep on their toes, understand?" He looked around, making sure they understood. "Okay, get his pressure suit off."

Van nodded vigorously, jumping to the task before Zeedo could change his mind. They worked together to get the suit off. They'd been taking them off all their lives, and it was second nature, but nobody had ever taken one off someone else. The suits by design were form-fitting. Braced against the wearer's body at each articulating joint location, the suit provided barely a half-inch of air layer above the skin. The pressure in the suit—and the entire Moon base—was kept at 5 psi, one-third that of Earth. The reduced pressure was compensated with a forty-percent oxygen mix. Under average exertion, the suit radiated about two hundred Watts of body heat into the vacuum of the lunar night . The suit would presumably quickly overheat during the day, but nobody went outside then, not since the Blast.

They started with Randy's head, and worked their way slowly down. Almost immediately Tyna began crying and turned away. This was the first time since they were little kids that Van saw her cry.

After ten minutes, he was sweating with the effort. "Does it have to come all the way off for the archive?" Van asked Zeedo, who stood by patiently waiting.

"The suits are precious," he replied. "You know that."

"Yes, sir. But does it have to come off for the archive? I mean, isn't there some sort of time limit? After all, his brain cells will start …"

"Decaying," Burl finished for him.

Zeedo didn't answer at first. He stared off at nothing a moment. "Finish taking it off. There's time."

With a final tug, the suit pulled away, leaving Randy lying on the floor in just his undergarment. "Genie," Zeedo said, "tell Julius and Louden to come." To Van, he said, "Okay, we'll take it from here. Thank you."

Van nodded and walked away, Burl and Tyna following. Van scowled. "I guess I'd better work out a new platform schedule before Meyer comes up with one of his own."

As union steward, it was his job to negotiate the work schedules for the twenty-three adult nexgens, those sixteen or older. The nine nexgens that were fourteen or fifteen had indoor union duty, mostly kitchen and facility cleaning, jobs originally handled by bots long since fallen into disrepair. The five remaining lucky nexgens spent twelve hours a week performing unpaid "community duty"—the lowest grade cleaning jobs—and were supposed to spend the rest of their time studying the complex base operation in preparation for adult contribution.

"It's not like you need to fill a very big hole," Burl said.

He was right. For the last six months, Van had made sure Randy had light duty—as light as Meyer would allow. It seemed disrespectful to hold the fact up for viewing, though. "Randy left a hole, however large. We'll all be doing our bit to help fill it."

"Uh-oh," his friend said. "I call bullshit." Burl denounced him when he thought he was talking a little too much like a Manager.

"I could accuse you of Earth drivel on that," Van said.

"The term has origins on Earth, but only in the same way that the word 'salary' is derived from the Latin term 'sal' for salt, which comprised a Roman soldier's pay. Neither require detailed knowledge of Earth to understand."

"Do you compose these little lectures ahead of time?"

"The fact that you view them as lectures demonstrates your gross ignorance."

"Thanks, Burl."

"My pleasure."

"That's exactly the problem, Wilson."

Tyna glanced at him. "Who's Wilson?"

Burl gave her a knowing look. "Wilson is his mentor's best friend."

"Wilson's head is filled with air," Van said. "That's the important point here."

Tyna looked confused a moment, then nodded, rolling her eyes. "I get it. That old movie with Tom Hanks—your idol."

Van snorted. "Ha. Idol. He just happens to be the best actor of the twentieth century. You two are jealous because I have historical perspective."

"You mean Earth drivel," Burl said. "You're infatuated with him. How many times have you watched *Cast Away*?"

"I have no idea."

"That's because it's been too many times to count. You've never missed his two movies on movie-night, either."

"I go every week. I haven't missed any movies."

"Which is another reason for your good friends to be worried about you," Burl said.

Van didn't argue with that one. He sometimes wondered why he religiously attended. The fact was that Friday movie nights was a weekly ritual for most nexgens, including Tyna and Burl, despite their ribbing. With only a eighty-nine movies cycling endlessly, it had long ago become simply a social event. It was the one time each week, particularly during the lunar night, when they were all together at the same time. During lunar days, when their schedules were more relaxed and limited to indoor maintenance and platinum processing, attendance fell off dramatically, but Van continued each week. As the oldest nexgen, he believed that the routine provided an important structure and foundation for the rest of the nexgens, particularly the younger ones. It was the one activity they did for themselves rather than AMC.

And he had to admit that he did revel in the infinitely varied scenes of Earth life. He'd always been fascinated by the magic of it, even if most of the movies were decades old, from the tens and twenties, the personal stash of one of the parents who'd made it a hobby. As children, all the nexgens were enamored with Earth. As they grew older, however, the difference between the real life portrayed in many movies and that of *The Lord of the Rings* remained blurred. Earth itself became a fantasy. So he could understand that more than a few nexgens, including his two friends, looked at him with some worry and suspicion. After all, he was supposed to be their leader.

"I remember that you enjoyed *Cast Away*," Van said to Burl.

"Yeah, once, which was enough."

"You would have watched it again if you weren't scared—"

Meyer came around the corner, on his way to the Lab. *Cast Away* was part of Van's hidden stash of unauthorized material—a small assembly of files he'd found on one of his parent's play devices that Management had missed when cleaning out the apartments after the Blast. Possession of unauthorized files landed an automatic three points.

As Van passed Meyer, he couldn't resist. "Did you hear? Your attempt to deprive Randy failed."

The Ops Head stopped and stared at him impassively. "Are you questioning my authority?"

Van shook his head. "Just stating the facts."

"The facts are that Randy took Troy's pack without permission. That's a point under any circumstances."

"Even circumstances where a person you'd known all his life just died?"

"Any circumstance means any circumstance."

Van nodded knowingly, as though the Manager had said all he needed to say. As the Ops Head walked away, Van couldn't stop himself. "At least Zeedo has a heart."

Meyer stopped and turned. "That just cost you two points, union steward."

"Only if Zeedo agrees," Van said.

Meyer turned and walked away.

Tyna touched Van's arm. "Zeedo's going to allow those points, you know."

"Yeah," Van agreed, shivering at the thought that he was now in misdemeanor.

Burl put his hand on Van's shoulder. "We'll all be doing our bit to help keep you alive," he said in his mock-Management tone. "How long until your two oldest points expire?"

Van tallied them in his head. "Three weeks."

"Oh, boy. These are going to be the longest three weeks of your short and undistinguished life."

Van sighed. As usual, Burl was right.

Chapter 2

Katlin tapped on the sill of the door to her father's tiny office. "Daddy, are you busy?"

Her father was sitting at his one meter square desk with his back to her, staring at the rough hewn basalt wall. He turned and smiled. "Never too busy for you, Peaches."

"Daddy!"

"Sorry. Sometimes I can't resist. Besides, as long as you're calling me Daddy, I should get equal privileges."

"Fair enough. Let's start over." She tapped again. "Cummings, sir, do you have a moment to speak with me?"

He turned his chair to face her and clasped his hands behind his head. "Come in, Cummings. Have a seat."

She sat on a short stool. The office was so small, their knees almost touched. She glanced around at the tiny space. The door hadn't closed in two years. The genie was fine, but something in the mechanical mechanism had failed. "Scientists of your status on Earth have offices ten times as large," she said. "Many have windows—with a view of trees."

"Is that what you came to tell me? That you've been perusing the library?"

"No. But that doesn't change the fact."

"Well, thank you for reminding me that we're marooned on an airless world a quarter million miles from the closest tree."

"That's not what I meant."

"Why bring it up, then?"

She just looked at him. She regretted bringing it up.

"Have you been to see Meyer?" he asked.

He knew her inside-out. "But Daddy! His office is twice as big as yours. *Four* times! It's just not fair."

"Not fair?" he said, raising his eyebrows. "Who made a judgment?"

"But you're his boss."

"The size of my office doesn't change that fact."

"He thinks so."

He touched the tips of his fingers together. "Where did you get that?"

"Everybody knows it." Dirk Meyer was a joyless taskmaster by nature—or by nurture, according to her father, who always reminded her that Meyer had a difficult childhood, having lost his father when he was very young.

Her father looked at her a moment. "What everybody 'knows' may actually be just what everybody believes."

"Oh, Daddy. You know Meyer thinks he should be running the base."

"He does run the base."

"You know what I mean. The *whole* base, not just the commercial production."

"Honey, I don't think Meyer wants to run the Lab."

"He doesn't think you should be his boss."

"That may be, and that's his prerogative. But what's brought all this up?"

"He's complaining that you countermanded Randy's point."

Her father gave a tight little grin. She could tell that he was finally getting a little irked. "I doubt he actually said that. He knows better than anybody that to be countermanded implies the authority to issue points in the first place."

"Daddy, I don't understand why he even has a job at all."

His brow pinched together at this. "Now who's being unfair?"

She blinked in surprise. "Oh, no, that's not what I meant. I mean, why do we keep harvesting? We have sixty tons of stored platinum. Even if Earth suddenly showed up, it would take them a year to ship it all back."

Her father's brow unfolded and his shoulders relaxed. "Platinum is why we're here, honey. That's why the company invested so much money."

"Nearly twenty years ago."

"That doesn't matter. It's still an investment." He stared at her.

She could tell he had something on his mind. "What, Daddy?"

He hesitated a moment, then said, "There's more to the history of the base than you know. It's time you understood the nuances."

Her pulse quickened. She'd thought that he was going to remind her of her responsibility to prepare for eventually assuming the base leadership, and then she'd have to yet again remind *him* that their future was on Earth, not the Moon—that a ship from home would eventually arrive. "Truth lies in the nuances," she said. "I'm all ears."

He seemed puzzled. "Who said that?"

"The ears, or the nuances?"

"That truth lies in the nuances."

She shrugged. "I did. It's obvious."

He smiled. "You remember what I told you about ICLM's rules regarding mineral rights? How they're coupled with colonization policies?"

She nodded. "The mineral rights are granted based on an 'intent of permanence.' That's why there's nexgens."

ICLM was the French abbreviation for the International Lunar Management Commission, established by the UN in 2036 to oversea development of the Moon. As of 2051, when contact was lost, the commission had administered the establishment of three bases—theirs, China's, and the Saudi consortium. Theirs was the only privately held one. AMC, the American Moon Company, decided that it needed babies born on the Moon, and only hired young couples. She remembered the "go-babies" inspiration posters, as though men and women needed urging to procreate.

"How about the provision on scientific investment?"

She shrugged. "I guess that's why we have the Lab."

The American base was located on the far side of the Moon because that's where a platinum-heavy asteroid had hit four hundred million years ago. The location was also ideal for studying the slow neutrinos left over from the big bang—they were easier to capture after passing through the entire Moon from the other side. On the Earth side of the Moon, energy noise interfered with detection.

He nodded, slowly, watching her. "It's the only reason the Lab exists. AMC has no interest in scientific research. It was an addendum, really, an unwelcome necessity. They have as much interest in neutrinos as whether Shakespeare really wrote his plays."

This was vaguely disturbing, her father just an unwelcome addendum. "I think you're exaggerating. Why would they have made you head of the entire base?"

Her father clasped his hands across his chest. Here came the nuances. "Construction of the base began in 2044. That's when Meyer arrived. It was understood that it would take a few years before the platinum would begin shipping to Earth, and a couple years more before the venture was profitable. That's a vulnerable time for a company. Being profitable is black-and-white. As long as you *are* profitable, the company advances. But during the development phase—the first handful of years—the metrics are more abstract, budgets are based on projections. Malleable budgets represent temptation."

"You're talking about corruption?" she asked.

He lifted his palms. "That's a harsh label. Let's just say that AMC's CEO took advantage of the situation to shuffle funds in order to artificially inflate the perceived value of the company. An artificial inflation has to eventually deflate, and when it did—six years into the venture—it caused a national economic crisis."

"One company caused a national crisis?"

"You're too young to remember. It was called the second space race, the rush to colonize and exploit the Moon. China started it, and we couldn't resist following. We were fading as a global economic power, and viewed this as a test. AMC was born, and investors flocked to contribute, to the eventual tune of six-hundred billion dollars. When the bubble that AMC had created burst, there was more than simply national pride at stake."

"AMC was too big to fail," she offered.

Her father grinned. "You've been reading about the Great Recession. Indeed. So the government stepped in. We'd wanted to show the world that pure capitalism would beat the phony China type, but it wasn't to be. The Lab—the scientific 'addendum'—had been partially funded by Congress from the beginning, and that program was now expanded. It was a ruse of sorts, but it was a ready means to infuse cash and quell investor fears."

"I think I understand," Katlin said. "Congress sent you to clean up the mess."

He chuckled and shook his head. "Not nearly. Ostensibly, I came to oversee an expansion of the Lab. At the last minute, they gave me the unofficial task of assessing the overall operation. They likened it to Richard Feynman's investigation of the Challenger explosion. It was too late to explain to the Congressional committee that I wasn't qualified, so I just sort of…went along for the ride."

He sighed and stared off, the way Katlin had seen him do when she was younger and giving him a hard time. He shook his head at whatever he saw in the invisible distance, looked back at her, and snorted. "I thought it would be fun for six weeks."

"You were only supposed to be here six weeks?" she said. The idea spun her mind. "I always thought we came to stay until I turned sixteen. In fact, I remember you telling me that. You said that Mom was supposed to join us—"

"I lied." He sighed again. "I didn't want you to feel like a castaway. I thought that ten years would be plenty of time for Earth to recover and return."

Katlin leaned back on the stool until she was resting against a cabinet. So much to absorb. "If you were only supposed to be here six weeks, why did you bring …"

"You along? Believe me, every minute of these last twelve years I've regretted that—and celebrated it. The selfish side of me thanked God you were here. I wouldn't have made it, otherwise. Your mom and I thought it would be a good experience for you. Also, she was finishing her dissertation, and, well, frankly, you were a handful back then."

"You brought me to get me away from mom?" she said, a little stunned.

"Whoa! Don't take away the wrong message, here. She didn't like it. It was mostly my idea. She cried all night before we left."

"I don't remember that."

"Of course not. We wouldn't let you see that. You would have thought something terrible was about to happen."

He laughed at that.

"Which did," she said. She gazed at her father, so different from the pictures taken when they'd arrived. A mature silvered fifty-three now, he'd been a youthful forty-one then. His ordeal was even harder than she'd imagined—his wife left behind, not knowing whether her husband and child were even alive. Based on the flux readings her father had gathered during the sun's super-flare—the Blast—scientists on Earth could easily have surmised that the lunar base had been wiped out. Most of it was. The scientists and Meyer only survived because they were inside. Otherwise every last adult would have been killed, leaving thirty-seven nexgen children—and her—to fend for themselves.

She shook her head, banishing the gloomy thoughts. "Sorry, Daddy, I'm even farther from understanding how you ended up as Meyer's boss."

He nodded. Time to get on with it. "It was the last message from Earth before the Blast. Meyer was challenging my investigations, and he'd appealed to Earth. The reply was 'Dr. Cumming's has priority.' Between you and me, honey, I've always thought that they meant this only as it related to my investigation activities, but Meyer took it as an overarching statement."

"So ...?" Katlin probed.

"So, what?"

"Did you find any shenanigans on Meyer's part?"

"Not at all. I didn't expect to. I don't think AMC did, either. The whole investigation was political. Everybody knew that it was the AMC executives that were the stinkers. Meyer may be difficult to work with, but he's a straight shooter. They couldn't have found a better operations manager."

"Or a more bad-tempered one."

"Honey, you have to let that go. That was months ago."

The wound was still felt fresh. Meyer was struggling with a kidney stone, which she discovered only after she'd accidentally tripped over a piece of equipment waiting for repair. She'd gotten a bloody shin, but she also broke off a cable harness, which caused additional delay. Her father had explained that Meyer's subsequent tirade was mostly his kidney stone screaming, but he'd said things that really hurt her. Once he allowed the med-genie to deliver pain relief, his mood improved, but he never did apologize for the insults.

Katlin leaned farther back and rested her feet on her father's knees. "Daddy, you and Louden have been collecting data for a dozen years."

"So?"

"Don't you ever get … tired? I mean, it must be tedious."

He rubbed his beard. "Honey, it's what we do. It's our lives." He studied her a moment. "Someday—any day—Earth is going to show up. When they do, don't you want them to be proud of us?"

She laughed. "We'll go back heroes." It was good talking about the day when they'd return to Earth.

"I'm just shooting for respect. They'll say that we were responsible, that we carried on, bringing to fruition the great investment that had been made in us."

"Sixty tons of platinum."

"We do have a lot of platinum," he agreed.

He'd said it sardonically. That wasn't what he'd been referring to. "And the neutrino background data," she added enthusiastically.

He sighed. "At least the platinum served us well in other ways."

His eyes dropped, and he studied the floor. She knew he wanted to change the subject. "Speaking of lessons," he said, looking up, "it's probably time you got back to them."

"We weren't talking about lessons, Daddy. You were talking about other ways that the platinum has helped us."

"I'm just rambling. It's nonsense."

She watched him. She wasn't going to let him get away with it this time. "You're talking about the nexgens, aren't you?"

He blinked and stared at her.

"Keeping schedules and quotas for platinum production is a tool," she said.

He blinked again. Rather than lie to her, she thought, he just wouldn't say anything.

"It keeps them in line, doesn't it?"

He sighed. "That's a crass exaggeration."

"It's true, then."

"Let's just say that it's an effective tool for maintaining stability. Idle hands are the devil's workshop, as they used to say. Without organization and dutiful purpose, a population falls into rivalry and chaos."

"And when you say 'population,' you mean the nexgens."

"They're part of it, sure."

"I don't think you're talking about Julius or Louden."

"They're educated professionals, scientists."

Julius was the Chief—and only—Engineer, who spent every waking minute maintaining the aging base. Louden Dulles was the neutrino expert, the focus of the base's research. Both of them, along with her father—and her, for that matter—were what the nexgens considered "Managers."

"What about me?" she asked.

"Same thing. You're on your way to becoming one." He gave her ankle a light slap. "You enjoy poking at your old man."

She pulled her feet back, and planted them on the floor. "Old men need poking now and then," she said. "Otherwise, they might become rivalrous and chaotic."

He gave her feet a playful sideways kick. "I have to check on the archiving. Get out of here, girl."

"You mean woman."

She got up and followed him out. "I looked up the history of the base's name," she said. "The Daedalus crater was named when the Lunar Orbiter missions of the sixties first mapped the whole Moon. Do you know who Daedalus was?"

"Of course. In Greek mythology, he was the father of Icarus."

She let that sit a moment. "Doesn't that ever worry you?"

He snorted. "I don't believe in ancient Greek myths. I doubt most of the ancient Greeks did."

She grinned. "The logic of science is a handy shield."

"Certainly. When it's against nonsense."

The archiving room was in the same direction as the library, so she walked along with him. When they came to the door labeled "Human Archiving," they stopped. Katlin had never been inside. It was kept locked. "This is the first one since ..."

"The Blast," her father said levelly.

He stood, apparently waiting for her to leave.

She wanted to put distance between her and Randy's body, but the curious part of her spoke. "Daddy, can I watch?"

Her father looked pained, a reaction she was used to. "No, honey. I don't think so."

"Okay," she said. For once, she didn't push it. A big part of her was relieved. "You know," she said, sliding her hand across the plastic printing on the door, "I have a vague memory of this room being something else a long time ago, when we first arrived."

His pained expression deepened. "You were just a little girl, and everything was new. It's easy to confuse things." He put his hand on her shoulder. "Katlin, there's something else ... I think you should be careful with the nexgens for awhile."

She wanted to take his face in her hands and wipe away the troubles that seemed to be haunting him. "They're adjusting to the situation with Randy. Is that what you mean?"

"Yes. They're probably traumatized. I had to give Van two points, and he's now in misdemeanor for a few weeks."

She hadn't heard about any problems. "What did he do?"

He shrugged. "Insulted Meyer."

"You put Van in misdemeanor for *that*?"

He looked like she'd smacked him. "It may sound trivial, but we can't allow respect for authority to erode."

She snorted. "Now you sound like Meyer." He just looked at her. "Those were his words, weren't they?"

He took a deep breath and said, "Besides, I had just refused Meyer's request for Randy's points."

She let it go. She wouldn't convince him to stand up to the sourpuss Scrooge. "Have you thought about a memorial service for Randy?"

He sighed. She'd just added a few more pounds to his burden.

"Would you like me to put something together for you?" she asked. "I could probably find something in the library to adapt."

He smiled. "Thank you, Peaches, but I don't want to distract you from your lessons. Besides, I don't think they're expecting anything."

"Why not?"

He shrugged. "There's nothing like that in the movies."

That was a rather strange answer, but she'd bothered him

enough already. She gave him a peck on the cheek and walked towards the library. Calculus awaited her—integrating hyperbolic functions—and she was in no hurry.

She stopped short when a thought suddenly struck her. She had referred to the Greek myth of Icarus in the abstract, but her father might have thought she was bestowing the name of Daedalus on him. If so, he surely would associate Icarus with the forty-four workers who had died twelve years before.

She gasped and put her hand over her mouth. Like Icarus, they had perished when the sun's power was ignored. Except that in Icarus's case, he, himself, carried the blame.

Katlin continued on to the library. She'd probably re-awakened the guilt she knew had plagued her father since the accident. She vowed to make it up by being extra nice.

But for now, calculus waited, and she wouldn't want her father to think of her as part of the uneducated crowd prone to rivalry and chaos. She smiled. Now that she thought about it, those were probably Meyer's words as well.

Chapter 3

"I can't do it," Tyna said. "I'm sorry."

They'd retrieved Randy's body from Julius at the Lab's side door, and were on their way to the recycler. "This is just a bunch of minerals and amino acids," Van said, pointing to Randy's body lying on the rolling lab cart. "Randy—the real Randy—is back in the archive storage."

She just shook her head, determined.

"Someday," he said, "you'll talk to him again, and you'll both laugh at how you were squeamish."

"That will be good," she replied. "And while we're at it, I'll remind him that it was you two who tore his molecules apart."

"Should I remind him that you wanted to let him decay?"

She sighed. "I know. It can't be helped. But I don't have to watch it. I'll catch up with you guys at class."

"Okay. See you soon."

He was going to make a crack about females and fortitude, but he guessed she wasn't in the mood for sparring.

They rounded a corner, and came to the cycling center. The formal label was Environmental Processing, and included not only the organic recycler, but also the materials recycler, water capture and purification, air filtering, and, perhaps most important, oxygen extraction, where the precious element was pulled from the metal oxides—mostly iron and magnesium—that they found alongside the platinum they were mining. Although they stored the de-oxidized metals, they were essentially a byproduct of the far more useful gas.

During lunar days, when the nexgen's work moved indoors, and the sun bathed the solar converters, delivering the massive amounts of electricity needed for some of the processing, the center was a beehive of activity, ringing with the clangs of machinery in motion and the shouts of irritated or bored colleagues.

Being lunar night now, the cycling center was empty, dark, and quiet, an appropriate mausoleum, albeit a short-lived one. Van flipped the switch to activate the organic recycler, and stood back. It would take a few minutes for the internal elements to get to temperature.

"The dead were never meant to be recycled," Burl said.

"What? How do you know?" Van asked.

His friend glanced around, even though it was obvious they were alone. "My father wrote about a crypt that they were scheduled to build. It didn't have high priority, and he wondered if they would finally get around to it when one of them eventually died."

All the nexgens had a secret stash of material inherited from their parents—a hardcopy photo, an audio com message, or an item of clothing. Burl had a journal his dad had kept, pen-on-paper.

"I guess the crypt would have been just another cave." Van said.

"Sure. In the vacuum, they could have just stood the bodies up in a row. Out of the sun, they'd stay frozen forever. The digging robots could have built it in no time."

"Meyer probably couldn't bear losing those few pounds of platinum."

Burl gave him side glance, as though checking to make sure he was ready. Van knew the look. "What?"

"This is cannibalism, you know," he said, pointing at Randy's body.

Van knew the term. It was what Julius did when he took parts from some equipment to keep others running. "I guess it is. It's molecules instead of circuits."

Still that sidelong glance. "Give it up, Burl," Van said. "What's on your mind?"

"On Earth this is a high crime."

"Really? How do you know?"

"Glenda told me."

"Ah. Her mother's novels." Van and Glenda had paired—had been intimate—for a short time a year ago. Talking to her now was strained.

"This one was called *Silence of the Lambs*," Burl said. "The point is that the bad guy in the story eats people, and this makes him a criminal of the highest order."

"You mean, he eats people, like, without going through a recycler?"

"Yep. He cooks their flesh and eats it like our parents ate beef."

Van tried to visualize that, and shivered. "That's not possible."

"I don't think Glenda's lying, at least about what she read."

"It's a novel. It's all a lie to start with."

"Novels were based on cultural norms. She said that the British navy had specific punishments for cannibalism. They wouldn't need to punish sailors for something that they would never do."

Van shrugged. "Earth was strange."

They always talked about Earth in the past tense, as though it had ceased to exist after the Blast.

"Exactly," Burl said, grinning.

Van groaned. His friend was playing the Earth game. Burl—and Tyna, for that matter—believed that he was obsessed with old Earth, and took any opportunity to prove it. The problem was, Van knew he probably was. Their home planet seemed so much more interesting than the Moon, though. He couldn't understand why they *weren't* fascinated.

The green light on the recycler came on, and Burl helped him lift Randy onto the feed belt. They were watching their dead colleague slide slowly inside, when Burl suddenly said, "Bye," and trotted away. Van grabbed the empty cart and took off after him, the wheels clattering and echoing among the dark crannies of the cavernous space. He didn't want to be close enough to hear Randy's body being rendered in preparation for soaking in enzymes, after which the vitamins and amino acids would be filtered out, and the rest ionized and atomically segregated.

Tyna wasn't a woman lacking in fortitude, she'd just been more prescient.

Once safely away from the recycler's racket, they slowed and Burl said, "Do you think we'll ever talk to Randy?"

They didn't discuss the archiving very much. With the threat of threshold points hanging over their heads—leaving open the possibility of forever missing out—there was an unspoken idea that talking about it might jinx them. Van suspected superstition was hardwired in humans. "If we don't screw up—or if Meyer doesn't screw us—sure."

"Then you do believe that Earth will someday return."

Zeedo had explained that archive retrieval was only possible with Earth equipment.

"Of course," Van said.

"After twelve years?"

"Why not?"

"Twelve years is a long time. Maybe the Blast knocked Earth back to the stone age."

"Zeedo said that's unlikely, and even if it did, it didn't take ten thousand years for Earth to build civilization. It took that long for it to learn *how* to do it. The knowledge wouldn't have disappeared."

"You sure?"

"You think the Blast might have knocked out all electronics? *All* of it? All around the world? Seems far-fetched. Besides, some of our parents brought books to the Moon. Obviously people still kept them."

"So, Earth is being rebuilt from novels…" Burt said.

His friend had a point. Novels were the only books any of them had ever seen. References and technical manuals—at least the ones they had access to—were all e-versions. It made sense. Nobody wanted to snuggle up in bed with a manual on platform realignment.

"Well, I still say that it's pretty unlikely that every piece of electronics on Earth was killed," Van insisted.

They turned a corner, and found Tyna waiting. "Who was killed?" she asked.

Van explained their disagreement over the likelihood of Earth's extinction.

"It killed our parents," she said.

Burl shook his head. "Come on, Tyna. You know that Earth's atmosphere protected it from the bad stuff."

"That's what they tell us."

"You don't believe it?"

She sucked her lip. She wasn't sure. Then she looked puzzled. "I wonder why we never sent a rover around the horizon?"

Just then, a blue jumpsuit came around a corner, and the three of them turned in anticipation. Managers seemed to find unoccupied nexgens unsettling, and often reacted by assigning them tasks. It was just Katlin, however, and though technically a Manager, she was free from responsibility for the base, and was more relaxed, although still somewhat removed. Arrogant, by Tyna's evaluation. "They talked about it," she said. She'd obviously heard Tyna. "But think about where the base is located."

She seemed to be waiting for an answer.

"On the far side," Van suggested.

"Of course, but where on the far side?"

Van had no idea what she was asking. "The Daedalus crater?" he said, with no confidence.

Katlin rolled her eyes. "Yes," she said patiently, what Tyna would call arrogantly, "but do you know *where* on the far side?"

Burl liked the young Manager even less than Tyna, and particularly hated to have his technical knowledge questioned. "The very center of the far side," he replied dryly. "Which puts us about fifteen hundred miles from a view of Earth."

Katlin nodded, seeming unaware of Burl's surly tone. "One thousand, seven hundred miles, in fact. One of the three rovers was inside and survived the Blast. Unmodified, it had a range of a hundred miles. Julius attached spare fuel tanks, oxygen and hydrogen, which doubled its range. He also added an insulated storage compartment. The plan was to set up depots along the way. A crew of two would set out toward the horizon during lunar night. Along the way, they'd scour the dark crevasses for hidden water. Once they reached the rover's range limit, they'd set up the depot, including solar panels and a water splitter. Then they'd return and wait out one lunar day. When they went back to the depot, their collected water would have been converted into fuel, so that they could start out on a next leg and another, farther, depot."

Burl looked intrigued, and torn. He hated to defer to her. "So, it would have taken maybe twenty lunar nights—two years."

She shrugged and nodded.

"Wait a second," he said, happy to have found a hole. "They'd have had to carry more and more fuel each time they set out—by the end, twenty times as much as the first leg."

"No. The plan was that they'd find enough water along the way so that each depot would have enough fuel to send them on their way towards the next one, and also have enough left for the return trip."

They stood in silence, contemplating this.

"Every trip," Van said, "they'd have to find the same amount of water along the same route. By the end, they'd have found twenty times as much water as on the first trip."

He couldn't finish the thought, to contradict a Manager, even if it was only Katlin.

He didn't need to. "I know, Van. It was an elaborate fantasy. They knew it, but didn't think they had a choice. Those first couple of years were pretty desperate. My father says that Julius was actually relieved when the third rover failed beyond repair before they could even start the program."

Burl and Tyna looked a little shocked. They weren't used to hearing details of Managers' conversations. Van was seven when the Blast swept across the face of the Moon, delivering a lethal dose of radiation to anybody not protected by layers of solid rock. His parents lived on as mental ghosts, indistinct forms in his memory— hands offering food, voices encouraging and reprimanding, bursts of unaccountable laughter when their friends came by for drinks, and Van was put to bed early, lying in the dark listening to the comfortable drone of adults socializing.

He realized that Katlin was talking.

"... even if they had made it all the way, it would have been pure luck if anybody on Earth would have been listening."

"Listening?" Van said, attempting to show he'd been paying attention.

"Sure. Their transmissions would only have been picked up if somebody on Earth happened to be pointing a high-gain directional antenna at them."

"Right. Of course."

Van had no idea what a high-gain directional antenna was. The antennas on their pressure suits were built into their backs, but he knew that when they were working on the ground beyond the platform and bent over, they could lose contact with the base. He guessed it must be something like that.

"My father says the failure of the last rover was the beginning of stability," Katlin said. "Once we accepted that we were on our own, we could get back to an operational routine."

"Except that your workforce was dead," Burl said. His tone was even, but Van knew he was itching for a fight.

Katlin looked at him levelly. If she caught his antagonistic mood, she ignored it. "It worked out in the end, didn't it? It took a few years to train the next crew."

That was unsettling—the nexgens were just the next wave of workers, the backups, brought out of storage after catastrophes. There was nothing to argue about, though. It was the truth. Van had begun working the platform at age twelve. It was all he knew.

Except for the repeating stories of Earth on movie-night, and, of course, their secret stashes.

"It worked out in the end," Burl parroted. "The platinum pile began growing again."

He was priming for a sarcastic volley, possibly attracting a point or two. Attempting to intercept the crash, Van said the first thing that came to mind. "It's like *Cast Away*," he said.

Unfortunately, the first thing that came to mind was a movie she wasn't supposed to know about.

Katlin nodded. "Yes, castaways, that's what we are."

She hadn't caught the slip, but now Van was nervous. His hand beat out a rhythm against his thigh.

Her brow wrinkled. "Wasn't that a movie? With … who was that actor?"

Tyna had been watching the trains on collision courses, and jumped in. "Wasn't that Tom Hanks? I love his two movies. He was so good with Meg Ryan."

She was talking about the two movies they'd all seen on movie-night, and she was lying about loving them. She thought they were silly.

Van could have kissed her, though. "He also played the part of our Columbus," he said, picking up the distraction ball.

They all looked at him.

"You know," he said, "Columbus discovered America, and Tom Hanks discovered the Moon. Well, he didn't discover it, but he—"

"What in God's name are you talking about?" Burl asked.

"You know. The previews for that other movie, where he plays Neal Armstrong."

Katlin burst out laughing. "You mean *Apollo 13*? Oh, Van, he's not playing Armstrong. That was the Apollo eleven mission. *Apollo 13* was about a follow-on mission that went wrong. Hanks played … wait, don't tell me—James Lovell."

She looked at them and blinked. Her smile melted. "Um, you don't know any of this, do you?"

They just stared at her. Van shook his head, embarrassed that he'd been so wrong. On the other hand … "How do *you* know this?" he asked.

She shrugged, and her brow crowded together. "Why, you know, it's a fundamental part of Earth history."

"I'm guessing that it is," he said, surprised at his own brashness, "but where did you find out about it?"

Her cheeks turned red. "I … well, I guess I knew it before I left Earth."

"At five years old?" Van asked gently. She was on the defensive, and he felt sorry for her.

She took a breath and looked at them. "I suppose so. Of course. Why not?" She pressed two fingers against the side of her head. She was listening to her implant, another legacy of Earth. Their parents had them. Everybody on Earth, apparently, had had them. "I have to go."

She turned on her heel and strode away.

They watched her until she disappeared around a corner. "She's going to make a fine Manager," Burl noted with his usual dryness.

"With Van licking her feet the whole way," Tyna added. It was an expression they used with no idea of origin. She looked at him critically. "I believe the boy's smitten."

"Cut it out," Van said, feeling his cheeks burning. "You two had better get to class."

His two friends walked off. "Does marrying a Manager make you a Manager?" Tyna asked Burl loud enough to make sure Van heard.

"Close enough to be permanently impaired," Burl answered even louder.

The rest of their joking was drowned by a clattering that turned a corner to reveal Linda, a fourteen-year-old nexgen, pushing a solar converter along on a dolly. She looked distraught. "That's the unit that failed?" Van asked when she reached him.

"Yeah," she replied, not stopping. "I'm taking it to the Lab. Julius thinks he has a replacement part."

"Why the worried face?"

Now she stopped. "I'm going to be late for class."

"Julius will give you a waiver."

"If I see him," she said, continuing on.

Van understood. If Meyer took it from her, he might just be a jerk and refuse a waiver. "Hey," he said, "I'll take it. I have to return this cart anyway."

Linda grinned and thanked him, then sprinted off, glad to not risk a point.

Van pushed the lab cart out of the way—he'd come back for it later—and set off, pulling the dolly behind him. At the Lab side door, the genie didn't wait for him to ask. "Doctor Dulles is on the way," she said.

Van waited, tapping his thigh. He didn't really need to be at the classroom, since the first lesson was for the mids—a misnomer for the twelve and thirteen year-olds, since they were now the youngest—but all nexgens scheduled for class duty were supposed to be on time. Meyer might eventually give Van a hard time about being late.

The Lab door opened to reveal Louden standing there with a plate of food in one hand, and the other feeding his mouth. Van liked Louden. The plump scientist performed the most important research (not that Van had the least idea what that was about), and yet treated everybody as equals, to Meyer's chagrin. "Well, hello, Van. What brings you to the hallowed halls of science?"

"Hi, Louden. Delivering equipment for Julius."

Van was ready to dash off to class, but Louden seemed in a quandary, holding his plate in front of him as though he'd just been handed a new-born baby. He glanced around, and, finding no flat surface to receive it, turned and walked away, motioning with his elbow for Van to follow. "I just saw Julius in his shop," he said.

Van hesitated, but saw no other choice and pulled the dolly along into the Lab. Sometimes Louden's relaxed disregard for social structure made Van nervous.

Van had been inside the Lab maybe a half dozen times that he could remember. This must be what immigrants felt when stepping onto new shores. He was intimately familiar with every well-organized inch of space in the rest of the base, the commercial enterprise, Meyer's domain. In here, everything was new and ... different. He had no clue what most of the equipment was for, and what he could see of the Managers' living quarters was, disconcertingly—he hated to admit it—messy. It was a little unnerving to think that all their lives were ruled by, were dependant on, these men.

Louden ushered him with his elbow into Julius's shop—yet more messiness. The engineer was sitting at a bench with his back to them. "Your crippled solar converter has arrived," Louden said.

"Right," Julius replied, absorbed in what was on the screen in front of him.

"Okay, Van," Louden said. "Thanks."

At the sound of Van's name, Julius spun around, his eyes wide with alarm. "What the hell!" he cried. "What's he doing here?"

Louden seemed mildly surprised at his distress. "Cool your jets, Julius. He's just delivering the converter."

Shaking his head in disapproval, Julius turned off the screen and said, "How many times a week does Arthur harp about this directive?" He glanced at Van. "You'd better get him out of here before Arthur sees him."

Louden shrugged and motioned for Van to follow. At the side door he nodded a goodbye. "Thanks, Van. Sorry about the rude reaction. Julius takes Arthur's authority a little too seriously."

As Van walked away, and then broke into a trot to get to class, he thought about the image he'd seen on Julius's screen. It looked like a 3-D diagram of some equipment, with parts identified, and paragraphs and paragraphs of text below.

He'd never really thought about it before, but it made sense. After all, Julius couldn't possibly keep all the thousands upon thousands of details about the workings of the base's equipment in his head.

It was an eye-opener, though. A mind bender. This stuff was more along Burl's line. Maybe even Tyna. What other wonderful instructive treasures did Julius have that would set Burl salivating?

There was no way to know.

Blaine C. Readler

Chapter 4

Katlin was engrossed in the material, and jumped when her father spoke behind her. "What are you doing, honey?"

She exhaled in exasperation. "Daddy, you scared me."

"Peaches, what's there to be scared of? There are no animals on the Moon."

"It's instinctive, you know that. And don't call me Peaches. I'm not a little girl anymore."

"You'll always be my little girl," he said as he leaned over her shoulder to see the screen. "Why are you looking at the workers' class outlines? Thinking of teaching?"

"No … actually, maybe. I was curious what they learn."

She'd never sat in on the nexgen classes, as she had her own program, using the Lab library files.

"Honey," he said, "they learn everything they need to know. Why the sudden interest?"

"No particular reason. They're not connected to the Lab repositories, are they?"

"No. Of course not. They never were. The Lab documents are secure. That's always the case with ongoing research."

"But the Lab's repository isn't just research material. It has *everything*. That's why Meyer spends so much time in here, even though his office is out with the nexgens."

"Well, sure. Before the Blast, his links were with Earth—the home office."

"Before our satellite was blown out."

"Yes. In fact, Julius had to patch together some programs to recreate Meyer's logistics routines—"

"Daddy, before the Blast, the nexgens—I mean, the workers—had access to the same Earth connection as Meyer?"

"Sure. So did the Lab. It was a base-wide network. Honey, what's all this about?"

"Nothing, really." She looked up at him and smiled. "I'll need to know this stuff someday when I inherit the management of the base."

She was joking, but her father didn't catch on. "Let's talk about that when the time comes. It's wasted brain cycles now, since Earth will surely arrive long before then."

"Of course, Daddy."

She used to share his optimism. Although she'd give anything to get back to Earth, she'd come to accept that each passing year made that scenario more unlikely. It might never happen, at least not in her lifetime.

Her father put a finger to his ear. "Time to go. You coming?"

"I'll be along in a minute. Do you know what you're going to say?"

He shook his head, looking tired. As the base leader, he was responsible for everything and everybody.

"It was inevitable, Daddy. You understand that, don't you?"

"Sure, Peaches." He put his hand along the side of her face a moment, and then walked off.

Katlin smiled as she watched him go. She was going to miss being called that.

ж ж ж

Van spotted Tyna and Burl in the sea of dull reddish-brown jumpsuits and worked his way to them, stepping through the crowd of three dozen nexgens sitting or sprawled on the supply hanger floor. The thirty foot by fifty foot receiving dock area was the base's largest cavern—the only room large enough for them all to assemble. None of the nexgens could remember the hanger doors ever being opened. There'd been no need once the last rover expired.

"What's this all about?" he asked, squeezing in between his two friends.

"Don't know," Burl said. "Must be important, though. Meyer was just getting rolling with his famous 'teamwork wins out over technology' lecture when he got the message, and told us to meet here. Where have you been?"

"In the Lab."

That had exactly the effect he was expecting. They just stared at him. "What do you mean?" Tyna finally asked.

"Just what I said. I was in the Lab."

"I got that. Why? How? Did you get caught?"

"Louden let me in. I delivered the broken converter to Julius. Louden *told* me to come in. Actually, his elbow sort of told me. Julius obviously wasn't too happy about it."

"Huh," was all Tyna said.

"What did you see?" Burl asked. "Robots waiting on them hand and foot?"

It was a running joke that the Managers still had some functioning machines hidden away inside their sanctuary. "Just Julius slaving away. I think I'd be grumpy all the time, too, if I was expected to fix everything that broke."

"How many times have I volunteered to help?" Burl asked.

"Dozens of times more than we wanted to hear," Tyna replied.

"I saw what he had on his screen," Van said, glancing around to make sure nobody else was listening. Louden, a Manager, had told him to enter the Lab, but he hadn't been given permission to relate what he saw.

"What?" Burl asked intrigued.

The nexgen chatter went silent at that moment as Zeedo walked in and stepped up onto a box. He looked weary as he scanned the assemblage as though searching for something. "We're here today to remember Randy," he said. "He was a friend and colleague, and we are saddened to lose him." He threw a quick glance at Meyer, who looked on stoically. "Randy's end was inevitable, written in his genes."

A murmur rippled through the seated nexgens, and Meyer's face hardened further.

Zeedo held up his hand for quiet. "We could have helped him had we been on Earth, but we are not. We must accept his fate, as he so bravely did."

"Bullshit!" somebody hissed.

Van recognized the voice, but he guessed Zeedo didn't, as his eyes searched the crowd for the outburst. He chose to ignore it. "So today we say goodbye to Randy. Would anybody like to add something—something constructive?"

Kim, a fourteen-year-old nexgen raised her hand and stood up. Looking around, she said, "It's not goodbye, but *au revoir.*" She suddenly seemed at a loss, as though she'd intended to say more, but had forgotten. She quickly sat down, and the crowd turned back to Zeedo.

Their leader looked even more tired, drained. "Yes, Kim's correct. Randy was successfully archived. And, we do hope to talk to him again someday, but as you all know, retrieval is only possible on Earth." He paused a moment and looked down at Katlin, who stood next to him. "We all look forward to that day, when contact is again established."

Another nexgen hand was waving. Zeedo looked pained as he said, "Yes, Glenda?"

A groan rose from the sea of nexgens. They all knew her reputation for arguing irrational points, seemingly just for the sake of arguing. Van was convinced that she'd lost the ability to distinguish reality from the fabricated worlds of her mother's novels.

Van couldn't remember why he'd been tempted to pair with her. Ever since their break, he had a hard time recreating his initial attraction to her.

"Maybe we should say a prayer…" Glenda said. The fact that she was so positive about this, so completely oblivious that her suggestion might not be enthusiastically received convinced Van that their break had been a gift.

"Uh-oh," Burl muttered under his breath.

Zeedo took a deep breath and stared hard at Glenda.

She apparently took this as encouragement. "People pray at funerals all the time—"

"No!" Zeedo bellowed, and the cavernous room carved from Moon rock went utterly silent. He continued mildly, "You can do that if you like in your own quarters, of course, but you know that sort of thing isn't allowed in public."

"I know," she persisted, "but this is a special situation—"

"Mr. Meyer," he said angrily, cutting her off again, "what is the penalty for public nuisance?"

This was Zeedo's euphemism for anything related to religion.

"One point for a first offense," Meyer replied flatly. "Two points if continued after a warning."

"Very well. Glenda, you've been warned. If you say one more word about prayer, it's two points. Well?"

She finally got it. Face red and lips pulled tight, she sat down.

The nexgens started clapping, but stopped when Zeedo made a cutting motion with his hand. He glanced around the room, as though searching for other troublemakers. "We're done here. Back to your schedule."

He stepped off the box and stalked away. Katlin caught Van's eye. She gave a little shrug, as though apologizing for her father, then turned and followed him.

The three friends waited as their fellow nexgens began filing out. "Glenda claims that public display of religion is not only legal on Earth," Burl said, "but actually guaranteed in the Constitution. I wonder why Zeedo is so bothered by it?"

"Who knows what goes on in the mind of a Manager," Van replied. "You've been spending a lot of time with Glenda, it seems."

His friend threw him an alarmed look. "No, no. Don't even start. She has some fascinating stories to tell from her novels."

"That's what they *are*." Van said. "Stories."

"You know what I mean," Burl said.

Tyna was smirking.

"What's up with you?" Van asked.

She nodded knowingly. "I saw that look Katlin gave you."

"What are you talking about?"

She watched him, grinning. "Your denial is just confirmation."

"You're crazy," Van said, but she was right. He'd felt a little thrill. "She was looking at all of us."

Tyna just grinned. Her unspoken accusation was louder than words.

Strangely, Van didn't like Tyna thinking that he was attracted to

Katlin, even if he was. He wondered why. The three of them were pals, had always been pals.

"So," Burl said to Van, "what did you see?"

Van wasn't sure what he meant.

"On Julius's screen, you low-gear."

"Oh, yeah!" He hesitated.

"You're afraid you'll get into trouble?" Burl asked. "It's Louden's fault, not yours."

Van nodded. "Yeah, okay." He glanced around again. "It looked like detailed instructions," he said quietly.

Burl raised his eyebrows in question. "Yeah ... and?"

"That's it. They were really detailed."

"You already said that. What were they for?"

"I don't know—how could I know that? Whatever he was working on."

Burl shrugged. "It makes sense. The equipment must have come with design explanations. Even before the Blast, they wouldn't have expected to haul everything back to Earth for repair."

"So," Van said, "what do you think?"

"What's there to think? Julius has information about how to repair equipment. Is that a surprise?"

"It was to me."

"It's commendable that you admit it."

"Right. Like you had predicted it?"

"I didn't say that. I'm just not shocked by the news."

Tyna shook her head. "No. Van's right."

"So there," he said to Burl. To Tyna, he said, "What am I right about?"

"This is significant. Maybe it's not a complete surprise, but think what it represents."

"What else do they have back there?" Van offered.

Tyna nodded. "Exactly."

Burl looked at each of them, and slowly nodded. "It's a good question." His eyes narrowed. "A really good question."

A single beep sounded through the halls of the base, marking the half-hour.

"We'd better get back," Tyna said. The nexgen crowd in the

hangar had thinned.

"Back to the grind," Burl announced. "I wonder where that expression came from?"

"Ask Glenda," Van said as they walked out. "Maybe from grinding wheat like our grandparents did."

"Our *grandparents*?" Tyna said. "Van, aren't you off by a few generations?"

He considered. "Yeah, it would have been earlier than our grandparents."

I should know this stuff, he thought. *It's our history.*

They joined the class that had broken for Randy's memorial. During lunar day, classes were held five days a week, but just two days a week during the night, and only half-days at that. Van, Burl, and Tyna—in fact, all the nexgens over seventeen—were done with classes, but they were often scheduled to help the younger ones. After the basics of reading and math were mastered, their education focused on the operation and maintenance of the base. Classes consisted of two basic types. In one they studied the various roles that human workers were originally slated to perform. The material for this was slick and well organized, since it was created on Earth during the base's conception. The other classes consisted of all the tasks originally performed by the now-defunct robots. This material had been pasted together by Meyer and supplemented by anecdotal instruction from older nexgens.

Today, Meyer was introducing platform operations to young nexgens. Specifically, how the probe bits worked to find the platinum layers. An array of up to two dozen super-hard nanodiamond bits were simultaneously drilled down into the Moon's crust. Each bit contained a thin metal band, which was electrically connected to a central processing unit on the platform control stage. Originally, a robot would monitor the bits as they dug deeper and deeper. Every hundred milliseconds, a high voltage pulse was sent to each bit, and all the other bits would listen. The robot's analysis program could correlate the information and construct a 3-D image of the platinum lode.

Meyer had been drawing on a board, and he paused and looked at the small group of young nexgens. "You are now that robot. Julius has rigged up a visual cue for each bit. At first, it looks like a random spray of colored lights, but with practice—a lot of practice—you'll learn to interpret it, and, like the original robot, construct a 3-D image in your head. The real trick comes down to remembering enough of it to be useful later."

He lay his hand on a screen. "We're going to play back an actual drill sequence that we captured." He gestured at Burl. "Mr. Jennings has mastered the whole process, and will explain how he interprets it as we watch. The sequence takes about ten minutes. Don't interrupt if you get lost. We'll repeat it as many times as it takes."

He motioned for Burl to step up to the screen.

As Burl walked over, he threw Van one of his sidelong glances. *Uh-oh*, Van thought. *That doesn't look good.*

The master probe drill operator reached to tap the "play" icon, but paused. He turned to Meyer. "Maybe we could dig up some supplementary material," he suggested.

The Ops Head looked annoyed at the delay. "What are you talking about?"

"I don't know," Burl said with exaggerated casualness. "Maybe some instructional support documents filed away somewhere."

"Cut the nonsense," Meyer snapped. "You know there aren't any. We would have been using them if there were."

Burl shrugged nonchalantly. "You're probably right. I just thought that maybe somewhere hidden away back in the Lab ..." Before Meyer had a chance to say anything, Burl tapped the icon and launched into the sequence.

Ж Ж Ж

After class, Van grabbed Burl's arm and waited while the room emptied. "Why'd you do that?" he asked. "You trying to get me a couple more points?"

"Relax," Burl said, carefully peeling away Van's fingers. "What was your crime? Not closing your eyes when Louden forced you into the Lab?"

"He didn't force me—never mind. But what did you think you'd gain?"

"Confirmation that you're not telling stories like Glenda."

"What are you talking about?"

Tyna came over to them. "I saw it," she confirmed.

"What?" Van said.

"Meyer's face," she said. "Didn't you see it?"

"Apparently not."

"He knew exactly what Burl was referring to. That man can't hide anything. His face is a puppet to his emotions."

Van looked at her and then at Burl. "Really? You think so? What's a puppet?"

"It's like the role John Malkovich is forced to do in the movie—you know, becoming him. But, definitely, Meyer knows about documents in the Lab."

Burt and Tyna walked away discussing how wonderful it would be if they had a technical understanding of the base's equipment.

"Huh," Van said, staring after his friends.

ж ж ж

At 2:50 PM Van positioned himself. He knew that Katlin usually took her shower at 3:00. The male nexgens had the showers on Tuesdays and Saturdays mornings, the females on Mondays and Thursdays. The Managers used them anytime they wanted, and usually that was the remaining mornings—Wednesdays, Fridays, and Sundays. Most people on the base typically took one shower a week, sometimes two during the lunar nights when outside work could be sweaty. Except Katlin. She took a shower almost every afternoon. Van had never thought about it before. It was just the way it had always been.

And nexgens didn't question Managers' privileges. As he stood listening now, though, he wondered what would happen if he asked Zeedo for additional shower time for nexgens. He could guess—a lecture about how precious water was, almost up there with oxygen. As efficient as their recycling equipment was, inevitably some tiny amount of water was lost to the microscopic pores of the rock beneath them. Also, the more they used the recycling equipment, the more likely something would break—eventually something with no spare part, and then what would they do?

So, he didn't ask.

He straightened. Katlin was approaching around the corner. Living together in relatively small quarters had tuned his senses to subtle patterns. He could recognize anybody just by the sound of their feet. He waited, timing his move. She was going straight toward the showers. When he guessed she was a half dozen paces away, he stepped out, as though he just happened to be coming from the side aisle at that moment.

"Hi, Van," she said from behind him.

He turned and smiled. "Oh, hi, Katlin. Off to the showers, I see," he said, nodding to her towel.

"Superb detective work," she said, grinning.

He took a breath. *Here goes nothing.* "Hey, I was thinking—I noticed in the preview to *Apollo 13* they don't mention the name of the astronaut—what was his name?"

"You mean James Lovell? The guy Tom Hanks played?"

"Yeah. James Lovell. Thanks." Van tried to sound totally casual, which was difficult with his pulse beating in his neck. "I searched through our class materials, and they don't mention the Apollo 13 mission at all. I'm embarrassed to say, though, that I did learn—was supposed to have learned—that it was the Apollo 11 mission that first landed on the Moon."

Katlin didn't look at him. She was studying the floor as they walked along. "That's okay," she said. "We all forget things."

She wasn't making it easy.

"Katlin," he said, stopping.

She stopped and turned. She looked apprehensive.

"You remembered the difference between Apollo 11 and 13, and you even remembered James Lovell's name from when you were five? After twelve years?"

She gazed at him for a long few seconds. "I probably read about it since then."

Van nodded. This was it. He waited for her to explain, but she just watched him. He shouldn't have expected her to volunteer it. "Which means that there's stuff—information—back in the Lab that we nexgens haven't seen."

She held his gaze. She could just walk away. He couldn't challenge her. She was a Manager.

"Yes," she said, finally nodding. "There probably is." She glanced around, as though hoping to find someone, or something, to distract them. "I'll—" she started. She blinked twice and nodded again. "I'll look into it, Van. I'll let you know."

She turned and walked away.
Van had expected she would be angry. He smiled.

Blaine C. Readler

Chapter 5

Van wagged his head. "No. Let's wait to see what Katlin has to say."

Tyna took his elbow and rested her head on his shoulder. "Please?" she said.

They all knew she was playacting, but it was effective. Van hesitated. He liked it.

"Looks like our fearless leader isn't so fearless," Burl said.

Van wanted to say, "Go away, Burl" but instead, he said, "I'm already one point over. Why don't *you* go?"

"Policy says that as union steward, you can ask Zeedo for anything. All he can do is say no."

Van sighed. He let Tyna pretend that she adored him a moment longer before facing reality. "Fine. I'll talk to Zeedo. If I get another point, I'm going to assign you both to recycler cleaning duty for a week."

Tyna immediately sat up. "Thanks, fearless leader," she said, and she and Burl walked off to suit up for their outside shift.

"I wouldn't do it for anybody but you, Tyna," he said. They'd already turned a corner, and he knew they couldn't hear.

ж ж ж

Van sat fidgeting, tapping his thigh.

Why are Managers always exactly three minutes late? Maybe they keep different time. Maybe they wonder why nexgens are always three minutes early.

"Mr. Wilkens," Zeedo said, coming through the doorway.

Van stood up, but Zeedo waved for him to sit down, as he took his seat. "What's up?" the boss of his boss asked.

Van swallowed. "Dr. Cummings, sir," he started, but a tickle in his throat set him to coughing.

When Van finally caught a clean breath, Zeedo said, "If it's about your point, Van, don't worry about it. If something should ... happen, I won't hold it against you. But you have to learn to respect Meyer. You have to set an example for the others, and respect for the line of authority is important. It could backfire on you someday, you know. Also, um, let's keep this between us. Don't expect me to be lenient every time."

Van stared down at his hands lying in his lap. *Damn.* Zeedo wasn't making this easy. It ran in the family. "Uh, thanks—thanks very much, sir, but that's not the reason I wanted to see you."

"Oh? What is it, then?"

Van looked up at the base leader. "You see, sir, well, I delivered the failed converter yesterday, and—"

"Ah, yes. Julius told me. It's fine, Van. Louden should have taken it, and I've talked to him. I appreciate that you're addressing it, though. That's leadership."

Zeedo started to get up.

"Um, sorry, sir, but that's not it either. I mean, it *is* about me delivering the converter but, well, it's just that I couldn't help seeing what was on Julius's screen."

Zeedo sat back down slowly. "I see."

He didn't say anything else, forcing Van to continue. "It was detailed instructions about some piece of equipment."

"Okay."

Van took a deep breath. "I, we, were thinking that maybe there's stuff—manuals, information, whatever—back in the Lab that, well, that maybe could be..." He looked Zeedo in the eye. "Shared?" He remembered Burl and Tyna's directives. "What we're most interested in is technical stuff—how all the equipment works, that sort of thing."

Zeedo just sat staring at him. Van squirmed. *Policy says that the union steward can ask anything,* Van thought. He was practicing the words, ready to deliver.

"I see," Zeedo said. "Tell you what, Van. Come with me."

And with that, the base leader got up and walked out. Van followed.

At the Lab, Zeedo entered and let the genie close the door behind him. He didn't even glance back—having no reason to believe that Van would follow him inside. Van stood in the hall, tapping out a rhythm on his thigh, a tune that Tyna was playing a lot lately on the com while they were working outside.

He tried to guess what Zeedo was doing, but gave up. He'd just have to wait and find out. If it was more points, he'd have already doled them out. Van was elated, freed from what he realized he'd really been fearing. Policy was all fine and good, but in the end, Zeedo controlled the archiving.

After maybe ten minutes, the door finally slid open, and Zeedo stepped out. He handed a clip to Van. The label was hand-written, and read "Loan to Wilkens."

"Bring it back when you're done," Zeedo said, "and I'll load it with more."

Van looked at the clip. "Uh, thanks, sir, but, I mean, could I—"

"That will be all," Zeedo said, and stepped back into the Lab. A moment later, Van was looking at the door.

ж ж ж

"He just handed it to you?" Tyna said. "No fuss?"

"Yes," Van replied, "and no."

He felt around at the back of the entertainment console. The clip wasn't the kind they used for movie-night viewing, and he wasn't sure the box even took it. "Ah, there," he said, and slipped the clip into the slot. The console screen lit up, showing the contents.

"Well, look at that," Burl said reverently, and flipped his finger along the screen to see farther down the list. He kept going, and the contents kept rolling down. "Wow! Look at that. Dozens and dozens of movies . . and books ... and ... 'symphonies'?" He looked up at his friends.

"It's music," Tyna said. "Old stuff, with a whole room full of musicians all playing at the same time. Where's the technical material?"

"Hold on," Burl said, continuing to scan. The end of the list rolled up the screen. He looked at Van.

"Maybe you missed it," Van said.

Burl started over, going more slowly this time. "Did you *tell* him what we wanted?" he asked when he got to the end of the list again.

"Of course," Van replied. "Maybe he forgot."

Burl sat back, disgusted. "Well, this is just a bunch of Earth drivel. I could get this talking with Glenda."

"Maybe he did just forget," Tyna said. "Can you go back and ask?"

Van wanted her to lay her head on his shoulder. It wasn't going to happen. "Sure."

They sat looking at him.

"I'm not going *now*," he said.

"Why not?" Tyna asked.

"I just got done bothering him. I don't want to drain the battery. I'll ask him tomorrow. Or the next day."

Burl tapped his finger on Van's hand. "I voted for you."

"So?"

"So, I expect a degree of service."

"I'm not your slave. I said I'll talk to him tomorrow. Or the next day."

His friend looked at him a moment, and then stood up. "Come on, Tyna. We lowly hourlies better get back to the grindstone." He nodded at the screen. "Maybe you can find out where that expression came from." He walked out, muttering about Earth drivel.

Tyna stood up and shrugged. "Do your best," she said, and followed Burl out.

Van looked at the long list of Earth material, and a warm desire filled his tummy. His shoulder was cold and lonely, though.

ж ж ж

Katlin knocked on the edge of her father's open door, then walked in. "What did you want, Daddy?"

Her father turned in his chair, and motioned for her to sit down. "I just met with Van. He saw a repair manual on Julius's screen yesterday." He shook his head. "I guess it was inevitable. Anyway, they're asking about technical information."

She chewed her lip. "Daddy, I ran into Van earlier this morning. We talked about, uh, movies. I as much as admitted that there was information in the Lab they didn't know about."

Her father's eyebrows rose.

She was blushing. "It was obvious that he already suspected. I couldn't just … lie." She searched his eyes for forgiveness. "I don't understand the harm."

He sighed. "Honey, it's a matter of stability."

"I'm not sure I understand."

"You will someday."

There it was again.

He was giving her that look. "What, Daddy?"

"You interact with them."

"Nexgens? Sure I do. You know that. Movie-night, game-night, in the *hall* on the way to shower."

He held up his hand. "You misunderstand. I'm not criticizing. Not at all. What I'm getting at is, well—you talk to them. You have a sense of what they're thinking."

She sat back and blinked. She couldn't believe what she was hearing. "Daddy …"

"Yes?"

"Are you asking me to spy on them?"

He flinched. "That's harsh. I'd just like a general notion of, well, their mindset, their mood."

She shook her head slowly. "Daddy, shame on you."

He looked like she'd stabbed him. "It's not like this is unprecedented," he said. "Before the supervisor genie failed, the workers were monitored continuously."

"In the public areas. Not in their quarters."

"I'm not asking you to go into their quarters. God, no."

"And, besides, back then they *knew* they were being watched."

He looked at her beseechingly.

She sighed. "I'm happy to share with you whatever sense I gain in normal activity, but I won't go out of my way to prod them."

He shrugged an okay. "Do what you can, Honey."

She looked at her father sitting there. He was doing his best in a situation he never asked for. A situation he'd woken to every day, hoping it would be the last. But Earth never came. She hated to have any rift, no matter how small, between them.

"I love you, Daddy."

He grinned. "I love you, Pea—uh—Katlin."

She laughed. "You almost remembered." She started to get up, then sat back.

"What is it, Honey?" he asked.

She laughed again. "It was just a couple of days ago that you told me to be careful around them."

He nodded sheepishly. "They took Randy's death better than I expected."

She wiggled her eyebrows. "I think Van kind of likes me."

Her father looked alarmed. "What happened? What did he say?"

"Calm down, Daddy. It's nothing—just that 'sense of mindset' you're so intent that I gather."

He relaxed a little.

"Besides," she added, "you've always promised that when I get married, it will be the biggest party ever seen in Sacramento."

The unspoken assumption was always that her husband was somewhere on Earth.

"I gave Van a lot of Earth material. Hopefully it will keep them satisfied."

"So?"

"So, they're now seeing a whole world—literally, a whole new world—of ideas and culture. They may be jealous once it sinks in you've had access to this material all along."

She smiled. "I understand, Daddy. I'll be careful."

Katlin walked away, thinking it would be nice to have someone to talk to about Earth. Like maybe Van. She grinned to herself. *Don't tell that to Daddy.*

Ж Ж Ж

Van turned when he heard familiar footsteps. "Hey, Tyna. How'd the shift go?"

"Like usual," she said, letting herself fall into the seat next to him. "The sifter jammed, and it took us over an hour to get it free. It's so bent, I don't know if it will survive another one."

"The same one we had trouble with last time?"

"Yeah. Remember it jammed really badly?"

"Oh, I remember. We had to jury-rig the feeder attachment. Meyer never did get Julius to take a look. Did he give you a break?"

"Lord Ops Head said it was our fault. But because he's a reasonable person—his words—he's going to split the difference with us."

"Meaning that he's reducing the harvest quota for this shift by a half-hour?"

"That would be almost reasonable, but, no, the quota remains the same. He's withholding one-sixteenth of the harvest percentage."

"But, with an hour's downtime, you couldn't even *make* quota. There *isn't* any harvest percentage."

"Looks like you picked a good day to take vacation."

"That turd. You want me to talk to him?"

"You think it would make a difference?"

"No. It might ease my guilt, though." He gestured at the screen. "It could be worse," he said. "We could be working the coal mines of England in the eighteenth century. Miners—often children—worked twelve hours a day, and didn't see the sun for months at a time."

She leaned forward to see the screen. "How's that different from us? We never see the sun."

"We only work eight hours a day, and we take vitamin D supplements so we don't develop rickets."

"Why didn't they?"

"They didn't know about vitamins. They didn't even understand the connection between rickets and the sun. The coal mine owners just assumed the miners were naturally prone to all kinds of diseases. England had a class system then, and the aristocracy believed that the lower classes were fundamentally inferior."

"And we don't now? Burl's worried about you, you know."

"How sweet."

"He thinks that anybody who'd take a vacation day to immerse themselves in Earth drivel should visit the psych genie."

"He listens to Glenda talk about her novels."

"He claims that's purely entertainment. You, on the other hand, believe that the Earth drivel is important."

"Where is the sweet man, by the way?"

She glanced around the entertainment room to make sure nobody could hear. "The com shack."

Van snorted. "He's going to get caught. Then both of us will be hanging free."

He automatically used the current expression for sufficient points to deny archiving. Van had found a radio manual buried deep in the Pulitzer Prize-winning book files. He guessed that somebody had accidentally dropped the document there years ago. He should have guessed that Burl wouldn't resist exploring what the contents might reveal about the com equipment.

"I'm going to go check on him," she said, getting up.

Van looked at the volumes and volumes of information still waiting his perusal. "I'd better go with you," he said.

None of them knew why the com shack was called a "shack." It was a small room carved out of the bedrock near the surface that contained the com-link radio equipment. The com-link was what allowed them to talk with each other while they were outside, suited, with Meyer inside. The radio units associated with this limited communication comprised just a small portion of all the equipment in the cramped room, but with no satellite to link to, the rest of it was only so much silicon and metal.

The door was closed when Van and Tyna arrived, and, glancing up and down the hall, they opened it and slipped inside. Burl looked up in alarm, but, seeing it was just them, turned back to the portable screen on his lap where the manual file was displayed. He reached over, adjusted a dial on some racked equipment, lay his hand against the earphones covering his ears a moment, then pulled them off. "I've got reception," he said, looking back and forth at them expectantly.

"What do you mean?" Van asked.

"What do you mean 'what do I mean'? I've got reception. I'm receiving a signal."

Van just stared at him. "Is the next shift outside?"

"I don't think it's ours," Tyna said quietly.

"Thank you," Burl said.

Van just stared. "Not ours," he said. The import was slowly

sinking in. Once the com satellite failed a dozen years ago, there was no longer a reason to listen. There was nothing above them but empty space. "It's … Earth?"

Burl gave him a sidelong glance. "I don't think it's the Mars colony returning." He paused for effect. "Whoever it is, they're not speaking English."

Blaine C. Readler

Chapter 6

Katlin turned a corner and saw Van come out of the com shack. She called to him just as Tyna emerged behind him. The two nexgens glanced at each other, and Van reached over and closed the com shack door.

"Hello, Katlin," he said as she reached them. He was looking at her strangely, as though expecting trouble. Tyna looked on somberly.

"Hi, Van, Tyna," Katlin said. "Is everything okay?"

Van recoiled slightly. "Of course. Why do you ask?"

"I don't know. You seem worried."

He shook his head. "No. Everything's fine."

"Something wrong with the com-links?" she asked, gesturing towards the com shack door.

"No. They're fine," he said, glancing again at Tyna, "Okay, here's the thing, Meyer just came down hard on us for jamming the sifter."

Katlin nodded. "Just now?"

He nodded. "Yeah. I guess we're still recovering."

"I understand," she said. "Hey, listen, I said that I'd get back with you about the Earth information in the Lab—"

"It's okay," he said cutting her off. "I already talked to your father. We, uh, have to go. Come on Tyna," he said and they hurried off.

Katlin watched them until they turned a corner. What to make of it? *Maybe Daddy's right.*

She passed Meyer coming out of her father's office. He didn't say anything, just scowled his usual displeasure at the world. When her father waved her in, she said, "Daddy, you've been with Meyer the last hour, right?"

He sighed. "More like an hour and a half. He's not happy that I gave Van the material."

"Well, it looks like you predicted the outcome pretty well."

"What did I predict?"

"That the nexgens could become jealous of me—what I've had access to all along. I just saw Van and Tyna, and they seemed sullen. Van made up some story about Meyer coming down on them for jamming the sifter."

"I think he did."

"While you were meeting with him?"

"No. Why?"

"Never mind." She waved it off. "Daddy, in the beginning, before the Blast, there was no need for a general library, was there?"

"That's right. We had a continuous link with Earth. Providing local storage would have been redundant."

"Why the Lab library, then?"

He smiled. "Scientists don't trust technology, I guess. We value information, we want to know it's safe and always at hand."

Katlin hesitated, hating to oppose him. "The nexgens' education is basically just the bare minimum required to operate the base."

He frowned. "I wouldn't say that."

"They learn virtually nothing about history—Earth history."

He sat back and clasped his hands across his stomach. "We're working in an emergency mode, honey. We're struggling for survival."

"It's been twelve years, Daddy. When can we finally admit that we're on our own?"

She immediately regretted that. He looked like she'd just thrust a knife into his chest. The belief that Earth would someday return was the only thing, other than perhaps her, that kept him going. "I'm sorry, Daddy. Of course they'll come. It's just a matter of time.

As you always say, they have to first recover from the Blast themselves."

He nodded. He looked tired. "Do you remember your first birthday here on the Moon?"

"Um, barely. I was only turning six." She smiled. She did remember. "You gave me a little stuffed monkey that Louden had made with the material generator." She still had it. It was a precious artifact now that the material generator had degraded to the point where it could only produce rough-weaved cloth, which they then had to cut and sew by hand.

"Do you remember that you cried?"

"No. I cried? Why?"

He grinned at his own memory. "Because you couldn't have ice-cream. You said it wasn't a birthday party without ice-cream."

She shook her head slowly. "No, I don't remember. I guess the bad memories fade more quickly with time."

"But do you see the point I'm making?"

She did. Suddenly. "I wouldn't have missed the ice-cream if I'd never had it. Daddy, are you saying that you've purposefully kept the nexgens ignorant?"

"That's an extreme way of putting it. I would say that I just haven't gone out of my way to show them what they're missing."

"I understand, Daddy," she said, toying with the pocket of her jumpsuit. "I'll have to think about it." Her head snapped up. "Daddy!"

He jumped. "What?"

"You've been educating *me* about Earth—completely!"

He frowned. "That's different."

"How?"

He sighed. "Honey, you're stronger. You can handle it. Besides, you have to be ready."

"And they don't?"

He didn't say anything at first. "Look," he finally said, "you have a place to step into back on Earth. Remember, the nexgens' parents came to the Moon with everything they owned. When they died, their children were left … in limbo."

"They're orphans."

"Exactly."

"They have years of harvest percentage saved up."

"That's true, and that might buy them passage back to Earth. But then what?"

"But, Daddy," she said, treading carefully. "Part of the reason they'll have difficulty is that they know nothing of Earth culture."

He lifted a shrug and held it a moment. "I'm doing what I think is best, Katlin," he said.

It was Katlin, not Honey, or Peaches. She decided to go with just one more probe. "But why hold back technical information about the base as well?"

His face became hard. "They don't have your intellectual level, Katlin, your abilities to comprehend. Partial understanding can be dangerous. They could cause serious damage if they start trying things outside their supervised program. Just today, Meyer told me they caused a serious jam in the sifter because they were messing with it."

They don't understand, because they've never been given the chance, she thought. She'd pushed as far as she could, though. She stood up, bent over, and kissed him on the cheek. "I know you're doing your best, Daddy. We're all lucky that Earth sent you."

As she walked away, however, she couldn't shake the feeling that they'd been inflicting a grave injustice on the children of the Moon immigrants. A thought suddenly struck her, and she stopped and looked back, as though her father might have followed her just so that he could counter the point. She'd been reading about the rise of cotton in the early nineteenth century, how Eli Whitney's invention had essentially ensured the expansive growth of slavery in the south by making cotton a profitable crop. She'd read that it had been a crime to teach a slave to read.

Different century, same reasoning.

ж ж ж

Van tapped Tyna's shoulder and pointed at the sky, and she nodded. All the nexgens knew where to find the dead com satellite among the stars. The tiny point of light remained fixed in position, while the blaze of familiar stars slowly moved in a weeks-long procession from horizon to horizon. Over the course of a year, the suite of constellations paraded in turn—Scorpius, Lupus, Vela, and the distinctive sword and belt of Orion.

Tyna tapped him back, moved her finger in a circle around the direction of the disabled satellite, and made a zero with her thumb and forefinger. She was indicating that there was nothing else there.

They were using hand signals in case Meyer happened to tune in. The ability to limit the com-link channel to speak one-to-one had long ago failed, so everybody on the link heard whatever was said, and Meyer often kept his com box on while working in his office. This wasn't Van and Tyna's shift, and they had no business being outside. Coming out was not allowed unless working, since every cycle through the air lock inevitably lost a tiny but non-zero amount of air to the Moon.

Tyna clutched his arm, and pointed.

He saw it.

Far down on the western horizon another, brighter, point of light was moving slowly away, slipping down over the horizon. An impulse tugged at him, and he looked to the east. Excited, he grabbed Tyna's shoulder and pointed. Rising towards them was yet another, moving so slowly that a quick glance would have mistaken it for just another star. But it was rising inexorably up the black dome, chasing the first one, a skies-width behind.

They gasped together. Up over the crater wall appeared a light so bright, Van imagined that it cast shadows. It hurtled upwards, catching and passing the slow-poke as though it wasn't moving at all. The blazing, awe-inspiring star rose in a straight, smooth line, never wavering in speed or direction, as if tracing a line drawn in the heavens with a perfectly straight edge. Up and over them it raced as they craned their heads to follow. Perhaps three minutes later, it plunged below the horizon to the west.

Van had a memory of Meyer speaking over the com-link. Ops Head had heard their gasp, and had queried the matter, but by now had given up, perhaps assuming it was just another stray burst of noise that plagued the system with increasing frequency.

Tyna motioned, and they headed for the air lock. Van had his hand on the seal at his neck, and ripped off the helmet as soon as the inner door hissed open. "What *was* that?" he exclaimed as Tyna shook out her hair.

Her eyes were wide with the same wonder. "Whoever Burl is

hearing, obviously," she replied.

A flurry of thoughts was bouncing around between Van's ears. Burl had suggested they go outside to see what they could see. What they saw was a miracle.

"What's going on?"

Van yelped in surprise. Katlin stood there, hands on hips.

"Nothing!" Van declared, louder than he'd intended.

Katlin folded her arms across her chest. "You saw something surprising outside, and Burl may be listening to whatever it is. That doesn't sound like nothing."

Van looked at Tyna, who shrugged. "We'd have to tell them sometime," she said. Tyna sucked her lower lip a moment. To Katlin, she said, "How about this. We'll tell you the whole story if you tell your father that it was me who was outside—and also it was me who decided to mess with the radio equipment."

Van started to argue, but Tyna placed her hand across his mouth.

Katlin frowned. "Radio equipment?"

"It's part of the story."

Katlin nodded in understanding. "Van is already hanging free. This might hang you free as well."

"No!" Van insisted, pulling away Tyna's hand.

Tyna sighed. "Will you shut up?" To Katlin, she said, "Well? What do you think?"

Katlin stared a moment, and then nodded. "No promises. Let's hear the story first."

Before they could begin, someone from the next shift walked by, and they moved away. Every time Van began, someone else came around a corner. "Oh, shoot," he said. "Let's go in the com shack."

When Van opened the door, Burl was sitting with his back to them. He turned, and when he saw Katlin, he jumped up, sending his chair clattering.

"She, uh, stumbled on us as we came in," Van explained.

"Actually," Katlin said, "I was looking for you, Van, and Glenda told me that she saw you heading towards the lock."

"You were looking for me?"

He felt his cheeks grow warm.

"That can wait," she said. "So, what's the story?"

Van explained about the wayward radio manual they'd found, Burl's interest in the Earth-link radio, what he'd heard, and his suggestion that he and Tyna go outside and investigate. When Van described the moving lights they'd seen, Burl sputtered with excitement, but, like them, had only questions to offer.

Katlin's eyes were wide with awe, but she was also nodding with understanding. "You know what they were?" Van asked.

Katlin looked him curiously. "You don't?"

Van's warm cheeks grew hot. "No, but I can guess."

He had no clue, but he didn't want to seem completely dense.

"What?" she asked, as he feared she might.

"Spaceships," he said tentatively. "From Earth." Flustered by the tension, he became confused, "Or Mars."

Burl groaned.

"No," Van corrected. He realized his mistake. "Not Mars."

Katlin tried to suppress a grin. "Yes, I expect the ship is from Earth, and this is the most wonderful news we've ever received. Perhaps. We have to figure out what language they're speaking, first."

"Um," Van said, "there are … three ships?"

Katlin seemed deep in thought, and she looked at him in surprise. "Huh? Oh, no. The last one, the bright one, was the ship. It was moving quickly because it was in low orbit. The other two are probably satellites placed in higher orbits by the ship when it arrived. There's probably a handful spread around the Moon."

"What are they for?"

"Communications, I suppose. They can link together and provide continuous coverage to any point on the ground, except, maybe close to the poles."

"Communication? With whom?"

She shrugged. "Somebody on the Moon, obviously."

The com shack settled into silence a moment as that idea seeped into stunned brains. "How do you know this?" Van finally asked.

She looked at him oddly. "Common sense. The lights you saw were obviously objects in orbit."

After a few moments of silence, she said, "You don't know

about orbits, do you?"

"Sure," Burl said. "They're ... circular paths around planets." He thought a moment. "The Moon is in orbit around the Earth," he added confidently.

"You learned that in, what? The third grade?" she asked, and then immediately waved her hand, as though erasing it from a board. "Sorry. This is actually what I was coming to talk to Van about. But that can wait. We need to find out what language they're speaking." To Burl, she said, "Are you still receiving transmissions?"

He practically hurdled back to his chair. "Yeah. It's almost continuous. The reception became crystal clear for just a few minutes." He paused and looked at Van. "I guess that's when the ship was overhead? Maybe ten minutes ago?"

"Yes," Katlin confirmed. "It'll be back in about two hours. Can I listen?" She held her hand out for the earphones.

Burl handed them to her, and she sat down. She leaned her elbows on the table and stared at nothing for many minutes, concentrating, sometimes adjusting the dial. Van whispered into Tyna's ear, saying she couldn't possibly take all the points for this, and Katlin held up her hand and shushed him.

After a couple more minutes, Katlin put the earphones down and turned to them. "He's speaking Mandarin—but he's not Chinese."

"How do you know?" Van asked, surprised at the amount of detail she'd gathered.

"He's speaking with a strong accent. And he's speaking slowly—pausing now and then as he searches for the right words."

"What's he *saying*?" Van asked.

Katlin looked as though she wondered why he would ask such a thing. "I can't *understand* it. I don't speak Chinese."

"How do you know he has an accent?" Burl challenged.

Katlin threw him a cold stare. She didn't like being tested. "The party he's speaking with is obviously native Chinese, and so the comparison is ongoing—the accent is revealed in juxtaposition. It's clear which one is the ship talking, since it's the much stronger signal.

Burl seemed stymied by the precise response. "But, how do you know it's Mandarin?" he challenged, a final, desperate stab.

She glanced around at them, considering. "I've looked through your lesson outlines, and the only history class I found was just broad brushstrokes, the sort of thing you might be taught in fifth grade. It didn't cover anything past the millennium. What do you know about the colonization of the Moon?"

Van looked at his friends and shrugged. "We're it," he said, gesturing around.

Katlin frowned, and shook her head sadly. "There were three original settlements, all based around mining the Moon's resources. The first was established by the EU, and—"

"Eee-what?" Burl asked.

Katlin blinked. "You don't know about the European Union? Hoo-boy. That'll have to wait. Anyway, the first one was set up by a … union of European countries, but it never became profitable, and they shut it down after six years. We—the USA—were the last to arrive, and we learned from the mistakes of the first two."

"Who was the second one?" Van asked.

Katlin looked at them each in turn, preparing the audience. "The second settlement was a Chinese venture, established to mine europium—all the rare earth metals, actually. It was—is—located in the Amici crater, two hundred and fifty kilometers east of us."

"Two hundred and fifty kilometers," Burl muttered, dazed. His eyes popped with understanding. "That's, like, only a hundred and fifty miles!"

Katlin crossed her arms across her chest again. "And that, Burl, is why I'm so confident that it's Mandarin they're speaking."

Her smug grin lost its grip as her arms slowly slid down along her sides, and she stared off at nothing. She looked up at them, as if having forgotten that they were even there.

"Earth has returned," she said, in amazement.

Blaine C. Readler

Chapter 7

Katlin jumped when a box beeped next to her, pulling her out of her amazed reverie. "What's that?" she asked, pointing at the blinking red LED.

"The com-link alarm," Van said, scrambling past her, and flipping a switch. "Van here," he said into the box. "What's the problem?"

Katlin looked questioningly at Tyna. "Somebody outside hit the alarm," Tyna explained. "Meyer will be on any second."

The voice—Katlin recognized it as Kim's—coming from the little box was saying, "... it's maybe a half mile away. It's not moving."

"Can you tell what it is?"

"Hold on. I'll see if I can zoom. It's so dim ... I'm not sure. It looks kind of like our rover, only ... huh, it looks like a silver ball ... with wheels."

Meyer's voice cut in. "What's going on?"

"Fill him in, Kim," Van said. "I'm on my way."

He vaulted to the door and sped away. Burl and Tyna ran after him. Katlin stared at the blinking red light a moment, and then sprinted off after them.

She caught up with them at the lock. Van was already nearly suited, and Burl and Tyna were peeling off their jumpsuits. Katlin felt something odd course through her arms and legs, something visceral she hadn't experienced since she was a child. The sensation came flooding back, nearly overwhelming her. For the first time in years, Katlin was facing something rarely encountered inside the base: adventure.

She went to a locker at the far end of the wall, a locker that she hadn't opened in over a year. From inside, she pulled out her pressure suit, and held it up. She felt a tingle in her stomach. Procedure called for her to pressure-check it, since it hadn't been used in so long. It could malfunction once outside. She would probably die if it did. She unzipped her jumpsuit and began pulling it off.

Meyer had arrived, huffing and puffing, and was giving instructions to Van, who seemed not to be listening. The Ops Head noticed Katlin off to the side. "Just what do you think you're doing, young lady?" he asked.

"I'm going out with them," she answered. She couldn't resist adding, "What does it look like?"

"I don't think so," Meyer said.

"Well, I do think so," she countered, trying to remember the trick to folding the suit so it could be easily pulled up over her knees.

"As Ops Head, I forbid you. At least until your father okays it."

"As Ops Head," she said struggling to pull the inside-out suit over her hips, "you have authority over hourly workers." She stopped and looked up at him. "Which I'm not."

"Hey, Meyer!" Van called from the air lock door. "This could be a momentous moment. I think a Manager should be on hand. You want to come along?"

Meyer glared at him. Neither Meyer nor any of the scientists went outside, not since the Blast. "Genie!" Meyer called into the air. "Give me Cummings." There was no response. "God damn this piece-of-shit base," he muttered as he stalked off.

All three of the nexgens stood waiting, holding their helmets. Tyna and Burl kept glancing at Van. The message was clear, *do we have to wait for her?* "Go ahead and cycle," she said. "I'll follow you."

Van handed his helmet to Tyna and came to help Katlin. His practiced hands pulled this way and that, tugging and twisting her suit until she was finally inserting her arms. "Have you gained weight?" he asked.

"Since I was fourteen when the suit was selected? Yes."

He grinned as he mounted her oxy-pack, and finally handed her the helmet. "Do you know how to put it on?"

She grabbed it from him and pointed at the air lock door. She was trying to appear miffed, but her excitement made it impossible to actually be angry. In fact, she enjoyed the sparring. She often joked around with Louden, but he was—old.

It was a tight fit in the lock with the four of them, and they bumped elbows getting their helmets locked. The three nexgens held up their thumbs one after another, and Katlin realized they were indicating they were ready. She jabbed her thumb into the air, even though she wasn't at all sure she was really, truly ready. Van lifted the safety cover, and jabbed the big red button, and Katlin heard the air pump thump to life. The sound quickly diminished, since the air that carried it was thinning, pulled away, back into the base. Simultaneously, her suit stiffened, and she felt the joint braces pressing around her knees, elbows, and shoulders. She worked her gloves, getting used to the constant force needed to move any finger. The whole effect was one of constriction and a loss of fine motor control. A tinge of panic crept in—claustrophobia, she guessed. She'd felt it each of the half dozen or so times she'd cycled through the lock, and, like each time before, she breathed deeply, calming herself. *They do this every day—day in, and day out.*

The outer door slid silently open, revealing a small swarm of bright pinpoints of light in the lunar blackness, the illumination of the platform shift operating a quarter mile away. The light in the lock dimmed and disappeared, and Katlin's eyes quickly adjusted until she could make out the contours of Moon rubble in the starlight. She was surprised that Kim had seen the alien object in the distance at all, and then remembered that she would have been using infrared. The Moon's surface slowly cooled to -240 degrees Fahrenheit over the course of the two-week lunar night, but the sensitive infrared viewer could still detect temperature differentials, particularly for metal equipment that would cool at a much faster rate.

The ground in front of her suddenly glared in stark contrast as Van flipped on his helmet lights, one at each temple. He turned to her, watching the ground. He reached up, still not looking at her, and tapped her arm, then pointed to the side of his head. Katlin knew why he watched the ground, it was simply to keep from blinding her. But what did he want? He tapped his temple again, with demonstrative sweeps of his hand.

Why doesn't he just tell me? she wondered, until she realized that she hadn't enabled her com-link connection. This was exactly what he was trying to tell her. She was glad he wasn't looking at her face, since she was sure she was blushing.

She reached up, and, clumsily, with stiff, resisting fingers, worked the display controls on her faceplate until Burl's voice was suddenly talking into her ears. "... she can catch up with us when she finally figures it out," he was saying.

"I've figured it out," she said. "It's been over a year," she added in defense.

"We're well aware of that," Burt replied.

She resisted taking the bait, and was relieved when Van took control. "Okay, let's go. Katlin, I'm sorry, but you'll probably fall behind. Any other time, we'd wait for you, but ..."

"No," she said. "Absolutely. Don't wait. Go!"

"Nobody gets left behind!" Meyer's voice commanded. "Somebody stay with her."

Katlin waved them silently away, and after a moment's hesitation, they were gone, three spots of light dancing away.

She was left in darkness, and, after a few more fumbling minutes, figured out how to turn on her own helmet lamps. She took off after the receding waltz of lights. She managed as well as anybody else in the one-sixth Moon gravity indoors. Now, however, not only was she wrestling against a protective cocoon that carried along a bit of Earth environment wherever she wanted to go, but she wasn't adept at the form of long-hop locomotion the nexgens used when not confined by walls and doorways. Although made with super-strong plastic, her faceplate could conceivably crack given a sharp enough blow, so Katlin erred on the side of caution and proceeded along in the short, loping gate she was used to indoors.

Along the way, she listened to the excited exchanges between Granden, the nexgen shift supervisor out on the platform, and Van.

The imperious directives from Meyer were mostly ignored. When she arrived at the platform, Van, Burl, and Tyna had already continued on, and the platform shift—twelve nexgens ranging in age from sixteen to Granden, the eldest at eighteen—stood with heads tilted down, watching her through the tops of their faceplates. They held up their hands to shield their eyes from her bright lamps, looking like a dozen shamed sea creatures. "Sorry!" she said, and turned away, following the others towards the alien visitor.

After a few minutes, the rhythmic dancing of the receding lights changed pattern, swinging back and forth, up and down. They'd obviously reached the machine. Katlin hurried her pace, risking a fall and loss of air. She hated the idea that she might be missing something vital—momentous, as Van had sarcastically suggested.

As she got closer, the swinging lights of the three nexgens revealed in flashing strobes the details of the "thing." It was indeed mostly a large ball as Kim had guessed, and did have wheels—six, if the far side matched the three Katlin could see. Their own defunct rovers had four oversized wheels, but an extra set in the middle allowed for better negotiation of uneven terrain.

Closer still, Katlin began to see that this vehicle, for that was clearly what it was, had seen better days. Because lunar soil is electrically charged, the dust sticks to everything, and it was an annoyance they were used to (each pressure suit included a thigh pocket containing a special cloth to wipe their faceplates without scratching), but the bulbous main compartment of this odd conveyance was caked with it. Machinery used on the Moon's surface required regular cleaning, since otherwise the microscopic dust eventually found its way past even the best seals, and once it reached moving parts, it acted as an abrasive, quickly destroying the mechanism. Without spare parts, the machine was done.

What she initially took to be a small dome on top of the ovoid cabin turned out to be just the tip of an equipment pack, probably a radio, that had sunk down into the flexible surface of the compartment as internal pressure was lost.

The vehicle was a deflating balloon.

Katlin was familiar with the concept. The main compartment could be formed from very light material—cheaper to ship from

Earth—and its shape formed by the pressure of the air inside. The lunar landers of the early Apollo missions were hardly more than inflated metal foil balloons. The downside, of course, was that the thinner, lighter material was susceptible to puncturing. This was why the engineers who developed their Daedalus base had chosen a more robust, if more expensive, rover cabin.

Van had already climbed a short ladder and was peering inside through narrow, smudged windows. Beneath the dirt and dust, the compartment material was silvered. That, and the narrow windows, spoke of a craft meant to be outside during the lunar day, an odd and troubling idea.

Van twisted his head back and forth, swinging his beams around the interior. "There's four of them. They're not wearing suits. They, uh … they look dead."

"Kim saw somebody flashing a light," Tyna said.

"Maybe it was an automatic indicator."

"Or a reflection," Burl added. "They could have been here for days without us noticing."

"It was a light," Kim cut in on the com-link. "I'm sure of—"

"Can you tell the nationality?" Katlin's father's voice was loud and clear. The command console in Meyer's office overrode all other conversations.

"They, uh, they look Asian, I guess. It's hard to tell."

Katlin had already reached up to wipe away the dust on different surfaces she could get at. "They're Chinese," she declared, finding some writing. "At least, this rover thing is. I think the Han characters say 'People's Republic of China.'"

"Katlin?" her father asked.

"Yes?"

"You're out there? At the intruder?"

"Yes. I wouldn't exactly call it an intruder—"

"I want you to come back. Now."

"Daddy, I—"

"Now. That's an order. Van, please escort her back."

He turned to look at her from his position perched on the ladder, and held up his hands in apology, then started down.

Katlin grinned. "Ow!" she cried. "Van, leave me alone!"

Van turned to look at her, and she held up the tip of her finger to where her mouth would be located inside her helmet.

After a moment, he nodded. "You heard your father," he said roughly from his perch. "You have to return."

"I'm … not … going," she growled, pretending to be struggling.

"Sir," Van said. "I'm afraid I may damage her suit if I continue."

The com-link was silent for a moment. "Katlin," her father finally said, "I'm asking you to please come back."

"I will, Dad—sir. Soon. I can be useful here in the meantime."

She heard him breath in, and then out. "Van," he finally said, "I'm counting on you to make sure she doesn't do anything dangerous."

"Yes, sir. I will."

"The batteries are dead," Burl announced from the back of the vehicle, where the drive mechanism was mounted. He wiped away some dust. "The temperature of their core is minus eighty. But that's centigrade—that's uh …"

"About minus one-hundred and ten Fahrenheit," Katlin said.

"Right. Let's see. One-ten. I'd say this rover has been here about eight hours."

"They almost made it," Tyna said.

"You think they were heading for us?" Van asked as he climbed back up to continue peering inside.

"Where else?"

"The chances that they weren't, and just happened to stop here," Katlin said, "aren't even worth considering. It's pretty clear they were coming to us."

"I wonder why," Tyna said. "I wonder if it has anything to do with …"

"With what?" Katlin's father asked.

The jig's up. "Sir," Katlin said, "we were picking up transmissions from a ship in orbit just as Kim's call came in. We're pretty sure they were speaking Chinese."

A breathless moment of silence, and then her father said, "What transmission? What 'we'? What in God's name are you talking about?"

Katlin saw all helmets turn to look at her. "I … I fired up the

Earth link radio. I, uh, had this crazy idea that some Earth transmissions might be bouncing off the dead com satellite." Burl was running his finger back and forth across the neck of his helmet, trying to tell her that the idea was nuts. She already knew that but she didn't have time to come up with anything plausible. "I asked Burl to help me," she added.

"I, uh, *told* her it was nuts," Burl said, playing along.

Another a moment of tense silence. "A *ship?*" Katlin's father said. "You *heard* it?"

"We, um, also saw it," Van said.

"When?" her father asked, incredulous.

"Tyna and I went outside. After Katlin and Burl started receiving transmissions."

Silence. "Why didn't you tell me? How long ago did all this happen?"

"It all happened so fast," Katlin cut in. "Just minutes before Kim's call. In fact, that was just about the time that Van said we needed to fill you in."

That came out of nowhere. She was a little surprised at her own fib.

"Hey!" Van suddenly yelled. "One of them moved!"

Katlin ran to the base of the ladder, joining Tyna and Burl. Five feet above them, Van peered intently through the window. "I swear," he said. "I saw one of them move his hand—there! He did it again. He's turning his head. Uh, it's actually a woman." Van turned to look down at them. "We have to do something!"

"Van," Katlin said, trying to sound calm. "You said they have no suits on."

He cursed under his breath. "That's right. No suits."

Katlin's father spoke. "I'm sorry. Katlin's right. There's nothing you can do."

"We have to just let them *die?*" Tyna said.

The com-link was filled with the silence of the uncaring universe.

Chapter 8

Katlin put her hand on Tyna's shoulder. The frustration of the moment was almost unbearable. She had an urge to climb the ladder and look inside. *If I do, the mental image will haunt me the rest of my life.*

"There has to be something we can do," Tyna insisted.

"Their batteries are dead, they're out of air, and they have no suits," Burl said. "It's terrible, I agree. The truth sucks."

"There *has* to be something," Tyna repeated, peering underneath the Chinese rover as though there might be something they'd missed.

"It's not possible to get them out," Katlin's father said. "You should all come back. We need to contact that ship in orbit."

"You want us to just leave them?" Tyna said, her voice rising in volume. "They've seen us. They'll die knowing that somebody came, and then abandoned them."

"Van," Katlin's father said. "Bring everybody back."

His voice was all authority, but Katlin knew that he was as heartbroken as the rest of them. This was his CTO persona speaking.

"I'm not leaving," Tyna stated.

"I'm staying as well," Katlin said, surprising herself again.

Her father cursed, softly, the words coming clearly over the com-link.

"Winch them."

That was Kim's voice. She'd broken protocol. Unless there was an urgent matter, workers on shift kept their silence. Otherwise, the com-link became jammed with colliding conversations.

What could be more urgent than people slowly asphyxiating?

"The winch cable is only a couple hundred feet long," Burl said. "Wait, I see. Maybe we could haul it in segments."

Katlin was generally familiar with the winch. They used it to reposition the platform. It was certainly powerful enough. "But it goes so slow," she said.

"It has multiple speeds," Burl replied with an edge of impatience. "The power is reduced proportionally at the highest speed, but this thing can't weigh more than a small fraction of the platform—"

"And it has wheels," Tyna said.

"I was getting to that," Burl barked. "Even at the highest speed, the winch will have more pull than that dinky rover motor they've been using."

"Kim," Van said, "bring the winch."

"Already on my way," she answered.

"Hold it!" came Meyer's voice on the link. "Kim, who gave you permission to leave your post? Van's not the supervisor of this shift."

"Oh, come on, Ops Head," Van said. "You're not going to stand on protocol at a time like this—"

"Quiet, Van. Kim, acknowledge."

The com-link was silent. Katlin wanted to say something—Meyer shouldn't be concerned about the loss of product, not with people's lives at stake—but suspected that anything she said would just confuse the situation and delay any rescue attempt.

Kim finally spoke. "Van, what should I do?"

"I told you," Meyer warned, "Van is not the supervisor—"

"Ops Head, *please!*" Van exclaimed. "Just one second. Kim, Ops Head is right. He has ultimate authority. You know that people's lives are at stake. It's your choice. It will almost certainly mean points for you. We could be there in five minutes to get the winch."

Nothing but heavy breathing. Katlin realized that it was Kim—she hadn't stopped transporting the winch. The device was self-propelled, but it required somebody to walk along behind, guiding it with two handle bars, and over the years it had gotten cranky, and needed serious manhandling to keep it on course.

"I estimate my ETA in five minutes," Kim said.

They had her answer.

"Van," Meyer said, "tell her to get back to her station."

"Can't do that, Ops Head. Tyna, go and meet her. She'll need help. Burl, what are you doing back there?"

Burl had opened up two different compartments at the rear of the rover, and was rummaging around.

"I need a wrench."

"What for?"

"This thing's in gear. We won't move it an inch if I can't disconnect the drive—"

"I can have someone run one out—"

"Here! I found it."

Katlin was impressed with Van. She'd never had a chance to watch him in his role as crew leader. "What can I do?" she asked.

"Katlin—right. Uh, tell you what, step off around two-hundred feet in their direction. They'll need to know where to plant the winch. I'll try to figure out how to get into the rover's compartment. We'll need to know that the minute we get air back into the hanger."

Katlin started off, counting as she went. She guessed that each step was about two and a half feet. This wasn't accurate at all. She'd have to err on the short side.

"Katlin," her father said over the com-link. "They don't really need you there. Why don't you come back?"

She didn't answer. *This isn't the time to get distracted by petty anger.*

"Katlin? You there?"

"Yes, sir," she finally said through gritted teeth. "I'm here. Despite expectations I am helping." *Okay, I failed.* "Let's leave it up to Van."

"Of course she's useful," Van said, running his hands slowly along the bottom of the bubble compartment.

That's all he offered, but her father didn't press it, so she put it aside. "Sixty-nine, seventy," she counted to herself, and stopped. The swinging, bobbing lights of Tyna and Kim were approaching.

From the position of their lamps, it looked like they'd each taken one of the handles.

"Katlin," Tyna said.

"Yes?"

"Your light."

"What about it?"

"It's in our *eyes.*"

"Oh!" she said, swinging her head down. "Sorry."

She cursed herself. *I'm not doing much to prove Daddy wrong.*

As Tyna and Kim arrived, the knife sharp shadows cast by Katlin's light softened, and the area around them glowed with a diffused light. One wheel and then the other of the winch spun as it momentarily lost traction on the uneven ground, kicking up a small cloud of dust, each tiny particle catching and reflecting the light from their lamps. They halted the winch next to Katlin, and seconds later, the shadows were knife-sharp again.

Without a word, Tyna and Kim began planting the anchor stakes that would hold the winch in place. "Shall I carry the cable to the rover?" Katlin asked, praying it wasn't a dumb thing to suggest.

"Yes," came Van's voice. "Do it. I'll meet you."

Katlin had never used the winch, and she couldn't see at first how to release the cable. "You need help?" Tyna asked.

"No, I've got it," Katlin said. *Judas! Where's the release?*

Kim's foot reached over and kicked down a lever on the side, and Katlin felt the cable come free. She wanted to thank her, but that would give away her lie. She grabbed the heavy hook and started off towards Van's approaching lights.

"It's nearly a mile back to base," Kim's voice said.

"Yeah," Van said. "Maybe three-quarters."

"That's, uh, about twenty spans of the winch."

Moving the winch twenty times. Twenty times replanting it, and hauling the rover another fraction of the distance, Katlin thought. It was going to take forever.

"Sounds right," Van said.

"I'm not sure the batteries have enough juice," Kim said. "In fact, I'm sure they don't."

Van was quiet a moment. "We have some time. Maybe we arrange some sort of auxiliary setup. I'll think about it."

The winch's batteries were probably unique, and making some sort of adapter would take more time than they had.

Since nobody else jumped in, she took a chance. "Maybe if we pushed, we could save some battery power."

The silence that followed made her heart sink. She met Van and handed him the cable hook. He said, "Pushing will save battery juice?"

"Sure. The less work the winch motor has to do, the less electricity it will need to draw."

"She's right," Burl said. "I'm just not sure how much pushing will help."

"We won't know 'till we try," Van said. "Every little bit helps. Good suggestion, Kat."

Smiling, she helped Van pull the cable to the rover. Long ago her father had let her join the rest of the kids at the workers' day-school. Kat had been her nickname there, but nobody had called her that in years. She had cried when her father wouldn't let her go anymore, after the Blast. Now she thought she understood his reasoning, at least a part of it. A week after the Blast, after each of the parents died, one after another, he'd been suddenly left in charge of dozens of pre-school children. At some point—maybe then, maybe months later—he'd decided that their education would be focused. No, the truth was that it had been limited. *Don't show them what they're missing.* She, on the other hand, was being prepared for re-entry to Earth life. It wouldn't do to have her mingling with the other kids, where she would be constantly demonstrating what she knew, and they didn't. From that day forward, her contact with nexgens had been tightly controlled.

She wondered how much Meyer had influenced her father in his decision to keep the nexgens so much in the dark. Ignorant cotton plantation slaves were thought to be more docile. Ignorant nexgens might be equally—

"Okay, Katlin," Van said.

"Oh! Sorry," she said, letting go of the cable. They had reached the rover. She watched Van attach the hook to a ring on the rover that was obviously intended for just such a purpose. He turned to look at her. "I thought you were going to push?"

"Yeah! Right!"

She walked around the three large wheels as Van told Kim and Tyna to engage the winch, first at low speed, and then if all went well, to maximum. By the time Katlin reached the rear, the rover was already inching forward. Then it began moving faster. Even with the winch pulling at full speed, Katlin only had to step forward every few seconds to keep up. Waltzing couples could have danced circles around it.

The rear of the rover was a large sloping cowling, a covering to keep Moon dust at bay. She planted her hands on it, pushed, and felt her feet slide away beneath her. This was a perennial problem on the Moon. At one-sixth Earth gravity, she weighed just twenty pounds, and even with the cleats on her pressure suit boots, twenty pounds wasn't nearly enough to dig a grip into the dust and rubble.

She tried again, and again her feet slipped away. The sloping cowling provided no way to push *up*, so that her feet pushed *down*.

"Having problems?" Burl asked, coming around the side with a wrench in his hand.

"Only if the goal is to push the rover."

"Here," he said, brushing her away with a sweep of his arm.

She stepped back, ready to smirk when he tried and failed. However, he reached underneath the lip of the cowling, fiddled a moment, and then lifted a cover—the one he'd had open earlier. Lifted, the lower edge of the cover hovered at chin level. He motioned her over, and together they pushed up against the cover. She felt her cleats dig firmly into the ground, but before she had a chance to push forward, the cover bounced up, and she lost her grip. Burl had been a little quicker.

Katlin positioned herself again, and this time it was Burl who staggered.

"Hold it," she said. "On three." She waited until he was ready. "One-two-*three!*"

The cover lifted a few inches, and they pushed off, stepping forward in sync. They managed five full steps before Katlin's feet lost their grip, and the dual-engine human motor disengaged.

"That's great!" Van said from up front. "Keep it up."

Wordlessly, Burl nodded to Katlin, and they took their positions. This time she just nodded the countdown—no need to clutter up the com-link continuously. Before long, they were managing a dozen steps and more before losing traction and re-positioning. Katlin had just started another push, when she saw something wriggle in the dust beneath her feet. It looked like the snakes she'd watched on the lesson videos. This was deeply puzzling, but not frightening, since an actual animal on the Moon was impossible. "The winch cable!" she exclaimed, understanding at last. They were outrunning the electric motor.

"You're heading off too much to the left," Van said. "Turn to the right."

Katlin looked at Burl. "You're obviously pushing harder. Here, switch places."

Soon, she saw dancing lights pass them by. It was Tyna and Kim at the winch. "You're ruining my great idea," Kim said, but there was humor in her voice.

After another minute, Van muttered, "Oh, crimps. Hold it, guys. I have to unhook the cable. You're dragging the winch. Also, now you're heading too far to the right."

Katlin had another idea. "Kim, can you detach the cable from the winch drum?"

"Sure," she replied. "Why?"

"Van," Katlin said, "you could go out ahead with the cable and lead us. You should be able to keep the front of the rover nudged in the right direction."

"Ah!" he said. "Brilliant, Kat."

"Watch it," Burl muttered. "It'll go to her head."

Katlin was tired and breathless as they resumed their coordinated tugboat roles, but she was smiling. This was a whole new experience, sharing a struggle with her peers.

The euphoria didn't last long. "Van, Katlin," her father's voice said, "check to make sure they're still alive."

"Why?" Katlin asked breathing hard.

"Think about it. This could be a problem. It could all be for nothing, and we could end up with a Chinese rover at our base full of dead Chinese. We'd have to answer for it. If you leave it where it is now, well, then we'd done our best to save them, but it was just too late. Nobody could blame us."

"Daddy—uh, sir," she said, "I don't understand. Why would anybody blame us just because we made it to the base, and they still all died?"

The com-link was silent a moment. "They would ask why we dragged the rover to the base, and left their countrymen inside."

"I still don't understand—"

"Sir," Van cut in, "let's talk about this later. We're bringing the rover in."

It was a flat statement. Van must be past worrying about his points.

"Kat," Van said. "You want to be spelled?"

"No," she replied with barely enough breath to speak. "I'm fine."

"How about me?" Burl asked.

"You want a break?" Van asked.

"No. I just wanted you to ask."

On and on they pushed the disabled rover. Keeping it moving, while maintaining a grip in the soil took a skill that she and Burl quickly learned. The slips and re-starts became farther and farther apart, and before long, they were pressing forward minutes at a time, sometimes only stopping to let one of them re-position their hands. From Van's occasional mutterings, she gathered that he was struggling just to keep ahead of them.

"How's your air, Kat?" Van asked.

"Fine," she replied.

She didn't really know, since the indicator on her suit had apparently failed at some point, but she figured that worrying about that now was just a distraction.

As they pressed on, Katlin watched the Moon glide away beneath her feet, every step representing a slightly improved chance that the people inside might be saved. Her breathing became the song of their rescue, long, deep intakes, storing power, and then blowing out, her breath pushing the car forward.

Out with the bad air, in with the good. With each breath, her lungs became bigger and bigger. More air to push the stagecoach. She wondered what happened to the horses. No matter. They had to get the coach to town. She and her cowboy partner, Van. No, it wasn't Van. It was Burl. Big, bad, outlaw Burl.

An annoying bird was flapping around her head, pestering her about air. She guessed that the bird must be a parrot, since it was talking. It must be Van's parrot. It was talking just like him. The parrot used its wings to grab her wrists. *Stupid parrot.* A huge bubble loomed in front of her. Somebody had cut off Burl's head and placed it inside. How sad. How strange—his head wasn't even dead. The eyes blinked, the mouth moved. It said, "Oh, yeah! She's done!"

I'm done, she thought. That actually sounded quite good. Done with pushing, done with worrying. Done. Done with everything. The only thing left was sleep.

She closed her eyes.

Blaine C. Readler

Chapter 9

"Dammit!" Van exclaimed. "What do you mean she's 'done'?"

"Done," Burl said. "Finished. Kaput. Either she's out of air, or she's had a stroke."

Van dropped the end of the cable and ran towards the stopped rover. "Katlin!" he shouted. "Can you hear me?"

"What the hell is happening out there?" Zeedo asked.

"Have the lock ready," Van said. "We're bringing her in."

Burl was already around the rover, carrying the stricken woman like Gort carrying Helen back to the flying saucer. Van grabbed her feet, and Burl slid his hands under her shoulders. They took off, side-hopping towards the base air lock just a couple of hundred yards ahead. She'd almost made it. "I should have guessed," Van said, "that she'd use more air than the rest of us. On top of that, all this exertion—"

"Van," Burl said in warning.

He knew what Burl meant. Zeedo and Meyer would be listening. No sense making a complete public confession.

Off to the right, a whole herd of swaying lights were heading towards the rover. The shift workers had given up all pretense of making product, and were coming to see the alien machine. As Van and Burl reached the protruding face of the base, Tyna was greeting the first arrivals, feeding quick instructions about taking up the transporting task.

Zeedo had somehow convinced the lock genie to open the outer door—a happy surprise—and Van dropped Katlin's feet so that they could squeeze her in with them. Van grasped the seal around her neck, and as soon as the green light came on, he unzipped it, and pulled up her helmet. He felt for her carotid artery. "She's okay," he said, based solely on the fact that he found a pulse, not mentioning that it was about 150 beats per minute.

The inner door slid open, and Zeedo pulled Burl roughly out, and then grabbed Katlin by her arms. "Honey! Peaches! Can you hear me?"

Her eyelids fluttered, and she opened her eyes, but then shut them again.

Zeedo drew her gently out, and gave her a quick hug before handing her off to Meyer. "Get her to the infirmary and on oxygen," he said. "Help him," he told Burl.

Zeedo then turned to Van, who was removing his own helmet. He'd never seen the CTO so livid. He shoved Van's chest so that he fell back against the wall. "That's going to cost you another five points, mister," he spat. "Hell, *ten* points. You were responsible for her."

"Look, sir," he said, unnerved by the base leader's intense anger, "she's okay. It was just a few minutes, and she wasn't completely out of air—she's not even convulsing. But we have people outside in real danger."

Van was still holding his helmet, and Tyna must have heard him, since her tiny voice inside the open helmet said, "We're almost at the hanger. Open the door!"

Zeedo took Van's helmet from his unyielding hands, flipped off the com-link, and set it aside.

"You never intended to open the hanger, did you?" Van asked.

He shook his head solemnly.

"That's why you didn't want us to bring the Chinese rover in."

The man's haunted eyes were answer enough.

"It's because of the weak evac pump, isn't it?"

Zeedo nodded. "Of course. Julius tells me it can only get the hanger pressure down to one-tenth PSI. We can't afford to lose that much air. That's thirty thousand cubic feet."

"It's *air*! These are *people*!"

"I'm responsible for *my* people, and air means life."

"We can recover the oxygen."

Zeedo shook his head. "Not without the excavation robots."

"*We* can do it."

"How? Are you going to give up your sleep? Without the robots, it would take years to recover the lost oxygen. Look, Van, I feel terrible about this, but I'm the one that has to make the decision."

The base leader was obviously feeling torn. But that comment about giving up sleep—"You'd expect us to keep up the production, wouldn't you?"

Zeedo shrugged. That went without saying.

"You're trading the lives outside for platinum."

He just looked at Van. The remorse in his eyes had turned to steely resolve.

Just then Burl returned. "She's fine," he reported. "She has a headache, but who doesn't after being outside for a shift ... ? Uh, looks like I'm interrupting something."

"Our CTO refuses to open the hanger door," Van said, keeping his gaze on Zeedo. "He doesn't want to give up precious air."

Burl nodded slowly, understanding. "That damn evacuation motor. It came up during last year's full-base equipment checkout. It's been on Julius's list ever since. Who knew that we'd need it—"

"You can give me all the points you want," Van said, making up his mind. He turned to Burl. "You up for some points?"

Burl grinned. "Sure. Risk is the spice of life."

Zeedo looked back and forth at them. "You're bluffing."

Van picked up his helmet and waved for his friend to follow. "Let's do it."

As they walked away, Zeedo called out, "This is beyond points! You're about to commit a felony crime. You'll be locked up!"

Burl waited until they were out of earshot to remark, "Locked up and not working the platform sounds great. Why didn't we think of something like this before?"

Van didn't answer. He was bubbling with emotion. Defying Zeedo was shaking his world. The man represented stability built on authority. Their disobedience could do irreparable damage to the order and security of the base, the only world Van knew.

Burl was still carrying his helmet, and he held it up to listen. "Tyna wants to know what the hell the holdup is," he reported.

Van took the helmet and spoke into it, "We're on our way."

When they reached the hanger, Van flipped on the lights, revealing the familiar meeting area that would soon be exposed to the raw vacuum of the Moon. It occurred to him that there were things stored there that might be damaged by vacuum—plastic containers could explode, for example—but he shoved the thought aside. Nothing in the room was worth a life.

Burl had stepped out into the inner receiving area, and was pushing boxes out of the way to free up the inside doors, which had never been closed in their memory, and Van helped him. It took them a minute to figure out how to release the doors from their restraining latches, pull them closed, and lock them tight, forcing the seals around the perimeter against mating surfaces. After nineteen years, the material of the seals was etched with fine cracks and imperfections. Anybody on the other side was going to hear the scream of air whistling through. So be it.

"Inner hatch doors are secure," the hanger genie announced.

Burl looked at Van. They'd never heard that before.

As Van shoved boxes and chairs out of the way to make room for the rover, Burl opened the control panel—again a first in memory—and studied the indicators. "Genie!" he called out. "Are you able to evacuate?"

"I am ready," she said. "All persons must be secure in pressure suits before I can begin."

She could see that their helmets were lying together on the floor. They picked them up, put them on, and held their thumbs up for her to see. Her voice now appeared over the com-link. "I am ready, pending failsafe confirmation."

Burl turned and looked at Van through his faceplate, and Van shrugged. "What's that, genie?" Burl asked.

"Failsafe confirmation is a requirement that a human must perform a specific mechanical step in order to ensure committed intention—"

"No. I mean, how do I do it?"

"It would break protocol for me to tell you."

"Oh, crimps!" Burl muttered as he peered at the control panel.

Van stepped over, and pointed at a green button.

Burl placed his faceplate against the panel and leaned in to see. "You mean the one labeled 'failsafe' in tiny letters?" He reached up, flipped open the clear plastic cover, pushed the button, and stepped back.

Nothing happened.

"Genie?" Burl inquired.

"The lockout has been engaged."

"What lockout? All I did was push the green button labeled—"

"This is an override accessed from the inner chamber."

"Who did that?"

"Doctor Cummings."

"*Dammit!*" Van cried. "I'm opening the inner doors," he told the genie, as he shoved aside the handle and pushed the heavy door outward.

Zeedo stood there staring at him resolutely. "I told you," he said.

His voice came through muffled by the helmet, giving Van the impression that the man was some distance off instead of right there in front of him. His presence was real enough, though, when Van pushed him back against the wall. Burl grabbed Van's arm before he could take a swing. Van jerked his friend's grip free, but before he could punch Zeedo, he heard Meyer shout. His boss came running, holding something out in front of him in both hands. Van couldn't make out at first what it was.

"He has a *gun!*" Burl cried, stepping back in surprise.

His friend was right. Van had only ever seen them in the movies, but this was unmistakably one. It looked like the marker guns they used on the platform, but this one had a hole in the barrel large enough for a bullet instead of a thin laser beam.

"Leave him alone!" Meyer yelled, stopping twenty feet away with the gun pointed at Van's chest. Meyer didn't exude confidence, and might fire the gun by accident. The danger didn't overwhelm Van. In nineteen years, the thought of being shot had never once crossed his mind. It was something that happened to actors in movies, like being attacked by spider-like aliens. For his whole life, vacuum had been the only real danger.

As he walked towards Meyer with clenched fists, Van knew the gun might fire, but the consequence of a bullet passing through his body was abstract, while his anger was very real. He saw fear grow in Meyer's eyes. He'd probably never considered a nexgen attacking him. The gun began to shake, and Van guessed that it would go off any moment. And then it did.

Even through his helmet, the explosion was shocking, stopping Van in his tracks. He wondered if the bullet had gone through him. In the movies, the actors played as though it was a traumatic experience, their faces twisting in agony. They either doubled over in pain, or dropped dead on the spot. He didn't feel anything, though. He guessed that the bullet had missed him completely.

Meyer seemed surprised that the gun had gone off. This didn't deter him, however, and he held it out farther with straight arms, aiming squarely at Van's torso. "I'll do it!" he shouted. "Believe me!"

Van did believe him, and it finally dawned on him that he could be killed any second. Furious, he took a step back to show his acceptance.

"No!"

It was Katlin's distant, muted shout.

She was running down the hallway. Her hair, normally layered in tight, overlapping curls, was jumbled from sweat and her helmet. It was a rough-and-tumble Katlin he'd never seen before. She could have been a nexgen.

"Get out of here!" Zeedo yelled. "Now!"

She shook her head, as she arrived, breathless. "You can't let them die out there," she said, sucking deep breaths.

"I have no *choice*!" Zeedo wailed, as though it was just a matter of them hearing what he was saying.

"But you do, Daddy," she said more calmly. She glanced around, and her eyes fell on a prominent red switch on the wall. The label beneath it read *emergency lock*. She nodded to Van, and gestured toward the open inner doors as she walked over to the switch.

Van glanced at Burl, and they trotted off into the hanger.

"Don't!" Zeedo called, but Katlin ignored him, and flipped the switch back up.

As Van pulled the door closed once more, he heard her tell her father that lost air didn't matter anymore. Earth had arrived.

What is Earth? Van wondered, though, as he secured the door latch and turned to give Burl the thumbs up to once again push the failsafe button. They'd always equated Earth with America. But what was the ship in orbit? Not American. Presumably Chinese. If so, why had the men in this Chinese rover set out on such a risky journey, a gamble with the odds strongly against them?

All of that would have to wait. Right now they needed to get the rover inside. Hopefully, answers would follow.

He heard a *clunk*, and then the whoosh of air being drawn from the room.

"Can I get an update?" Tyna asked after a minute of silence.

"The hanger's evacuating," Van replied.

"It will take about eight minutes," came Meyer's steady, no-nonsense voice, as though nothing had happened, as though this was just a routine exercise. He must have returned to his office where he could monitor things.

"Eight *minutes*—" Tyna started, but cut herself off. She knew there was nothing else they could do.

Van watched the clock on the wall as it crawled along its endless sequence of seconds. His suit stiffened slowly, a different sensation from the bathroom-sized personnel lock, where the joints practically popped in the sucking outrush of air. The whooshing sound diminished along with the thinning air.

After just five minutes, Meyer came back on. "You might as well open up. That motor isn't going to draw much more. Genie, lock tight," he instructed.

"Locked tight," she reported, indicating that she'd closed the outlet valve, preventing air from rushing back in.

Burl was at the outer door, hanging onto the handle with one hand and leaning inward. There were no latches to release—the air pressure in the base normally held the large, braced doors solidly closed with over fifty tons of force. Burl's leaning demonstrated that the evacuation motor had indeed not completed its job. The meager remnant atmosphere still mashed the doors closed with over a thousand pounds of pressure.

Van knew the answer to this one. The little round portal near the side of the door had always intrigued him. The label underneath read simply, *flush*. He'd never imagined he'd ever use it. Only one foot in diameter, the little door was held closed by just ten pounds of pressure now. He pulled aside the safety arm and tugged at the portal, but it didn't budge. "Genie," he said, "is the little flush door unlocked?"

"I have no control over that," she replied.

"It might just be stuck," Burl said. "Eighteen years is a long time."

Van braced his feet against the large hanger door, and gave a good tug. The door swung open, causing Van to lose his balance and fall backwards. From the floor he watched as the door swung closed, then slammed shut. Burl held it open while the last of the air exited into the lunar darkness.

Suddenly a face appeared in the opening. "You finally ready?" Tyna asked.

"The hanger door seals are probably stuck as well," Van said, getting up. "Tyna, push from the outside, while Burl and I pull."

The bottom corners gave way, and from there, they worked the seals open along the rest of the perimeter. Swinging open the fifteen foot-high doors was like merging the two worlds that had always been kept carefully separate. The base contained no windows. Despite the bright lights inside the hanger, the stars shone crystal sharp in the night sky beyond. The scene was deeply surrealistic, and Tyna broke the spell by waving her hand in front of his faceplate. "You fall asleep?" she asked.

He shook his head, and tried to ignore the disquieting juxtaposition of life and airless Moon. The alien rover waited just beyond, a hulking monster, manmade, but made by men as alien to him as Klaatu and Gort. He took up the cable again. "I'll pull, and Burl, you and Tyna push it in."

"Keep the dust off the floor seal," Meyer said.

He meant the lip running along the floor holding the seal. Dust and debris would compromise the seal's integrity. Van would ignore that for now. First things first. The combined force of six arms and legs quickly dragged the distressed craft inside, where it sat squat and motionless, like the stranded sea mammals Van had seen in a documentary. A heart might still beat inside, but the outward appearance provided no evidence.

"Farther," Burl said. "We need room to close the doors."

Van had to move to make room. He helped push the behemoth another four feet, leaving just enough room to open the inner doors a few feet. "Not enough," Burl gauged. "Push it right up against the inner doors. We can move it back after the outer doors are closed."

Zeedo's voice came over the com-link. "The floor seal has to be cleaned before the outer doors can be closed. We can't afford to evacuate a second time to clear a leak. This is non-negotiable."

"*Sir?*" Tyna exclaimed.

Communicating via the com-link offered no indication of the location of the speaker—whether near or far, the volume was the same. Van turned to find the bright blue pressure suit of a manager. He knew this in theory only. He'd never before seen one actually worn. "CTO?" he asked, but he could see Zeedo's face inside the clear face shield, smooth and unblemished, unlike the faceplates of their own battered suits.

"He's there to help," Meyer said. "Don't get in his way."

Van looked at Burl, who wiggled his eyebrows in amusement at the irony. It was obvious that Zeedo was uncomfortable in the suit. He moved slowly, cautiously, almost clumsily. They'd have to be careful to keep him out of harm's way—both his and theirs.

Zeedo walked to the south wall, moving as though pushing his way through syrup. He opened a panel and removed the folded white fabric they used as the movie screen. Burl tapped Van's arm and shrugged. He wondered what Zeedo planned to do. But the base leader dropped it, shoved other small items aside, and reached deep inside to extract a three-foot cylinder equipped with a trigger handle.

"A static gun!" Tyna said, surprised.

She was right. They kept a smaller version near the personnel lock, which they took along when they needed to clean away dust while servicing the mechanical innards of machinery. The daytime solar wind left the lunar dust energized with a negative charge, and it stuck to everything like it was alive and hanging on for dear life. Without help, it was impossible to wipe away—a static gun produced a stream of positive charges that neutralized the dust, allowing it to fall away.

Zeedo waded through the vacuum to one side of the doorway,

pointed the gun at the floor lip and pulled the trigger. Tyna grabbed a towel and joined him. "Sir," she said, "here's how we do it." She held out the cloth for him to zap with the invisible positively charged ions. She then wiped along the seal, collecting the Moon debris. It was a sight Van never imagined—the base leader in his clean, crisp blue suit, assisting a work-worn nexgen on her knees.

Van turned to help Burl. They moved crates to stand on, and found the outlines of the rover door among the seams of the geodesic structure, but the interlocking supports were bent at odd angles. They were going to have a problem getting it open. "The frame is designed to support the internal pressure in a vacuum, and probably applies downward tension," Burl said, pressing his palm experimentally against the center of the door. "With its internal air leaked away, it collapsed, became deformed."

Burl bounced his fist against the door while watching the edge.

"Do you really want to do that in the vacuum?" Van asked.

"You think it's that fragile?"

"Do you want to take a chance?"

The debate was terminated when Zeedo announced that they'd finished, and the hanger doors could be closed. Van jumped down and closed the small flush door as Zeedo ran his fingers along the edges of the doors, making sure they set properly. "Genie, pressurize one-half PSI," Zeedo said.

Van didn't understand. "Why just one—"

"Standard procedure," Zeedo explained. "Once we know the hanger can hold pressure, we'll bring it up to normal 5 PSI."

"Uh, how long will that take?"

Zeedo nodded. "You're right. This isn't a standard situation. Genie, can you tell if there's a leak as you bring it all the way up to 5 PSI?"

"I can currently only tell if the pressure is holding steady," she replied. "I don't have the empirical data to perform this dynamically. But, given four or five trial exercises—"

"Can it, genie. Just bring it up to full 5 PSI."

The first indication that the room was re-pressurizing was a perceptible loosening in the joints of Van's suit. Then, he heard the sound of inrushing air, at first a faint, distant rumble, swelling to a close, pervasive roar. As the gale tapered off, a thumping sound replaced the roar. Burl was pounding on the rover door. He reached back and swung down with his hands balled together, and the door caved inward. Van tore off his helmet and jumped up to join his friend, but staggered backwards.

The stench wafting from inside reeked of death.

Blaine C. Readler

Chapter 10

"What did he say?" Katlin asked.

"That the woman has a pulse, I think," Meyer replied, leaning in so that his ear was close to the com-link speaker. "They took off their helmets," he added, explaining what was already obvious, why the voices were so distant.

The other managers—Julius and Louden—hovered outside Meyer's office, waiting for news.

"Did you hear *that*?" Katlin asked, astounded.

"They found a young boy," Meyer confirmed.

From the hallway, Louden asked, "Is there a reason why we don't open the hanger doors?"

Katlin looked at him. "Judas. Because my brain's in overload, I guess," she replied, pushing past the scientists and running off. She heard the patter of their feet following her. Off-shift nexgens stared as she ran past the worker apartments. They wouldn't leave their area without Van or Meyer's blessing.

Arriving at the hanger, she turned the door handle and pushed, but it didn't budge.

"It's latched from the inside," Julius said.

She knocked on the door, then pounded. "They have to open it anyway," she explained, suddenly self-conscious about being disruptive.

She heard scraping, and the doors swung outwards. She stepped back as Tyna's flushed face appeared. "There's two," she said. "We need to get them to the infirmary."

"Just two?" Katlin asked, surprised.

It took a moment for Tyna to understand. "Two of them *alive*. There's two more that are dead."

Van appeared, carrying the woman. Katlin stepped aside. The woman was small. Her arms and legs dangled limply around Van's arms. Her clothes were strange. Katlin had vague memories of shirts and pants, something other than jumpsuits, and she'd seen the combination plenty of times in movies, but here in three dimensions, they reminded her of the doll she'd had as a child. The woman's clothes—worn and stained like the nexgen's jumpsuits—brought home the reality of the situation.

The woman's dark, matted hair fell away from her face as Van passed. *She's not Chinese*, Katlin thought. Her face was thin, and her skin smooth, the color of milk when just a teaspoon of chocolate is added. Except for a slight epicanthic fold—the misnamed Asian eye slant—she could easily have been mistaken as Caucasian. In any case, she found the woman beautiful, but something else about her was strange. Her age. In all her years of vivid memories, Katlin had never seen anyone older than nineteen and younger than fifty. This woman of perhaps thirty years was a new breed.

Burl followed, carrying the semi-conscious young boy, whose wider face and bleary, unfocused eyes bore a more distinct Chinese heritage.

Katlin stepped inside the hanger and joined Tyna, standing beside the crates Van and Burl had placed for access into the rover. Tyna seemed uncertain, gazing at the open rover doorway suspiciously. She looked at Katlin and scrunched her nose. Katlin smelled it. "It's terrible," she whispered, as though the two dead men in the rover might be insulted. "What is it?"

"Van thought it was the dead men at first."

"There wasn't time," Katlin said.

"Right. It takes, like, days," Tyna agreed. "Doesn't it?"

Katlin nodded. "How long do you think they were in there?"

"You said the Chinese base is a hundred and fifty miles away. I don't imagine this thing does more than five miles-per-hour over rough terrain. So, maybe a couple of days?"

"That's assuming they came from the Chinese base, which seems almost certain." Katlin tried to imagine herself bouncing along over endless Moonscape in darkness hour after hour. "What sort of bathroom facility do you think it has?"

Tyna sniffed again. She looked at Katlin and nodded. "Of course. That's it. Crimps. Those poor people. Suffocating, while putting up with that."

"Maybe it was the smell that killed them."

Tyna glanced at her uncertainly.

"I was joking," Katlin said. "Which is cruel at a time like this. I'm sorry. The two men, are they Chinese?"

Tyna scrambled up onto the crates. Now that she understood that the nasty smell wasn't rotting flesh, she showed no hesitation. She peered into the open doorway, then reached in, turning one of the men over. "I guess so. At least, they look like Chinese people in the movies. Why do you ask?"

Katlin gave a quick shrug. "No reason. I wonder why only the woman and child survived?"

"You didn't hear?" Tyna asked as she jumped down. "They had oxygen masks lying nearby. The men more or less sacrificed themselves."

Katlin raised her eyebrows. She'd read stories of such chivalry, but had always assumed they were just that—stories.

Her father appeared in the hanger doorway. "Tyna," he said, "see that those dead men get to the recycler ASAP," then walked away.

"Sir!"

He came back.

"ASAP," she said, "like immediately?"

"Yes," he said and started to leave.

"But, sir."

This time he had a stern look when he came back.

"Shouldn't we, um …"

"Shouldn't we what?" he asked. "Give them a memorial?"

"No," Tyna stammered. "I just thought … in the movies there's, like, an investigation. I don't know. Maybe collect evidence?"

"Don't be ridiculous. There's no foul play. It was just an

accident. Now get to it."

Tyna gave up, and just watched him walk away.

Katlin knew her father was having trouble with this. He never ordered the nexgens around like that, preferring to follow protocol, and let Meyer and then Van disseminate the directives. "He's worried," she said.

Tyna looked at her. "About what?"

Katlin wasn't exactly sure. It was more a sense. She knew her father well enough to almost read his mind. "I guess about the Chinese. We weren't exactly cooperating when we built our bases. Did you know that America and China came close to war twice in the last ten years—I mean the ten years before we lost contact?"

Tyna shook her head. "No."

Dumb question, Katlin thought. *How would she know?* "He's just being careful. I bet he wishes the rover had never made it this far."

"Which means," Tyna said with one eyebrow raised, "that he wishes they'd *all* died somewhere out there far from our base."

"No! That's not what I meant," Katlin said.

Tyna went off to get help, leaving Katlin alone in the hanger. She glanced up at the open rover doorway, shuddered, and hurried away.

She had lied to Tyna. She had no doubt that that was exactly what her father was wishing.

ж ж ж

"Do you think they'll be okay?" Van asked.

Louden studied the two patients. The boy stared up at him over the oxygen mask impassively, while the woman's brown, soulful eyes followed him carefully—fearfully, Van thought. "They're conscious," the neutrino scientist said, "and there's no obvious physical damage. I think the main question is whether there's been brain damage." He glanced at Van, and shrugged. "I'm not a doctor. My opinion's no better than yours."

"How long before they're ready for the med-genie?"

Louden laughed. "You have to believe me. My doctorate is not in medicine. I'd say if they're able to walk the fifteen feet, then they're ready."

It was just the two of them. Burl and the other Managers had gone off to gawk at the foreign machine filling most of the hanger. Van pointed at the boy's leg where his pants cuff had inched up, exposing some of his skin. "That doesn't look good."

Louden bent over to look at the rash and shrugged again. "Could be any number of causes. Perhaps the boy is allergic to suffocation."

Van didn't respond. He knew Louden well enough to guess he was joking.

"But," the scientist said, "that seems like a convenient reason to take the boy first."

Louden gently lifted the oxygen mask off the boy's face, and waited to watch the reaction. The boy blinked, and then smiled. "I think our first patient's ready," he announced.

Louden motioned for the boy to climb down off the bed, and then put his hand up to stop the woman who started to sit up, her eyes suddenly showing alarm. "It's okay," Louden said to her soothingly as the boy slid off the bed and stood.

The boy seemed a little wobbly, so Van walked next to him to the complicated array of dangling sensors and actuators of the med-genie. The boy looked up at him expectantly, and Van motioned for him to climb into the machine, which consisted of simply turning around and climbing into the seat. There was a time when the med-genie would have taken it from there, but the various robotic mechanisms had failed over time, and Van and Louden manually attached the cuffs, pads, and straps that someone had labeled with a marker. When Louden flipped the switch and told the genie to begin, the machine came alive with the sound of pumps and whirring sensors. At this, the woman sat up, her eyes wide with fear. One of the machine's operations involved making a pin-prick in the shoulder, and predictably, the boy gave a little yelp. The woman went mad. She launched herself off the bed with a torrent of unintelligible wailings. She was still weak, however, and stumbled, and Louden reached out and grabbed the small woman, keeping her from falling. This only seemed to excite her more, and she flailed her arms and pounded her ineffectual fists at the rotund scientist's head.

"She's afraid for the boy!" Louden shouted. He spun her around so that she could see the med-genie. Van didn't know what to do to assure her. He held his hand out over the boy, like a magician demonstrating that his attractive assistant was complete and whole after being sawed in half. The boy said something, and the woman slowed her frantic struggle, he said something else and giggled, and she stopped. She asked something, he answered, and she looked at Louden and Van and asked something else.

"What do you think?" Louden said, with his arms still wrapped around her.

"I don't know. We can't risk her damaging the genie."

Katlin had arrived. "Why don't you ease her back to the bed. Van and I will stand on each side of the genie in case she breaks loose."

"Why not in front?" Van asked.

"You don't come between a mother bear and her cub."

Van had never heard the expression, but he could guess what she meant. "You think she's the boy's mother?" He asked positioning himself next to the genie.

"It's just a guess. She's not Chinese—Vietnamese, probably. The boy has some of her features. Look at his eyebrows, and the crease above his eyelid."

Both the woman and the boy indeed had a pronounced eyebrow arch. "What eyelid crease?"

"You take it for granted. Most ethnic Chinese don't have it."

"But Vietnamese do?"

"It's a European feature. I think she has a European ancestor. Maybe an American soldier during the Vietnamese War."

Van glanced at her. "How did you gather all this?"

"I have eyes."

The boy spoke. "American?"

Van and Katlin's eyes met. "Yes, American," Van said. Van guessed him to be maybe seven years old. "Do you speak English?"

The boy nodded with enthusiasm. "English."

"What's your name?" Van asked.

"Name?"

"Yes. Your name."

"Tuan," he said, dragging the arm cuff to lay his hand on his chest.

"Tuan?" Van repeated.

The boy grinned.

"Looks like we're in luck," Katlin said.

Van nodded. "I hope he knows more than just two words." Van pointed at the woman and said to the boy, "Your mother?"

He nodded. "Mama."

The woman said something, and the boy replied.

Katlin's brow furrowed. "Let me try." To the boy, she asked, pointing to her own hand, "What's this?"

"Hand," he replied, happy to be so successful.

"What is it in your language?"

"Shou."

"Hmm," she murmured staring at the floor.

"What's wrong?" Van asked.

She looked up at him. "They're speaking Chinese—Mandarin."

"So? Oh, I see. Your theory is that she's Vietnamese."

She nodded slowly.

Van turned back to the boy. "Where's your father?"

"Baba," he confirmed.

"Yes. Where is Baba?"

"Where?"

"Yes, where?"

The boy thought for a moment, then looked at the door. He shrugged.

"Uh-oh," Katlin said.

"What?" Van asked.

"Louden," she said, "can you hold her a minute?" When he agreed, she took Van by the arm and led him out into the hall. "Did you see him look at the door?"

"Yeah. You're thinking that his father is one of the dead men in the rover?"

"He's expecting him to arrive any minute." She chewed her lip.

Van sighed. "Yeah. Let's not tell him yet. We'll have to eventually, but …"

"We need to pump him for information first?"

She sounded sarcastic. "No. I was thinking that his mother is on the verge of hysteria already. She may not know either, and this could really throw her over the edge. We should have the med-genie ready with a sedative."

Katlin gazed at him and smiled wanly. "Sorry. You're right." Her smile broadened. "Now let's go pump him for information."

When they returned to the room, Louden held up his hand for them to be quiet. The med-genie was just finishing her report, something about imbalanced electrolyte levels.

"What did she say?" Van asked.

Louden scowled. "She's stuck in pro mode. Med-genie! Report, lay mode."

"Patient, presumed a child, is malnourished in specific areas. Most pressing, the patient is gravely deficient in vitamin C, and is suffering the early stages of scurvy."

"Scurvy!" Van exclaimed, but stopped when Louden held up his hand so he could hear the rest, mostly vitamins and minerals that she urged be disseminated at the earliest opportunity.

"Genie," Katlin said, "can you tell the patient's ethnicity?"

"Based on DNA profiling, the patient is deemed to be Asian. This assessment holds a seventy-eight percent probability."

"Uh, anything more specific than just 'Asian'?"

"Anything more specific would hold a probability less than seven percent."

"Never mind."

"Genie," Louden said, "can you deliver a dose of vitamin C for the boy?"

"Negative. My organic synthesis program is currently blocked."

Katlin tsk'd. "The med-genie should have been at the top of Julius's list of repairs."

"Meyer has kept him pretty busy on production maintenance," Louden said. He snorted. "You'd think Meyer was just keeping Julius away." He sighed. "Fine, genie, then enumerate foods high in vitamin C."

"Listed by quantity of vitamin C per weight: guava, fruit; bell pepper, vegetable, all colors; kale, vegetable—"

"That's enough."

"You want me to run down to hydroponics?" Van asked.

"Please," Louden said. "A couple of bell peppers should do it— more if they're not mature. Grab some strawberries while you're there."

"She didn't mention strawberries."

"They're not for the boy."

"Right."

Zeedo was very strict about pilfering from the farm. This extended even to Managers, but everybody knew that Louden "tested the crops" on a regular basis.

Van shaded his eyes with his hand when he entered the large, humid room. During the lunar night, a quarter of the base's stored solar energy went to the painfully bright sun lamps (most of the rest to the platform operation).

"Unauthorized entry," the farm genie announced. "This will be reported."

"Fine," Van said. "Stick a carrot up your virtual butt while you're at it."

The genie didn't respond. Van sometimes wondered if the AI programs weren't a lot smarter than they gave them credit for. They always knew when he was joking.

The humid heat made him sweat, and he quickly gathered the food in a basket. Sweating was an unfamiliar and unpleasant sensation next to the cool, dry air of the rest of the base. He wondered about the vitamin C. From the movies and Glenda's novels, he was familiar with scurvy, and he'd always considered it one of those long ago Earth diseases, like Malaria. He'd heard about vitamins, but never understood what they were for. Long-depleted vitamin bottles were common throughout the base—full of loose nuts and bolts. Their parents had eaten the vitamin pills every day, but now everybody, supposedly got all they needed from the farm. Why did their parents have to eat the pills? It was one of those things that remained a mystery.

A long list of these sort of questions were filed away in his head, fed out sparingly to Louden and Julius. If he asked too many questions at one time, they got annoyed. Or, Julius got annoyed. Louden continued answering, but at a certain point, the explanations became nonsensical, like when he told Van that the Moon orbited around the Earth because platinum exhibited anti-gravity, and if they mined too much, the Moon would fall into the Earth. Or the time that he'd told Van that neutrinos passed all the way through the Moon, from one side to the other.

When he returned to the infirmary, Louden was helping the

woman out of the med-genie. She seemed calmer, but still suspicious, her wary eyes following and watching them every second. Katlin informed him that her name was Mai Dung, and that Tuan had explained that this meant beautiful flower. This was appropriate, as the woman was indeed beautiful. On the other hand, how could her parents have known this when she was born? Another one of those questions.

"She's also vitamin C deficient," Louden said. "Give them each one of the bell peppers." He casually took the basket from Van and began eating the strawberries.

Mai Dung hesitated only a moment, sniffing at the pepper and throwing Van a warning glance before taking a tentative bite. Surprise filled her eyes and she began devouring the green vegetable, practically shoving it whole into her mouth. Tuan took the cue from his mother and dove into his offering, holding it to his face with both hands.

"They're even eating the seeds!" Katlin said.

"Whoops," Van added. "There go the stems."

Louden was holding the basket in one hand, and a fat, red strawberry hovered halfway to his mouth in the other. He put the strawberry back, and handed the basket to Mai Dung. "They seem to be a little hungry."

Mai Dung took one strawberry, and handed the basket to her son, who immediately started popping them into his mouth whole, leaves and all. The juice ran down the sides of his mouth. His mother seemed to commune with her offering a moment before closing her eyes and placing it slowly in her mouth.

"Why don't you take them to the mess?" Louden suggested. "I'll wrestle with the med-genie and see if I can get more information that's not delivered in Latin gibberish."

Van and Katlin collected a following of curious off-duty nexgens on the way to the dining area. They met Zeedo as they turned the last corner. "How are they?" he asked, nodding at the two oddly dressed guests.

"Hungry," Katlin replied.

Zeedo glanced at them and nodded. He seemed not at all curious. If anything, maybe irritated at their presence. "We've recycled the other two," he said.

"Daddy!" Katlin exclaimed.

He raised one eyebrow.

Katlin glanced at Tuan. "Our young visitor understands some English," she remarked casually, but threw Zeedo a knowing look.

He didn't seem to get her message. "That's fortunate, I guess," he said. "Everything in the rover is in Chinese. The men didn't even have any identification on them—"

"Daddy!" Katlin cried again.

"What!" he exclaimed. "What's wrong with you?"

She composed herself, placing her hand on Tuan's shoulder. "The progenitor of our little friend is visiting the farm," she explained.

Her clever communication was impressive. "Progenitor" must mean "father." The output of the recycler was fed directly to the hydroponics processing.

Zeedo understood the meaning, but apparently not the nuance. "One of those dead men was his father?" he asked, surprised.

Katlin put her hand to her head.

"Baba?" Tuan said. "Baba dead?"

Blaine C. Readler

Chapter 11

Katlin held out the protein bar to Tuan yet again, and he finally took it. His hysterical crying had subsided, but he chewed the bar morosely. She had expected Mai Dung to go ballistic as well, but the woman must have already suspected the truth, as she only seemed to sink deeper into her suspicious funk.

Though her father's faux pas was uncharacteristic, Katlin couldn't blame him. He was managing the most extraordinary event since leaving Earth. Okay, she admitted, since the Blast.

"How's he doing?" Van asked, sitting down next to them.

"Better than I would have guessed," Katlin replied. "Maybe his age is working in his favor."

"Yeah. Kids are pretty resilient."

Tuan watched them as he chewed the soy morsel. Katlin wondered how much he understood. Her father appeared at the mess entrance and motioned to her. "Have you found out where they're from?" he asked quietly when she'd joined him.

"He only stopped crying just now. They're starving. We have to let them eat first. I'll let you know when I think they're ready to be grilled."

He looked uncomfortable.

"What is it, Daddy?"

"Could you do it? The interview?"

"Why me?"

His brow furrowed, and he stared off, searching for words.

"Daddy, it wasn't your fault. He had to find out eventually."

He took a breath and let it out. "Thanks. But I think you'll do a better job. You're good with children."

She laughed. "Now, how would either of us know that?"

He grinned, a sheepish surrender. "I just know. You have your mother's touch."

At this, his grin fell away.

Katlin put her hand on his shoulder. "Sure, Daddy. I'll see what I can find out."

She motioned to Van. "Could you leave for a little while?" she asked when he came over. "Maybe stand right outside and keep everybody away."

"Sure, I get it. He'll be more at ease without big, scary men around."

She was grateful that he understood. "It's more for Mai Dung."

"Yeah. She's definitely on edge."

"She doesn't trust us. Maybe I can find out why."

She returned to the two survivors and gave them some space to eat. The two of them talked together in Mandarin in subdued voices. After a while, Tuan leaned against his mother, and she stroked his hair as she consoled him in soothing sing-song rhythm.

Katlin hated to intrude, but the world—everything in her world—waited. "Tuan," she said, sitting down next to them, "do you mind if I ask a few questions?"

He just looked at her, and she wondered if he understood. "Some questions?" she repeated, and this time he nodded solemnly.

"Where did you come from?"

He looked up at his mother and said something, and she replied. He looked at Katlin, shrugged, and said a word that was Chinese, or at least not English.

"Is that the name of the place?" she asked.

He nodded.

She filed the word away in her mind. Perhaps her father knew the Chinese name of the other base. "Is that another Moon base?"

Again Tuan consulted with Mai Dung, and again he nodded.

"Why did you leave?"

This time the consultation took longer. Twice Tuan suggested something, and both times Mai Dung seemed to reprimand him. "It was time," he finally said.

Katlin sighed. "Why was it time?"

When Tuan translated, Mai Dung sat up straight and stared at the far wall.

So, Katlin thought, *secret motives*. She took a guess. "Did they force you out?"

She realized immediately that her wording was too complex for a six-year-old with limited English. His perplexed face confirmed this as he translated, and his mother's reaction indicated that he'd gotten the gist turned around. She panicked, hugging Tuan and jabbering hysterically until Katlin held up a hand for her to stop. Mai Dung pulled her son in closer and stared defiantly at Katlin. She spoke one sentence, and Tuan translated. "Refugees—don't force out."

Katlin shook her head. "You misunderstood," she said. "You can stay," Katlin said. "Tell her that."

Mai Dung's face relaxed a bit, turning to cautious waiting.

"Refugees," Tuan repeated.

Katlin smiled. "I get it."

Tuan looked confused.

"I understand," Katlin clarified, and let him translate. "You must tell us, though," she continued, "why did you leave?"

This was followed by an intense back and forth, until Tuan finally said, "Hungry."

"You were hungry?" Katlin asked, surprised. She could understand that they'd be hungry after days in the rover without provisions, but she couldn't imagine why they would have been hungry at their base. Tuan appeared well-fed. If anything, he could afford to lose a few pounds. Mai Dung, on the other hand, was thin, and looking at her in this context, Katlin saw that the woman's cheeks seemed sunken, her arms and hands nothing but skin, tendons, and bone.

"Did your mother work hard?" she asked.

This elicited energetic nods from Mai Dung. She held up her hands to show Katlin, who gingerly felt the woman's fingers. The skin on the tips were hard, as though stiffened with thickness. These must be calluses. She had read about them. Because the nexgens always wore their gloved suits when they worked, they never developed them.

They needed answers, even if it meant giving pain. "Tuan, did your father work hard as well?"

She was relieved that he didn't break down crying. He simply translated. When he was done, though, he seemed to sink into himself a little.

Mai Dung looked alarmed, wary. She said something that Tuan translated as, "Yes. We all work hard."

She seemed to consider her answer, however. She looked at Katlin as though trying to read her. She said something else. Tuan said, "Refugees. All refugees."

"You're saying that you are all refugees? That everybody in the rover—in the transport machine—were refugees?"

Tuan didn't have to consult his mother. He nodded.

Katlin carried on with her idea. "Is your mother Vietnamese?"

Mai Dung understood that. Her face hardened and she nodded—chiseled stone in motion.

"Your father was Chinese, wasn't he?" she asked Tuan.

Katlin thought Mai Dung's face was going to crack. Her eyes flashed anger.

Tuan didn't have to translate—Katlin had her answer. "That was a problem, wasn't it? Tell your mother that I understand this."

Mai Dung seemed to debate this. She looked at Katlin, and then at her son, and back to Katlin. She spoke, and Tuan said, "Refugees."

Katlin worked to suppress a grin. It was like piecing together a puzzle. "The leaders at your home, the people in charge—they made trouble because of this?"

She had to repeat the question, breaking it down into pieces. The answer that came back through Tuan was, "Yes and no."

The frustration on Mai Dung's face probably matched Katlin's own. The woman spoke softly to her son, placed a hand on his shoulder, and then stood up. She walked towards the doorway, stopped, turned, and motioned for Katlin to follow.

Outside, Van looked surprised to see them. "What's up?" he asked.

"I think Mai Dung doesn't want her son to know something,"

Katlin said. She turned to the woman and held out her hands, indicating she was ready.

Mai Dung made a motion of putting something in her mouth.

"Food," Katlin guessed. "Eat?"

Mai Dung nodded and repeated, "Food."

So, Katlin thought, *she knows at least a little English.*

The woman thought again, and then said, "Baba."

Katlin nodded. "Tuan's father."

Mai Dung nodded, repeating "Father." She again mimed eating, and then pointed at Tuan.

"Baba and Tuan hungry?" Katlin asked.

Mai Dung's brow furrowed, and she shook her head. She was getting more frustrated. She again made the motion of eating, then held her hands cupped a moment, and finally again pointed at Tuan.

"Baba was giving food to Tuan," Van said.

Katlin looked at him and blinked. *Of course.* "Perhaps food was scarce, maybe rationed." She turned back to Mai Dung. Time for some pantomime. "Baba," she said, then mimicked Main Dung's motion of eating, pretended to put food into her cupped hand, and finally held her hand out as though handing it off to Tuan in the next room.

Mai Dung nodded confidently. With her finger, she drew a line across her throat.

Katlin guessed what this meant. She repeated the American version and slid her finger across her throat. "Baba would be killed for this?"

Mai Dung nodded gravely. "Baba be dead," she said.

"Stealing food is a crime worth a death sentence?" Van said wonderingly.

"It was in the British navy during the eighteenth century," Katlin said.

"No kidding?"

Actually, she wasn't really sure, but she'd read of punishments so brutal that some men must have died. She decided that was close enough.

Louden showed up and asked how things were going. "Looks like we have some refugees as guests," Katlin said.

Mai Dung nodded. "Refugees."

Katlin explained their theory, and Louden shrugged. "Yeah. I can see that. Hydroponics is a tricky process. The base is a closed system, and balancing the continuous cyclical flow of hundreds of elements and minerals, let alone the oxygen and carbon dioxide, is beyond human ability." He snorted. "You know, the day that either the 'cycler or 'ponics genies give out is the day we break out the cyanide pills."

"Uh," Van said, "isn't cyanide, um, poisonous?"

Katlin nudged him with her elbow.

"Oh!" he exclaimed, then became thoughtful.

"I dug through the file archives," Louden said, "and found that we have a translator pad. It includes Mandarin."

"I forgot about that," Katlin said. "I remember running across that folder years ago—there were genies for dozens of languages. Louden, you're a genius."

"So claims my mother. If our refugee guests are finished eating, maybe we can take them to the Lab and get a conversation going."

They all turned at the pounding of feet. Morg, one of the younger nexgens came tearing around the corner and stopped in front of them. "There's lights!" he exclaimed.

"What lights?" Van asked.

"Dunno! Just lights!"

"What the heck are you talking about?"

"Outside!" he cried, exasperated. "Lights! In the sky!"

"Crimps!" Van hissed. "Come on," he said, running off.

Katlin looked at his receding back. She desperately wanted to follow. She couldn't. She knew that Mia Dung and Tuan probably saw her as their liaison.

She sighed. "Let's get them to the Lab," she said to Louden. "Finding out what they know might be even more important than we thought."

Lights in the sky, she thought. *They're obviously not talking about stars.*

ж ж ж

Van was glad he was still wearing his pressure suit. He'd left his helmet in the hanger, and sped off to get it, telling Morg to hold the lock for him. Two minutes later, they were waiting for the air to evacuate. Inside the helmet, Van was now tapped into the flurry of voices outside. He kept quiet, even though he was bursting with questions. Com-link etiquette—you don't talk unless you have something vital to say.

He gathered, though, that whatever the lights were, they seemed to be getting closer. "Van here. All lights out. Repeat, I want all lights out."

This launched multiple excited queries and comments, all interrupted by Ops Head, who must have been monitoring in his office. "Van's right. All lights doused, immediately. No sense advertising our location until we know who, or what, this is."

The lock finished cycling, and Van stepped out just in time to observe what he'd never seen before: the huge banks of lights over the platform went dark one after another. Seconds later, he stood surrounded by vast darkness, enveloped by a stunning spray of seemingly millions of stars so piercingly sharp, he could almost feel them pinging on his retina. It was a sight he rarely experienced, only when some business took him beyond the view of the platform, and it was so achingly beautiful, he couldn't imagine a life without the opportunity, or at least the possibility, of seeing it.

The darkness wasn't total, however. There were the scattered, dancing lights from nexgen headlamps a quarter-mile distant, but also far stronger lights, clustered close together, and dancing a much slower, coordinated waltz. These were located off at an angle from the platform, and the entire tight group periodically blinked out for a few seconds, and then back on. This was an intruder. It must be at least a few miles distant, and the periodic blanking would be caused by the occasional ridges and peaks that got in the way.

"Everybody listen," Van said, but the chatter continued. "Quiet!" he called, and there was silence. "Everybody turn off their headlamps and stay where you are."

The silence went on—everybody would be contemplating his order. This was truly unknown territory. One by one, the small cloud of manmade stars winked out, until Van was left seeming to float in space below a vast bowl of heaven's infinite blaze. A lone whimper on the com-link put voice to the mutual sense of desolation Van knew they were all feeling. A harsh "Shh!" squelched even this last shared connection.

He jumped when something pressed his upper arm. He spun to

find Tyna's ruddy face swimming inside her helmet, the red overlay of her heads-up display bathing her in an ominous glow. She winked off her microphone, pressed her face against Van's faceplate, and waited. He knew the drill. Originally the com-link had comprised multiple channels, but Julius had long ago consolidated them as various channels failed on different suits. The nexgens did this all the time now when they wanted one-on-one conversation.

"What's up!" he called loudly, once he'd winked off his microphone. The downside of this technique was that only yelling created enough vibration to be heard through the other helmet.

"It's coming from the same direction as the rover!" she shouted.

She was right. They'd headed off to find the rover at about the same point on the horizon—roughly ten degrees to the right of the star Vega, one of their standard seasonal landmarks.

"Do you think it's another rover?" she asked.

He broke away to look at the enigma again, then pressed back against her faceplate. "If it is, it's huge! It's still beyond the north ridge! It would have to be at least a hundred feet high to be visible from here!"

This time she broke away, and then re-connected. "Yeah! I see what you mean!"

"Crimps!" came someone's voice over the com-link, followed by a complete breakdown of the silence as everybody began chattering at once.

Van pulled back and looked. The waltz of powerful lights had climbed higher, like the Tyrannosaurus Rex in the old movie raising its gigantic head to roar in victory as it surveyed the human morsels below. A moment later the entire cluster of lights blinked out, leaving behind an indistinct elongated violet-white pencil that extended up from below the horizon, and ended sharply where the cluster of lights had disappeared. The ghostly pencil paused a moment, tilted, and then vanished completely below the horizon.

The com-link once again burst forth in tumbling jabber.

Van winked his microphone on. "Quiet!" The maelstrom subsided, but immediately rose back to full, chaotic volume. "*Shut the hell up!*" Van shouted, and this time was greeted with quiet. "Burl, you there?" he asked.

Meyer's voice said, "He's with Julius at the rover."

"Ops Head, did you see that?"

"The visual feed hasn't repaired itself yet," Meyer replied dryly.

Van had forgotten that the fiber connection carrying the combined feeds of all the outside video had gone down a couple of weeks ago. He never used it, since if he wanted to know what was going on, he just went out and looked.

"What was it?" Meyer asked.

"Lights," Van replied. "Off where we found the rover."

"What's the status now?"

"They're gone."

"Gone out, or gone away?"

Van resisted taking the time to describe what they'd seen. Ops Head was master of the platinum mining, and Van respected that. But unlike Zeedo, in Van's eyes he didn't command authority beyond that. "Not sure," Van replied, purposefully vague. "Tyna and I are going to go and investigate." At this, she gave him a surprised, but willing nod.

The com-link bubbled with activity. "Etiquette!" Van reminded, and the link went silent. He waved to Tyna, and they set out.

The first few hundred yards were easy, since the ground was as familiar as the hallways inside the base. Beyond that, they slowed, keeping one eye on Vega, and one on the terrain below their feet. As their eyes adjusted to the darkness, the starlight provided enough illumination to see the ground. The problem was that since the light came from all directions, there were no shadows, and thus no sense of depth. Van was constantly catching his foot and stumbling.

He stopped, and Tyna bumped into him. "What's wrong?" she asked.

"One of us—probably me—is going to crown."

This was nexgen shorthand for falling and cracking a faceplate. Van had a vague notion that the expression came from an old nursery rhyme.

"What do you want to do?" Tyna asked.

"It looks like we either need to go back, or use our lights."

Ops Head's voice came on the com-link. "You're not sure if the intruder's lights are gone, or just gone out," he reminded him. "If it's dangerous to continue, then you should come back."

Van winked off his microphone, and Tyna did the same. "I think it left!" he shouted, mashing his faceplate against hers.

She nodded. "Why don't you want Ops Head to know?" she yelled back.

Good question. "He gave us a hard time with the rover! If we listened to him, we'd have four dead people instead of just two!"

"He is Ops Head!" she reminded.

"This has nothing to do with platinum mining!"

He winked on his microphone, flipped on his headlamp switch, and walked off. A second later, he saw Tyna's light dancing around his feet.

"You coming back?" Ops Head asked.

"Negative," Van replied, and then ignored the Manager's further demands.

With the aid of the headlamps, they practically ran forward. After awhile, he felt a tap on his shoulder, and looked where Tyna was pointing off to the side. The marks in the dust were unmistakable. "The rover," he said. The wide, patterned tracks ran parallel to their destination, ten degrees to the right of Vega.

"Quite a coincidence," Tyna remarked, and gave Van a knowing look.

They proceeded on, following the tracks, reversing the rover's journey, since it obviously led them where they wanted to go. The tracks took them up over the south ridge, and down into the remnants of an ancient, shallow crater. Suddenly, Van stopped short, and this time Tyna fell into him so hard, they both stumbled before regaining their feet. They stared at what lay in front of them.

"What in Judas's name *is* it?" Tyna asked.

"A snake," Van said. He knew it wasn't, but it was the first thing that came to mind.

"What in God's name is going on out there?" Zeedo's voice came over the com-link.

Ops Head he was willing to ignore, but not Zeedo. "I think we found the intruder … I mean, traces of it."

"What is it? What do you see?"

Van glanced at Tyna. *How do I describe it?* "Sir, it … it melted the Moon."

Chapter 12

"Just make sure they stay here," Katlin told Morg. Guilt nagged at her for leaving the two "refugees," but she couldn't bear not hearing the details. Julius had only said that Van and Tyna had found traces of a new intruder, one that was apparently able to fly, and had been following the tracks of the rover.

She sped off to the Lab, where her father and Julius were debriefing Van and Tyna. Two alien craft in twenty-four hours, and nexgens allowed into the Lab as though that was a perfectly normal thing. Katlin's mind reeled as her world was turned upside down.

"... two snake tracks headed off to the east," Van was saying when she arrived at Louden's lab, the largest area within the wider "Lab." She had to peek around Louden from outside, as even that room wasn't large enough to fit them all. Van still wore his pressure suit, which added to the sense of strange doings, as suits were generally left at the lock to avoid tracking Moon dirt around. She noticed the contours of his youthful body, normally hidden under a loose jumpsuit. Here in the Lab, conversing with Julius and her father as though on equal par, he appeared mature and capable—and attractive.

"But you picked it up south of here," Julius confirmed, "beyond the south ridge."

"That's right," Van replied. "It had turned north—towards us—just before it stopped and went back."

"Which just supports the idea," her father said, "that it was following the rover's tracks."

"I don't think there's any doubt of that," Van said.

Katlin noticed that he hadn't added "Sir" to the statement, but she seemed to be the only one who had.

"Why do you think it turned back?" her father asked, addressing Julius.

"It probably saw our base," he replied. "Whoever it was, they weren't ready to deal with us."

"Maybe not," Van said. The two older men looked at him. "They were following the rover's tracks. They would have been focused on the ground below. Their bright running lights would be nearly blinding, and I don't think the platform was very visible from where they were. They shut off their lights and rose higher as they left, but we were dark by then."

"And thank God for that," Katlin's father said.

She shared his reaction, but why? They automatically assumed that the new interloper was malevolent. The Americans had finally accepted Mai Dung and Tuan as refugees, so whoever was pursuing the two must be their enemy, and by association, the Americans' as well.

"Then, why did they stop and go back?" her father asked Van.

"Maybe they were running low on fuel."

Her father nodded. "You could be right. What about that?" he asked, pointing at a six-inch plastic cylinder lying on the bench.

Van lifted his shoulders. "We found it just lying there on the ground. It must have fallen off their ship."

"So, you think it was a ship—that it was flying."

Van lifted his shoulders again. "We saw it rise into the sky as it left."

"Of course it was a ship," Julius said. "But things don't fly on the Moon, that requires an atmosphere. Here, rocket ships would hover."

Katlin was used to Julius's lectures, and like everybody else, she just ignored them. Besides, in this case she wasn't even sure he was correct.

Louden spoke up from his position just outside the door. "That snake you saw—"

"That's only what it reminded me of," Van said.

"I understand. Do you think this might be the result of the ship's exhaust?"

Where Julius lectured, Louden invited dialogue.

Van nodded. "That's what I was thinking."

"How wide would you say it was?"

Van thought a moment, and glanced at Tyna. "Maybe four or five feet wide?"

She nodded agreement.

"Hmm," Louden murmured.

"What are you thinking?" Katlin's father asked.

"It looked like glass, you say," Louden confirmed with Van.

"Yes. It was pretty obvious that it was Moon soil that had melted. At the end point, where the ship must have stopped for a minute, it looked like a pool—maybe ten feet across."

"Hmm," Louden mulled again.

"Come on," Katlin's father said, "give it up. What are you thinking?"

Louden nodded. "Van, you said that when it lifted and took off, they turned out all the lights and you then saw what seemed like a slender pencil."

"Yes. That would have been the rocket exhaust, wouldn't it?"

"Most certainly. But you didn't notice it until all the other lights went out."

"Right."

"Louden—" Katlin's father urged.

"Here's the facts," the neutrino scientist said, cutting him off. "One—the intruder ship has been following the rover tracks presumably all the way from the Chinese base, one hundred and fifty miles. Two—the ship's exhaust is a pencil-thin beam, barely visible, that melts Moon rock—rock that's very cold, nearly minus four-hundred degrees Fahrenheit—in seconds."

"I see what you're getting at," her father said. "this isn't the rocket technology of the Earth we left twelve years ago."

"Rocket lift is proportional to the total instantaneous momentum of the exhaust, which in turn is a product of the exhaust mass times its velocity. If you want to fly—excuse me, hover—slowly for a hundred and fifty miles, you need enough momentum in your exhaust to last that long. That either requires a whole lot of fuel exiting at a relatively low exhaust velocity—"

"Or a smaller amount of fuel at a higher velocity," her father finished, nodding. "In this case, a very high velocity, which, of course, translates into the temperature of the exhaust gas."

"A *very* high temperature. So high, it's able to melt cold Moon rock, and is almost imperceptible."

"The radiated 'color' is in the ultra-violet range."

"Or even higher. What Van and Tyna saw was the small percentage of molecules that cooled enough to radiate in the visible range."

Katlin's father shook his head in awe. "The amount of energy—" he said.

"Indeed," Louden said. "There's only one source that can produce that sustained temperature for hours on end."

Her father just stared at him, brow furrowed.

"Anti-matter," Katlin blurted, and then blushed. It was like a puzzle game, and she had to get the answer out before somebody else.

"Yes," Louden said. "Probably anti-protons, since you'd want the anti-matter to be charged so you could contain and direct it, and electrons have almost no mass."

Julius snorted. "Come on. Do you realize the technology it would require to create that much anti-matter, let alone harness it for practical use? We've only been out of touch twelve years."

Louden just lifted his shoulders in answer. Katlin's father smiled thinly.

"Bah," Julius uttered.

"Other theories are always welcome," Louden offered mildly, but Julius just chewed the tip of his little finger. The technology-expert scientist probably knew they were correct, and was already working through the industrial development principles involved.

The de-briefing broke up, and Van asked how the two guests were doing. "Mai Dung is opening up," Katlin said, "but only slowly. She's wary, almost paranoid. I don't understand why."

"She's at the mercy of people she doesn't know, and can't even understand," Van said. "Mind if we come along?"

Katlin, concerned about overwhelming Mai Dung, would have

turned down anybody else but she impulsively agreed. "Sure," she said. "Um, maybe you should stay off to the side, and not ask questions at first."

She was a little annoyed that Tyna was tagging along.

On the way, she told them what she'd learned from Mai Dung so far—that her husband had been a mining engineer, the other dead man was his brother, that her husband had been teaching Tuan English, and that he hadn't expected to find any Americans alive at their base.

"Did she explain what they hoped to find here?" Van asked.

"Questions like that just produce 'Refugees!' I suspect she's filtering for the sake of our communication channel."

"Tuan."

"Yes. For example, she said that many of the workers on their base are Vietnamese, and I got the sense that the Vietnamese are a type of second-class citizens. But when I asked whether that was so, she said no, that Chinese leaders treat everybody equal."

"A propaganda line. Why would she want to hide this from her son?"

"I thought about that. Mai Dung keeps repeating 'refugees,' as though she's trying to convince us, so that we let them stay."

"Ah, I see," Van said. "She's hedging her bet. If we somehow send them back, she doesn't want Tuan to be spouting anti-party ideas."

"Sounds right."

Morg was standing outside the spare adult apartment where Katlin had brought Mai Dung and Tuan. "Remember," she warned Van and Tyna, "avoid anything that might seem intimidating." She knocked, and then opened the door slowly.

Tuan looked up from the game she'd dug out for him. "Where's your mother?" she asked, and he pointed at the bathroom. At that moment, Mai Dung walked out wearing one of Katlin's jumpsuits. She seemed self-conscious, rubbing her hands down the front and along the sides. Katlin imagined the clothes must feel as foreign as the discarded ragged pants and shirt would feel to her. Her hair was wet, and fell along her shoulders in loose curls—another legacy of her American ancestor.

"You took them to the showers?" Tyna asked, surprised.

"No," Katlin said. "She must have bathed here."

"How?"

She smiled at her naiveté. "It's called a sponge bath."

"We don't have sponges, do we?"

"It's an expression. She probably used a towel. And we're going to make her uncomfortable with so much attention."

Tyna glanced at Van and gave him a backhanded whack. "Speaking of staring, she's twice your age, bub."

Mai Dung had taken the belt from her pants and cinched it around her waist, accentuating her slim figure. *More like half again his age*, Katlin thought. She was glad that Tyna had smacked him.

"Are you still hungry?" Katlin asked Tuan.

He translated, and fear filled Mai Dung's eyes. She looked at Van, and bowed her head, then reached behind Tuan and held four carrots out to them, her head still bowed.

"Oh no!" Katlin exclaimed. To Tuan, she said, "Tell her that it's okay—she can have all she wants." To demonstrate the misunderstanding, Katlin went over and put her arm around the woman, feeling her soft wet hair on her arm.

To Van, she said, "She thinks you're an authority, here to punish her."

He smiled and shrugged. "Hey, Tuan, tell her I'm another second-class citizen."

"No!" Katlin cried. "Don't translate that!"

Tyna gave him another whack. "Behave yourself, or leave."

"I have a better idea," Katlin said. "Van, bring back more carrots. That should ease her mind."

He looked torn, obviously wanting to stay.

"The sooner you go, the sooner you'll get back," Katlin said.

Van left at a trot, and Katlin and Tyna sat on the padded bench across from Mai Dung and Tuan. "Tuan," Katlin began, "I'd like to make sure I understand—your father didn't think there would be anybody alive here at our base. Is that right?"

The boy nodded, and a brief exchange with his mother followed. "Baba promised," Tuan related.

"Promised?" Katlin repeated, surprised. "Your mother didn't *want* anybody to be here?"

During the exchange that followed, Mai Dung avoided looking

at Katlin. She seemed a little agitated. "It safer," Tuan finally said.

"Safer for you if this base was unoccupied—was empty?"

Tuan nodded.

"Why? How would it be safer?"

As Mai Dung responded to her son in Chinese, Katlin realized that what she had thought was agitation was in fact embarrassment. "Bad stories," Tuan relayed.

"Bad stories about *us*?"

The boy nodded.

"What kind of stories?"

Mai Dung hid her face in her hands after talking. "Americans eat people."

Katlin blinked. She looked at Tyna who seemed more amused than mortified. "I guess it could come to that if the hydroponics failed."

A thought came to Katlin that disturbed her. They were indirectly eating people by placing Randy in the recycler. *That's not the same*, she told herself. *We didn't* kill *him in order to* eat *him*. "That's ridiculous," she said to Tuan. "Tell your mother that it's not true. Do you know what ridiculous means?" The boy shook his head. "Tell her that the idea is so wrong that it's almost funny. Can you tell her that?"

Tuan nodded.

As he translated, Tyna said, "Food was a problem on the Chinese base."

"You heard about … what the father did?"

Tyna glanced at Tuan, understanding the delicacy. "Yes. If food was such a problem on their base, it would be natural to think of things like this—eating people. We never thought of it, because there was no reason."

This was impressive analytic thinking, particularly for nexgens who had been given such a limited education. Katlin didn't let on, though, since that would point out that she'd been expecting less. "I'll bet the idea had some help, however," she said.

"What do you mean?"

"History is replete with examples of authority feeding on people's fears."

"You think the Chinese Managers told them this?" Tyna asked.

"Let's find out."

Mai Dung emerged from her embarrassment to nod enthusiastically at this question, glad to have the blame passed on.

"You know," Tyna said, "I'll bet this is why she was so scared when you put Tuan in the doc-genie."

Katlin hadn't thought of that. Again, she suppressed letting on that she was impressed. "Mai Dung probably thought we were checking out our next meal." She chuckled. "This explains why Tuan's father promised Mai Dung that our base would be empty. Even if he wasn't in a position to know for sure, it was a good bet—from his perspective."

"I don't get it," Tyna said.

"If you think about it, it was unlikely that we'd last twelve years on our own."

The base was all the nexgens ever knew, it was their entire world. Tyna's perplexed expression demonstrated this. Katlin's father—all the scientists—would have avoided talking about their precarious situation.

"Huh," is all Tyna said, clearly contemplating this disturbing thought.

"There's one mystery, though, that I haven't figured out." Katlin turned to Tuan. "Do you know how your father planned to get into the base if there was nobody inside? You had no pressure suits."

It took some back and forth to get those ideas across. Mai Dung explained that there were actually emergency pressure suits. They were located in the rear floor. From what Katlin could gather, one slipped into it from above, and then an air-tight panel closed above it, and another opened below, to drop you to the ground.

"Ingenious," Tyna said. "Burl is going to be jealous when he hears this."

"But, how did your father expect to get into the base?" Katlin asked Tuan.

The response to this was an apologetic shrug from Mai Dung.

"Maybe he was going to just wing it," Tyna suggested.

They heard voices outside.

A knock was followed by Louden's head peering around the door. "I have the Chinese translator ready," he said, holding up a pad, and stepped inside.

Meyer followed. He gazed at the two guests impersonally. Joyless assessing stares were standard for him, but his dour intensity could seem menacing. If anything, he seemed even more grumpy than usual. Maybe it was another kidney stone developing.

Katlin wished he'd leave. They were just beginning to make headway putting Mai Dung at ease.

"Tyna," Katlin said, "why don't you take Tuan to the resistance gym? That used to be the nursery—I'll bet you can dig out some more games for him."

Tyna looked at her, and then Louden. "Sure. Come on, Tuan. It'll be fun."

Katlin put her arm around Mai Dung's shoulder again and tried to reassure her. She seemed on edge now that these new men with obvious authority had arrived.

Van returned, and Tyna took the carrots from him and handed them to Mai Dung, then snagged him by the arm and shepherded both him and Tuan off. Katlin heard Tyna say, "If I can't stay, neither can you."

"Why get rid of the kid?" Meyer asked.

Katlin glanced reflexively at Mai Dung, and then remembered that she didn't understand English. "There's things she doesn't want him to know."

"Like what?"

Katlin was used to his brusque manner, but it still annoyed her. "We think they left the Chinese base because Tuan's father—Mai Dung's husband—was in trouble for giving his son extra food."

"So, they're criminals."

"That depends on your perspective. It wouldn't be a crime here." She didn't give him a chance to argue the point. "Besides, I doubt that's the only reason they left. That's what we want to find out."

Meyer grunted.

Louden had laid the pad on his lap, and patted the seat for Mai Dung to sit next to him. She looked to Katlin, who nodded that it was okay. He then poked at the screen a few times. "What are you doing?" Katlin asked, leaning over to look.

"There's no genie for this," he replied, poking again.

Different icons appeared with each poke he made. "Huh," she said. "It died?"

He looked up and grinned. "This program is old—very old. Maybe from the thirties. They didn't have genies back then, at least not commonly."

"How do you know it works?"

"I don't. We'll soon find out." He hovered his finger over the screen, and gave one last push against it, and the pad announced itself as the Core-ex Corporation's Transvox English/Chinese translator, version 9.7. It then repeated this in Chinese, and Mai Dung's face lit up.

"How does it work?" Katlin asked. "I mean, without a genie?"

"Not sure," Louden replied. Let's find out." Into the pad, he said, "How do I operate you?"

The device just sat there.

"Um," he tried again, "how do you work, translator?"

Silence.

"Maybe it doesn't know you're talking to it," Katlin suggested. "Let me try. Transvox—how do you work?"

After a moment, the pad asked if she was done, and when she affirmed, it instructed that in the future, she could just say "translate." It then chattered out something in what seemed fluent Mandarin.

Mai Dung's response was surprise. She blinked a couple of times and replied. The translator device said, "Translation: 'I have mostly operated machines that processed the raw ore, but I am competent in a wide range of skills.'"

After a second of baffled silence, Louden laughed. "It translated 'how do you work?', and Mai Dung thought the question was for her."

"Can we get on with this?" Meyer groused. "That ship is going to return any time, and we need to have these two ready."

"What do you mean, 'ready'?" Katlin asked. Her heart sank. She could guess what the Ops Head had in mind.

"To hand over, of course."

"We can't just hand them over. They're refugees!"

Mai Dung has trained me well.

"Refugees, hell," Meyer snarled. "They're criminals, by their own admission."

"We don't know that yet. We don't have the whole story. Heck! We haven't even started a valid interview."

"You're the one that's missing the whole story, young lady. This is our chance to make contact with Earth. For twelve years we had no idea whether the Chinese survived the Blast, and now we know they did. They not only survived, but they're obviously in contact with Earth."

"That's your theory," she retorted.

"Don't act stupid. That ship uses technology far in advance of what existed before the Blast. There's absolutely no way in hell the Chinese could have developed that on a remote Moon base."

"The action of stupidity is manifested in the narrow, false perception of the listener's mind." She was impressed that she'd gotten them all out in the right order. "A drive based on anti-matter is obviously Earth-developed. Indubitably. Your unacknowledged assumption is that the ship is Chinese."

She let that much fester, and enjoyed watching him fume. She didn't often butt heads with him, mostly because they avoided each other.

"Like father, like daughter," he muttered under his breath. "You obviously know something I don't. If you're done with your guessing game, we can get on with it."

Fair enough. "The personnel of the ship in orbit—probably the transport companion to the shuttle Van and Tyna saw—are not Chinese. They speak Mandarin, but they're clearly not native Chinese."

This furrowed Meyer's brow. "That's based on the radio contact you heard?" he said. "It could be just one person who's not Chinese."

"That's possible. Sure. But, if so, it means that Chinese culture has changed a lot since the Blast."

He just nodded. It was well known that the Chinese entrusted important roles only to loyal Chinese. Vietnamese might labor in the mines, but a spaceship crew would be state-educated Chinese.

Meyer nodded at Mai Dung, who sat wide-eyed listening to the foreign angry words. "Maybe she knows."

Katlin suppressed a grin. "Good idea. Let's get on with the

interview."

Meyer snorted at her sarcasm. "Transvox," he said, looking sternly at Mai Dung, "a shuttle—a small spaceship—came looking for you. Do you know who they are? Translate."

As the pad relayed the question in sing-song Mandarin, Mai Dung's face spread with alarm, and then panic. She burst forth with a stream of imploring chatter. After a few seconds, the pad began translating, but it was impossible to make out what it said in the jumble. Meyer held up his hand. "Hold it! Hold it!"

Mai Dung understood, and stopped. She sat frozen, staring at them.

The pad dribbled something about blame and hunger, and admitted that it probably didn't get it all.

"You're scaring her silly," Katlin said, but Meyer held up his hand to her, too.

"Transvox—Mai Dung, speak one sentence at a time. Do you understand? Translate."

Mai Dung nodded when the pad was done.

"Okay. Transvox—do you know who is in that shuttle? Translate."

Mai Dung looked at Katlin, who nodded, then said something that consisted of two words. The pad was silent a moment, and then reported that it had no translation.

"Damn!" Meyer muttered.

"Wait," Katlin said. "I have an idea."

She ran to the resistance gym, where Van, Tyna, and Tuan looked up in surprise from the game they were playing. "No time to explain," she said, and rummaged through the cupboards until she found the globe.

"That's broken!" Van called as she ran out.

"I know," she yelled back. "But it's good enough."

When she got back, Meyer said, "Good idea. I thought that was broken, though."

"Yeah, yeah," she said, "I know. It should still give us what we need."

She'd played with the globe for hours when she was a child. The image was originally full 3D, but sometime down through the years, one of the stereo channels gave out. Although an educational tool,

Julius considered it a toy, and it didn't even make it onto his fix-it list.

She set it down next to Mai Dung and flipped it on. A curved, two-dimensional image of Earth appeared on the surface, with national outlines shown as glowing lines. Mai Dung looked at Katlin, and picked it up, obviously familiar with the operation. "Transvox," Katlin said, "show us where the spaceship people come from. Translate."

Mai Dung nodded, and used the tip of her finger to spin the image. North America slid down, and the Atlantic Ocean moved across the top. She slowed when the peninsulas of Italy, and Greece glided by. She stopped when Iraq rested at the top. She seemed confused, and looked up at Katlin, who just shrugged. She studied the globe, and used the tip of her finger and thumb to expand the area, then moved it back and forth, as though searching. She thought a moment and nodded, understanding. She looked up again at Katlin, and then outlined a broad area with her finger, being careful not to touch the globe.

"She's indicating all of the Middle East!" Meyer said, disgusted.

"Hold on," Katlin admonished. To Mai Dung she said, "Again. Slow."

She understood this without the pad and repeated her tracing, carefully following the outer outlines of a group of countries.

"Not all of the Middle East," Katlin said. "Just Syria, Iraq, and Iran."

"How is that any better?" Meyer asked.

Katlin thought a moment. "I think I understand. Transvox—is this all one country now? Translate."

Mai Dung nodded. "Yes," the pad replied.

"Holy crimps!" Meyer whispered, mixing in the nexgens' expletive.

Katlin had another idea. "Transvox—can you point to the capital of this new country?"

Mai Dung searched carefully, expanded more of one area, and delicately pointed.

"Tehran?" Meyer exclaimed. "The ship is Iranian?"

Mai Dung's eyes widened in recognition. "Iran!" she repeated.

Meyer's face went red. "Son of a bitch!" he cried.

Blaine C. Readler

Chapter 13

Van heard his name, and looked up to find Louden motioning to him from the doorway. "I'll be right back," he said to Tyna, and stood up from the card game they were playing—one of the few children's pastimes that still worked.

"You probably arranged to have him come and pull you away," she said, lying a card down. "Tuan, take a peek at his cards when he leaves."

"Is that cheating?" the boy asked.

"Normally yes, but in this case it's considered fair punishment."

"She's evil, Tuan," Van called back. "She's just trying to get a look at your cards." To Louden, he said, "What's up?"

The scientist gestured for him to follow. "We need a pow-wow. Things are moving quickly. I sent Morg to get Burl."

Louden told him about Mai Dung's revelation, that both the ship in orbit, and probably the shuttle that was following the rover's tracks, were Iranian—or, rather, from Greater Persia. She'd explained that for the first six years that she'd been working on the Moon, the Chinese brought regular supplies, and returned home with processed ore. But there never seemed to be enough food, because—her husband had confirmed this—the Chinese managers kept the greater share of it for themselves. Many of them held it back, and traded it with the workers for favors.

"What kind of favors?" Van asked, to which Louden just

looked at him critically. "You're talking about *sex*?" Van squeaked.

Louden lifted his shoulders. "Mai Dung married early on, so she was spared. After a while, the Chinese transports began missing their schedules, and the situation became truly dire. Even the Managers were starting to lose weight. It's been nine months since the last Chinese shipment. Now, suddenly, a Persian ship arrives and demands all the available ore. The workers were getting desperate, and some trouble arose."

Louden stopped just short of the apartment where Meyer and Katlin were interviewing Mai Dung. "There's something you should probably know," he said quietly. "Meyer has no love for Iranians."

Van nodded. He wasn't exactly sure who or what Iranians even were.

"Let me re-phrase that," Louden said. "Meyer detests them—I've heard him curse their nation. I don't know the specifics, but apparently they wronged him at some point."

"Uh-oh."

"Exactly."

Mai Dung stopped when Louden and Van entered, and then went on. "There was much arguing," the pad translated.

"Transvox—Arguing?" Meyer asked. "Like people disagreeing across a table? Translate."

While the pad translated, Katlin leaned over to Van and Louden. "She's explaining what was happening at their base when they left in the rover," she whispered.

When the pad finished, Mai Dung looked at Katlin, and then back at Meyer. The pad translated her response, "Conflict."

"Ha!" Meyer exclaimed. "I knew it. Transvox—fighting? Translate."

"Yes," came the answer.

Meyer nodded, as though this is what he would have expected. "Transvox—physical fighting? People getting hurt? Translate."

Mai Dung looked scared and glanced at Katlin for guidance. "Yes," came the response.

"Transvox—this is why you left? In the rover? Translate."

Mai Dung took a moment. She looked to Katlin, but found only patient attention. Mai Dung asked the pad something, and it replied. Finally, the pad relayed, "Yes."

Meyer stood up and turned to Louden. "Well, there you have it."

Burl came in. "The rover's old and clunky, but serviceable. If we can get Julius to fix the hanger evac motor—" He looked around at the assemblage. "What's going on?"

"The Iranians attacked the Chinese base," Meyer said.

"What Iranians?" Burl asked.

"Now, wait a second," Katlin protested, "she never said they attacked the base."

"Transvox," Meyer said, "did the Iranians attack your base? Is that why you left? Translate."

While Mai Dung and the pad conversed, Van gave Burl a three-sentence summary. "Sounds like some excitement has found the Moon," Burl said.

Mai Dung seemed to be pleading with Katlin through simple eye contact as the pad responded, "Yes."

"Son of a bitch!" Meyer hissed. "Son of a bitch."

"They think the shuttle uses anti-matter for its drive," Van told Burl.

His friend nodded. "I heard the exhaust melted rocks in its path. That would make a wicked close range weapon, eh?"

The room suddenly went silent.

"Son of a *bitch*!" Meyer exclaimed. "We're sitting ducks!"

"You're jumping to conclusions," Katlin said. "The Iranians have no reason to attack us—"

"You can't assume that. They attacked the Chinese. They're obviously aggressors."

"We don't know why they attacked the Chinese base, if they even did—"

"Do you realize how easily they could destroy us? Do you grasp how vulnerable we are to their drive? Burl, maybe you can explain it."

Van was surprised. Meyer clearly grasped Burl's technical bent, but Ops Head had never before asked his opinion, let alone even acknowledged his friend's capabilities. It was a savvy move, however. How convincing, if even a nexgen recognized the danger.

"If the hot gas of their exhaust could melt rock," Burl said, "Then it could easily melt the metal doors of the personnel lock or hanger. Even a glancing pass would probably warp them so they lose their seal."

"The base wasn't built as a military installation," Louden said. "We have no backups for the two locks, even if the inner doors manage to hold their seals."

"The apartments have airtight doors," Katlin reminded, as though hopeful this might represent ultimate salvation. Van thought of her as a wellspring of rational intelligence, next only to Zeedo for direction, and he found her borderline fear far more disconcerting than Meyer's dire warnings.

"True," Louden replied. "That was meant as a fallback in the event the base lost pressure. They were only intended as safe havens while repairs were made." He looked at her apologetically. "The apartments have no airlock capabilities."

"So, we'd be trapped in each apartment," she said, "until the oxygen was used up."

Van glanced around the little apartment, imagining them crowded inside with the door sealed shut, each breath becoming deeper, more strained, until the carbon-dioxide built up and induced convulsions, unconsciousness, and, finally, death. He shuddered.

"Where the hell is Julius?" Meyer barked. "We need to devise a defense."

Burl tilted his thumb down the hall. "He's still in the rover—"

"I'm here," Julius said impatiently. Everybody shuffled around to make room for him. Van slid farther into a corner to make room for Zeedo who followed soon after.

"With airlock doors so vulnerable," Meyer started, "our only defense is an offense. We can't let them get anywhere near the doors."

"Before we start talking about going on the offense," Zeedo said, "shouldn't we try contacting them?"

Meyer clearly didn't like the suggestion, but it wasn't something he could discount out of hand. "Sure. We'll try to make contact as soon as they become visible, but we don't delay our defense waiting for a response. If they reply, fine, but let's consider it just a courtesy call—maybe a warning."

"It's important to find out what they want," Katlin said. "And use diplomacy. If we jump the gun, the whole thing could escalate."

"Diplomacy has always been a tool of manipulation," Meyer said, "a trap for weak fools."

"'Always'?" Katlin challenged.

"Diplomacy might work when both sides have something to gain, and something to lose. What the hell do they have to lose?"

"What do they have to gain?" she countered, but then blushed and glanced at Mai Dung, who sat quietly listening to words she didn't understand.

"Don't worry," Meyer said. "They're not Chinese. I doubt they care at all about whatever crime she committed at the other base. Besides, I wouldn't hand anybody over to them. They're animals."

That brought silence down on the room. Van felt embarrassed for Meyer, expecting an apology, or at least a retraction, but the Ops Head just glared at Katlin defiantly.

Van smelled something. Something awful that he'd encountered before, and it was always bad news.

"Hey," Burl said, "you smell that?"

Julius took a sniff and cursed. "Oh shit," he muttered, "there goes something else." Using his nose, he searched around, but the odor permeated the whole room. He eyed the pad in Katlin's hands and took it from her. He sniffed it, and jerked his head back. "Damn!" he said, poking ineffectually at the screen, and then tossed it back to her. "It shouldn't come as a surprise from forty-year-old circuitry," he said, "but it's still heartbreaking. I guess that burns your attempt to contact them, unless they happen to speak English."

"Somebody on the ship in orbit was speaking Chinese," Katlin said. "Maybe Mai Dung can translate."

Meyer nodded, but Van could tell that the Ops Head had already discounted the whole idea of contact. "They could return any time," Meyer said. "We need a plan."

"Where the plan is offensive defense," Burl said.

Meyer just looked at him. He knew Burl well enough to guess the nexgen might be setting up a joke.

"Meaning, we need a weapon," Burl added.

Meyer nodded cautiously.

"A weapon that could bring down a shuttle."

Meyer nodded again, this time curiously.

"How about pokers?"

One of Meyer's eyebrows went up, and then his eyes popped. "By damn! It just might work! Wait, how many bits are left?"

Always thinking about production, Van thought. "About a dozen," Burl said.

Meyer was obviously torn, happy to have a potential weapon on one hand, but worried that it might curtail yield on the other.

"If you're thinking of using it as a gun," Julius said, "remember, you can always retrieve any bits that miss their mark. Heck, you could even retrieve them if they do hit their mark. It would be messy, rummaging through the wreckage, but possible."

Count on Julius to be practical to the bitter end.

"Let's do it!" Meyer enthused. "Julius, don't you have a poker in the Lab that you've been working on?"

"I won't be able to get it working in time," he replied, "but we could use it as a model—figure out how to modify the others."

Julius and Burl filed out, heading off towards the Lab. Meyer started to follow, but turned and pointed his finger at Katlin. "And I don't want these two intruders near the med-genie again without me, understand?" he said, and headed off after the other two.

Ops Head had become protective of the automated medical facility lately. Van didn't know why, but it wasn't out of character for him to assume authority over anything he could get his arms around.

Van looked at Katlin and shrugged, then sped off to join them. Inside the Lab twice in one day. The world was changing at a dizzying pace.

ж ж ж

Katlin found her father at his desk, staring at the tips of his fingers pressed together like a teepee. Her knock broke into his reverie. "The nexgens have returned," she reported. "They removed two pokers from the platform."

Her father nodded. She couldn't tell if he truly approved of the mad rush to develop weapons capable of bringing down space shuttles. "Daddy, do you think this is right?"

"Using pokers from the platform?"

"No. I mean the idea that our only defense is to immediately attack."

"Julius is going to attempt to contact them first," he reminded.

"I'm sure that will be our saving grace in history books."

"That's sarcasm, I presume."

"Daddy, I'm not sure I would stop Meyer, even if I could."

He gazed at her a moment. She sometimes wondered if he was admiring her, or questioning how somebody so dumb could have come from his DNA. "You're experiencing a crisis of conscious," he said.

He was so confident. *Why can't I be like that?* "A crisis of conscious. That sounds exactly right."

"I didn't originate it. You abhor the idea of taking lives through unbridled aggression, yet you fear the consequences if we don't. I share your crisis. We really are as vulnerable as they said."

Katlin plopped down in the guest chair. He hadn't invited her, but she didn't care. "Do you think much about how we'll be viewed in history books?" she asked.

She hadn't intended to ask that. She would have taken it back if she could, assuming the question was insulting in some way.

He managed a weak grin. "Constantly. It's become my guiding force."

"Really?" she blurted.

If the question wasn't insulting, then her surprised reaction must have been, but he just laughed. "It's the perfect moral compass. What better judge than the collective assessment of your broad progeny? It forces you to take a long view, avoid squandering limited resources for short-term gain."

"Like keeping the nexgens semi-educated so that the base can continue to be operational for decades after all contact is lost."

She bit her tongue too late. She was tired. She should just keep her mouth shut.

Her father's grin wavered. "I guess, yes." He shrugged. "It could be worse."

"We could have all starved to death long ago," she said, trying to find her way out of the quagmire. "Like the Chinese base seems to be doing."

He just nodded. He knew she was just placating him. She

needed to change the subject. "I don't understand how the Chinese could have been in contact with Earth without a com satellite—I'm assuming, of course, that they have been in contact all along."

"I think that's a good assumption." He took a deep breath, and let it out slowly. "My guess is that they do have a com satellite up there—probably the original one. Remember, our base was established as a private venture, but theirs was—"

"Government," she said. It was making sense. "In China, that meant essentially their military. So their equipment, including the com satellite, would have been weapons-grade—hardened against radiation. It could have survived the Blast."

His grin returned. "That's my girl."

"But that means ... um, why haven't we intercepted their communications?"

He just raised his eyebrows. The answer should be obvious. If it was military equipment ... "The transmissions would have been encrypted, but we would have at least heard the scrambled gibberish."

"There's a lot of ways to hide the meaning of a transmission."

"Wait," she said, not wanting to lose the game. "I know. They're using some kind of spread-spectrum transmission."

His grin blossomed. "I should have turned the base over to you already. I wouldn't have even guessed the idea of spread spectrum if Julius hadn't explored the possibility. Within a year after the Blast, after we'd gotten back on our feet—or at least back on our knees—he searched the frequency bands for transmissions, any transmissions."

"On the far side of the Moon, anything you pick up is somewhere above you."

"That's right. He thought he had some nibbles, but they were transitory and marginal. He thought that he might be detecting the occasional bursts of carrier as the encoding technique jumped around almost randomly, but without an appropriate spread-spectrum receiver, let alone the frequency hopping encoding key, it was just conjecture."

"They've been transmitting all these years, and we didn't even know."

He just shrugged.

"Daddy, they never even came to check on us. They didn't know if we were dead or alive."

His look was the old one that told her she already had the answer, if she just looked. "We didn't try to check on them, either," she said.

"Of course. Both sides were concentrating on surviving."

She frowned. "There's one big difference. While we were completely isolated, they were in continuous contact with Earth. They had *transport* ships coming and going."

"So?"

"It's one thing to be unwilling to risk a rover on a dangerous cross-country journey just to find out if another base is alive, but they had *space* ships!"

That look again. But she really was tired. "Why didn't they come to check on us?" she asked.

He sighed. She'd let him down. "I suspect that the anti-matter drive is new," he said. "It's not even theirs."

She saw it. She should have seen it right away. "Of course, chemical rockets don't carry a lot of margin—the first American lunar lander had just seconds of fuel left. Any Chinese transport wouldn't necessarily carry enough fuel to go poking around for another country's base that may or may not be dead."

"And I don't imagine the economics of space flight changed much—at least not until the new anti-matter drive."

She scowled. "Economics. Do you think the Chinese would have been willing to check on us if the American government had paid them?"

He shook his head. "I'm not going there. We have no idea what happened after the Blast. There's nothing to gain from conjecture."

Her smile was sardonic. "I guess we'll let history decide whether our own government did the right thing."

"I guess," he said blandly. He didn't like it when she criticized her homeland.

She stood up and stretched and was about to leave, when another thought came to her. "Meyer really went ballistic when he found out that the shuttle was Iranian. He seemed almost irrational."

Her father's face clouded. "Meyer has, let's say, a history with

Iranians."

"If there had been a lawyer present when he was questioning Mai Dung, he would have been shouting 'Leading the witness!'"

He sighed, and motioned for her to sit back down. "There's no reason you shouldn't know, I guess. In the teens and twenties, the Middle East was one continuous war zone. You may recall that there was a long civil war in Syria—in the area that used to be Syria, I guess. Meyer's father was part of a special forces team fighting there. He was killed when Meyer was just a baby. But, here's the thing—Meyer has always believed that his father was killed by subterfuge. Do you know what that means?"

"Sure—deception or trickery. He thinks the Iranians were behind his father's death?"

"It's not unthinkable. Our countries—America and Iran—were essentially at war with each other. It was mostly covert, but that's what special forces are all about in the first place."

She nodded. It was a lot to think about. She stood up again to leave. "Fifty years is a long time to hold a grudge."

"Not when it's over your father's life."

Katlin felt tears welling up, and her vision became blurred. She leaned down and gave her father a long hug. "I love you, Daddy."

She let go, but he continued to embrace her. "I love you too, Peaches."

Chapter 14

Van hefted the jury-rigged weapon. It was odd holding it pointed out in front of him. For all his life, the pokers had been an integral part of platform work, always pointing *down*. They were one of the most dangerous components of production, and the nexgens treated them with respect. Nobody had ever thought of them as anything other than something to stay well clear of when they were about to fire.

Until now. Now Van was gripping it in his hands, and it gave him the willies. It was like holding a vial of nitric acid above his face when he was young just to scare Tyna. There was a memory he wished he hadn't dredged up.

"Have you loaded a bit?" Meyer asked.

"No," Van said. "I was going to wait until I was outside."

"Do it now," Meyer said.

"It's kind of dangerous—"

"Now!" Meyer growled.

Normally Van would have pushed back, but Meyer's anger was like a loaded poker that Van preferred to avoid firing.

Tyna handed him a bit from the bag she carried, and he dropped it into the chamber and closed the lid. He then pulled the lever that moved it into the firing chamber.

The bits were titanium-encased iron slugs the size and shape of a pine cone. As part of the platform operation, an explosive charge sent them hurtling from the mouth of the poker to embed themselves into the lunar bedrock a few feet below. A cable attached to a ring set in the blunt end was then used to winch the bit out, leaving a hole into which a first-stage drill could get a bite. A key modification had been to remove the cable, allowing the mining bit to fly free in its new life as a cannon shell.

Van handed the poker to Tyna to hold while he put on his helmet.

"You forgot the charge," Meyer said, imperatively.

Once the explosive capsule was in place, just a touch of the jury-rigged trigger would fire the powerful weapon. If it didn't blow a hole through somebody's body, it could damage the airlock door with catastrophic results. Van looked at Meyer's twitching eye and decided to risk it.

Van had just loaded the charge capsule when Zeedo arrived. "Is the work shift still outside?" he asked, concerned.

"Oh, crimps!" Tyna muttered.

"Uh, yes sir," Van replied. He'd forgotten all about them in the mad rush to prepare a defense. Shame burned him as he spoke the order into his open helmet to come inside.

Zeedo gestured at the poker. "That's not loaded, is it?"

"Uh, yes."

"Well, unload it, for God's sake," Zeedo ordered.

Van looked at Meyer, saw his mouth working in concert with the twitching eye, and decided not to correct Zeedo about whose idea it was.

"Are there enough charged oxy-packs for all the pressure suits?" Zeedo asked.

"Um, I'm not sure," Van replied. "Why?"

"Shouldn't we all be in pressure suits? In case the lock seals are compromised?"

"Would it really do any good?" He'd just contradicted the CTO. "I see your point, though, sir. The suits would be invaluable in the event the lock seal could be repaired—assuming enough air was still left inside."

Zeedo shook his head. "No, you're right. Putting everybody in pressure suits would be a waste of valuable time."

Burl and Kim arrived with the second modified poker.

"Remember," Zeedo said, "the goal is to keep the intruder away from the lock doors. Van, use your judgment here. The safety of the base takes priority."

"If there's any doubt at all," Meyer added, "shoot the bastards. The hull probably isn't armored, but they may be in pressure suits. If they land, don't let them get away on foot."

Zeedo, looking slightly annoyed, gave a little wave, downplaying Meyer. "Use your best judgment, Van. Remember, you don't want to damage their drive. We'll be here if you want advice."

It all seemed a bit surreal, like the poignant moment in the movies before charging off into battle. And, that's exactly what they were facing—a battle. "Sir," Van said, "um, can I talk to you a moment?"

Zeedo frowned at the delay, but said, "Okay. What's on your mind?"

"Um," Van said, "can we talk in private?"

Now Zeedo nodded with obvious annoyance, and stepped away down the hall, with Van following. "What is it, Van? The clock is ticking."

Van had never heard a clock tick, but he knew what Zeedo meant. "It's about my … uh, points, sir."

Zeedo stared at him, as though trying to fathom what he was talking about.

At that moment, Katlin came around the corner, followed by Mai Dung and Tuan. "Oh! Daddy—uh, hi, Van. The work shift has seen the orbiting transport coming up over the horizon. We're going to see if we can make contact."

Zeedo nodded, seeming a little dazed at the onslaught of changing events. "You're off to the com shack, then. Good. Van, so, you're worried about your points somehow?"

"Sir. I'm currently in misdemeanor."

Zeedo just stared, as though waiting for more.

"If I'm …" Van swallowed. "If I'm, um, killed out there …"

Zeedo stared a moment longer, and then his eyes widened in understanding. "You're worried about archiving!"

"Yes, sir. Sorry."

He waved his hand, dismissing the subject. "Don't worry about *that*." Zeedo blinked, looked at his shoes, and sighed.

"Okay," Van said. "Thanks ... I'd better get back."

Zeedo looked up and nodded, his eyes looking tired. Or maybe sad.

Before turning back to the lock, he glanced at Katlin. She was watching her father, and she seemed concerned. *No, not concerned. More like skeptical.*

ж ж ж

Katlin leaned back, giving Julius room to fiddle with the transmitter dial. She resisted objecting that she'd been doing okay on her own. There was so much in the base that they were totally dependent on him to maintain, and he worked so hard trying to keep up, she wasn't about to knock him even an inch off his pedestal.

"Daedalus base, here," he continued to repeat into the microphone as he twiddled the dial back and forth in tiny increments. "Can anybody read me?" Under his breath, he muttered, "Hell, it's been a dozen years since we used this. I can't even tell if the power stage is working."

The heavily accented lilting voice that had been emanating Mandarin from the receiver speaker suddenly changed tone and velocity, sounding excited. Julius froze and looked at Katlin expectantly, who in turn looked at Mai Dung.

The refugee woman listened intently. After a moment, Tuan said, "He say that he think somebody speaking English—"

Mai Dung cut him off, and they exchanged hard words. Tuan went silent, moping. He'd probably gotten a scolding. Mai Dung said something else, and he just stared at the wall. She repeated it, and he finally said, "I made a mistake."

Katlin glanced at Julius, who shook his head skeptically. "What do you mean, Tuan?" Katlin said. "What mistake?"

The boy looked at her, clearly not happy. "That man didn't say that."

This was followed by another heated exchange between him and his mother. She was probably making sure he was towing the line.

"She doesn't want us talking to them," Julius whispered.

"What did the man say, then?" Katlin asked.

Tuan just shrugged. He looked defeated and angry.

"Tuan," Katlin said, "tell me what the man said."

The boy looked at his mother and said something harsh. Her response was angry, but Katlin saw fear there as well.

"Tuan," Katlin said seriously, holding him by his shoulders in front of her so that he was forced to look into her eyes, "you must tell me the truth. Otherwise, we'll have to send you and your mother back. Tell her that."

As he spoke, Mai Dung's face twisted into outright panic. She erupted with a string of bullet-fast words, looking between Katlin and her son. Katlin caught phrases repeated. Mai Dung suddenly stopped, stared at Katlin a moment, and then hid her face in her hands. Katlin heard her sobbing softly.

"Tuan," Katlin said softly. "What was your mother saying?"

The boy seemed concerned for his distraught mother. He watched her, waiting for direction, and when she didn't look up, he turned to Katlin. "She said that we were attacked. We had to leave. We had no choice."

"Tuan," Katlin said as gently as she could, "is that the truth? Did the Iranians attack your base?"

He glanced at his mother, as though making sure she wasn't watching, and then looked at Katlin and shook his head quickly.

"Oh, damn," Katlin whispered. She turned to Julius. "She exaggerated what happened when the Iranians arrived—she just followed along where Meyer was leading her."

"Clearly," Julius said, disgusted. To him, accuracy was a moral indicator.

Katlin's mind was spinning. "We have to get word to the nexgens," she said.

"That would be prudent," Julius agreed, offering no help. Katlin hadn't expected any. He was always on the outside, looking in.

"Can we tap into the com-link from here?"

He nodded, reaching around Mai Dung.

"Don't!"

Meyer stood in the doorway, looking as though Julius was proposing to short the main battery banks. Katlin wondered how long he'd been standing there.

"Why not?" Julius asked, annoyed.

"The boy's lying."

"Be serious, Meyer. Look at her," he said, gesturing at Mai Dung, who was still crying into her hands.

"I am," Meyer said darkly, "and I see a woman who's been traumatized."

"She was afraid we'd send her back," Katlin said. "It's obvious. She was desperate that we think of her as a refugee."

"So? That's my point exactly. She's terrified of facing Iranians again."

Katlin tripped on her next thought. Mai Dung *was* afraid. Perhaps Meyer was right.

No! "Mai Dung lied about Iranians attacking the Chinese base."

"You don't know that."

"We can't take the chance. We have to call off the nexgens."

"You have it backwards. We can't afford the risk of calling them off. You heard how vulnerable we are."

"Well," Julius said as he reached again for the com-link switch, "we can at least fill them in on the possibilities."

Katlin yelped as Meyer plunged forward. He knocked her sideways, and she realized that he was going for Julius. The momentum of his lunge threw Julius off his chair, and he fell sideways, crashing against the rack of equipment.

"Jesus *Christ!*" Julius yelled, holding his head. "What the hell's the matter with you?"

"I'm not going to let anybody compromise the safety of the base," Meyer said, backing away to give Julius room. "It's my responsibility."

"I think the base is my father's responsibility," Katlin said softly.

She thought Meyer was going to punch her, but he turned back to Julius, who held up both hands in surrender. "I'm only the engineer," Julius said. "I'm not responsible for the base, just every last goddamn piece of equipment that keeps it running." He held out his palm towards Meyer as he used the other to lift himself to his feet.

From behind Meyer came the voice of Katlin's father. "What's going on here?"

Meyer spun to face the CTO. "Nothing," he said.

"No, no," Katlin said as her father came in. "Not nothing. We think that Mai Dung is lying—"

"Keep me out of it," Julius said, rubbing the bump on his head.

"Okay," Katlin continued, "*I* think that Mai Dung is lying about the Iranians attacking their base."

Her father nodded. "I was wondering about her myself."

Meyer's face was red as a tomato. He glared back and forth between Katlin and her father. "Of *course* you're going to believe *her*," he spat.

"I don't *believe* anybody," her father said levelly. "I'm simply expressing that I've had my doubts about her story."

"Daddy—sir," Katlin said, "we have to call the nexgens back. Or at least tell them to hold their fire for now."

Her father rubbed his chin as Meyer backed up against the wall, fumbling in the black shoulder bag he often carried. "I suppose you're right," her father said. "Maybe we could keep them in position, but hold off firing until we're absolutely sure—"

"No!" Meyer yelled.

He was holding his gun, waving it back and forth between Katlin and her father.

"Christ!" her father said, "put that away, Dirk. What's the matter with you?"

"I will not let you jeopardize the base," Meyer said through gritted teeth, holding the gun level at him. "It *is* my responsibility."

Her father looked worried, maybe even scared. "Dirk, put the gun down. Use your head, man. You're not making sense." Her father's eyes flashed with understanding. "Dirk, have you been pulling drugs from the med-genie?"

Just then Louden's voice yelled from down the hall, "What the hell?"

Surprised, Meyer swung the gun towards him, and an instant later, Katlin's father sprang forward. An explosion like nothing Katlin had ever experienced made her jerk back in shock.

Meyer's wide-eyed face was staring down at the floor—at her father!

Ж Ж Ж

"Ops Head," Van called into his helmet microphone, "you

there? Katlin?"

"They're probably busy getting the shift crew settled," Tyna said.

From their defensive position a hundred yards west of the locks, they'd watched the last of the work shift nexgens cycle through the lock just minutes before.

"Or they feel too guilty to talk to the sacrificial lambs," Burl said from somewhere an equal distance east of the locks.

"You don't even know what a sacrificial lamb is," Kim's voice said.

"I think the word 'sacrificial' says it all," Burl replied.

"Okay, cut the chatter. We're loading our charge," Van said, holding the makeshift gun sideways so that Tyna could drop the capsule into the slot. "Remember what Julius said—"

"Yeah, yeah," Burl said. "He didn't have proper springs for the triggers he made. If we're not careful, we'll blow holes in each other instead of the stinking Iranians."

"Burl, can we be serious for once?"

"Okay. Just this once. No, I've changed my mind. Did you hear the one about the nexgen who mistook his pillow for his helmet?"

"Burl! Please. Ops Head, are you there?"

Silence.

Van sighed. Managers were always in your face until you actually wanted them. "You guys ready for lights out?"

"Ours are already out, chief," Burl said. "The stinking Iranians can probably see you all the way from the terminator."

"Okay," Van said. "Tyna, you've got the next bit and charge ready?"

She held them out into her light for him to see.

"Good. You'll feel my hand reach out. When you do, place the bit in it first. Then I'll need the charge."

Van struggled to keep his voice from trembling. Talking it through brought home the fact that they really were preparing for battle, risking their lives.

"Right, chief," she said, dousing her head lamp. They called him that when they were joking around, but now it was nervous energy.

He reached up and flicked the switch, and lunar night snapped down around them.

Van tried to let the brilliant sprays of stars work their soothing magic, but the thumping in his throat made a tiny, repetitive little warning. *Danger! Danger! Danger!*

"Do you think they can hear us?" Burl asked in the darkness.

Van had no clue. Julius might know, but everybody inside was too busy to tune in. *We're only out here risking our lives for them.*

"I don't know," Van said. "But from now on, we won't say anything that would give away our positions, or … what we intend to, uh, do."

"Roger-dodger," Burl replied. "Iksnay on the infoyay."

They settled into silence. For once, Van would have welcomed Burl's irreverent chatter, but his friend was clearly uneasy about the darkness harboring enemy ears.

"Oh, crimps!" Burl whispered.

"What?" Van whispered back.

"I think I saw it!"

Van strained to see, watching to the south, where the melted-rock snake ended. His eyes watered from the effort.

"Yes!" Burl whispered again. "There it is!"

"I don't *see* it," Van hissed frantically.

"You're probably looking the wrong way."

"Crimps!" Tyna and Kim said together, and Van spun around.

There it was. A long violet ghost pencil high above the crater wall. It had snuck up on them from the opposite direction!

Van swung his gun around and aimed at the top of the pencil. He swallowed and slowly shifted his finger away from the trigger. *Easy there. It's still too far.*

The pencil just hovered, above what Van guessed was the very center of the base buried underneath, inside the crater wall. What was it waiting for? Far below it, another ghostly cloud formed, billowing out from all sides. He realized that this was lunar dust, blown aside by the ship's exhaust. *Of course*, he thought. *The hot propellant would splash on the ground even if the ship was a mile up.* The exhaust had to be travelling really fast. How fast, he had no clue.

"What's it doing?" Kim asked.

"We wait and find out," Van replied.

The com-link hissed with a collective gasp as brilliant lights appeared above the thin translucent column, pointing down and splashing on top of the crater wall where they couldn't see. The violet pencil, almost invisible next to the lights, tilted, and the ship moved to the left. A moment later it moved to the right.

"It's *watching* us," Kim whispered.

Van had the same eerie feeling, and it sent shivers galloping inside his pressure suit. "No," he said, "it's ... looking for something."

"For what?" she asked. "For the prisoners?"

"They're refugees—and no, they wouldn't be looking for them up there."

"Then, what?"

The image appeared in his mind out of nowhere.

"Burl," Van said, "did you see that plastic cylinder Tyna and I found when we went to investigate the ship's first visit?"

"I heard about it. Julius was going to dissect it, but I doubt he's gotten to it yet— ah, I see. You're thinking that it's some kind of location beacon."

"It could explain why they're poking around up there."

"They're picking up the signal from inside the Lab. It would also explain why they came in from the north."

"Right," Van said, "They were on a straight-line course from the Chinese base to the beacon. That would explain why they dropped it in the first place."

"Hey!" Kim exclaimed.

Van saw. The violet ghost pencil had tilted again and the ship eased forward, towards them. The com-link was silent as they all held their breath. The lights swiveled this way and that, searching, searching. Van caught glimpses of the sides of the ship, silvery metallic—shiny and cleaner than anything he'd imagined. The ship slid out over the rim of the crater, and large, probing circles of light slipped down along the crater wall, and prowled the crater floor. Here, the lunar soil was a complete jumble from their production activity, and the ship halted. The probing spotlights moved in smaller arcs, studying the human indications.

"What'll we do?" Burl whispered.

"Wait," Van said. "The locks aren't in danger yet."

To his relief, the ship glided east along the crater wall, away from the locks. He realized that he'd been holding his breath. He relaxed his hands, cramped from clutching the poker.

The probing ship stopped. The signs of human churning diminished the farther it moved along the crater wall. The platform, invisible in the darkness, sat out in the crater floor, away from the base. The ship's pilot interpreted the signs and reversed direction. The billowing dust, within which a new melted rock snake was forming, moved back, retracing its path. It came to its original position, and kept going. One of the spotlights angled up, and a blinding circle of illuminated crater wall raced along ahead. The spotlight fell on the small personnel lock, and froze there. The ship stopped as well, hovering in place.

"Shit!" Burl hissed, invoking a Manager curse.

Van lifted his gun so that he was sighting along the tube towards the locus of spotlights floating above the violet pencil. He waited, holding his breath again. He was ready in case the ship decided to attack the locks.

Suddenly he heard Burl huff, and one of the spotlights went dark. "Did I get it?" he called excitedly.

"Burl!" Van yelled. "Did you *shoot*?"

"Yeah! Didn't you see? It was aiming for the lock."

"It was shining a *light* on it, you idiot!"

"Gimme another load," Burl said to Kim.

"Burl!" Van yelled. "Hold it!"

The ship had swung its remaining lights up, parallel to the ground, and was sweeping them back and forth, looking for whatever had knocked out one of its eyes. Inside one of the beams, Van saw a flick of motion, Burl's next shot. "Burl!" Van yelled, "for crimp's sake! *Hold it*!"

It was too late. The ship must have seen the titanium shell as well. All the lights turned in that direction, and the pencil leaned hard over. The cluster of lights moved quickly towards Burl, gaining altitude as it went. Other lights joined the spotlights—these tear-shaped lights were all pointing downward.

Burl and Kim's frantic, nearly unintelligible, calls of panic filled the com-link. "Crimps, oh crimps," Van muttered as he swung his poker cannon, paused to aim, and then fired. Another spotlight went dead, and he saw a shower of glinting debris briefly hover for a moment next to the intruder menace. It was like hundreds of stars had descended to grace the Moon.

An instant later, the shimmering jewels disappeared, and the few remaining spotlights seemed to be splitting up, moving away from each other.

Van realized that this was an illusion.

The ship was surging towards him.

Chapter 15

"Run, Van!" Tyna yelled.

"Wait!" he said, grabbing her arm. "You can't outrun it."

Besides, there was something odd about the monster as it approached, something unexpected. It came to him. The ghostly violet pencil was gone. Suddenly Van was blinded as one of the spotlights found him. He put his arm up to block the brilliant onslaught. He heard Tyna whimper. They seemed to stand there, bathed in the overpowering beam, for an eternity before the light was gone. Van blinked, willing his eyes to recover. The ship had moved off and stopped, hovering a hundred feet away. It was much smaller than he'd thought—laid sideways, it could probably fit in the hanger. It was the super-heated pencil exhaust that had made it seem gigantic. The teardrop shaped lights were actually small rocket engines, probably providing just enough thrust for landing.

"Van," Burl's voice came over the com-link. "You alive?"

"Yeah. It's good to hear you are, too."

"I don't understand why. When it came over us, I felt a lot of heat, but we should have been vaporized."

"They turned off the main drive—the anti-matter thing. They're using small maneuvering rockets now."

"Aha. Lucky for me."

"I don't think it was luck. They turned it off to spare your ugly skin."

"The chemical rockets could do the job just as well if they got close enough."

"But they didn't. They don't want to hurt us."

"I don't know about that. I wouldn't take any chances."

"We wouldn't be out here in the first place if that were the case—oops!"

"What?" Burl asked.

"They're moving."

The small ship lifted, tilted, and came towards them. Tyna clutched his arm, but Van held still, waiting. Fifty feet from them, it stopped, and settled to the ground. The four rockets rimming the bottom went dark, and then the two undamaged spotlights went out in quick succession, leaving utter impenetrable darkness behind.

"What are they doing?" Tyna whispered.

"Dunno," Van replied.

In the darkness, a rectangular light appeared, the size of one of Glenda's hardcover novels. "It's a window," Tyna said softly

Something covered the opening from the inside, blocking the light, and then pulled away a few inches.

"It's a word," Tyna said. "They've written something. What does it say?"

It looked like the letters had been formed by smearing grease with a finger. The writing was stylized, slanted and continuous, the letters connected to each other. Van recognized it as cursive writing, something he'd seen in movies.

"I think it says, 'Americans,'" Tyna said tentatively. "They're *Americans*? Crimps!"

"No," Van said. "Hold on. Isn't that a question mark at the end?"

"Uh, yeah! You're right. Ha! They're asking if we're American. Um, how do we answer?"

As if responding to her question, one of the spotlights flashed once, and the window went dark.

"What are they *doing*?" Tyna said.

"Just wait," Van replied. "They're up to something."

Darkness reigned. Starlight glinted here and there on the eerily clean skin of the shuttle—for that's obviously what it was. He jumped when the spotlight flashed once. A few seconds later, it began flashing on and off, like one of the lights in the showers did before it failed completely.

"What are they doing?" Tyna asked. "Do you think they have a problem?"

Immediately, the light began flashing regularly, where before it had seemed random. Then it went dark. After a moment, it began the same seemingly random flashing.

"I think they're trying to communicate," Van said. "Maybe it's some kind of code."

Instantly, the flashing became very regular as before, and again went dark.

"It sure seems so," Tyna said, and the light flashed once.

"Crimps!" Van exclaimed. "It's as though they can hear us."

The light flashed once.

Van froze, absorbing what was happening.

"Guys," Burl's said. "They're probably tuned in to the com-link."

The light flashed twice.

Silence.

"And they understand English," Tyna observed.

The light flashed twice.

"But they don't say anything," she added.

Darkness.

"Which means," Burl concluded, "that they can hear us, but, for whatever reason, they can't transmit on the com-link band."

The light flashed three times.

"Crimps," was all Burl said.

After a moment, the light again began the seemingly random flashing.

"It's obviously a code of some sort," Van said, and it flashed and then went dark.

"It's a code, then," Van said, and the light flashed once.

"And you think we should be able to understand it," he added, talking directly to the ship now. The light flashed once.

"Burl," Van said, "any ideas?"

"A simple code would be to count the order of letters in the alphabet, but the pattern doesn't seem to follow that."

"Is that true?" Van asked. "I mean that this is not the code."

One flash.

"It would be pretty cumbersome," Tyna said. You'd have to count pretty high on some letters."

One flash.

"But, you're pretty sure this is a code we should know?" Van asked.

Two flashes.

"Huh," Van said. He knew the answer. "We need Katlin."

ж ж ж

"Blood is highly conductive," Julius said.

Katlin glanced at him. She wanted to ignore him. He knew no more about medical issues than she did.

But she couldn't ignore the blood. It seemed to be everywhere. There was a long trail tracing the path Julius and Louden had taken as they carried her father. Both men were covered in it, although that didn't seem to bother them. Blood continued to ooze from the wound in her father's side, pooling on the med-genie table, and smearing the multitude of sensor arms.

She guessed what Julius meant. "What are you implying?" she demanded, forcing him to put words to his callous concern.

"It's just an observation," he replied.

"You're afraid my father's blood is going to damage the med-genie?"

"Like I said, it's just an observation."

The first thing the genie had done was anesthetize her father, and he already looked dead, lying there limp and pale. Her fear became anger. "You think my father's going to die anyway, so why damage your precious machine, that's what you're thinking, isn't it?"

"I didn't say that. And in any case, the 'machine,' as you call it, isn't mine, and it could save your life someday, assuming …"

"Assuming what?" she said, practically yelling now. "Assuming my father doesn't damage it?" She pushed Julius as she said this.

"Chill!" Louden said. He was acting as the genie's long-defunct hands, holding a sensor in each fist and moving them along her father's body as the genie gave him verbal direction. "I can't hear her instructions above your arguing."

One of the nexgens appeared in the doorway and froze in horror at the sight.

"What do you want?" Julius asked harshly.

The girl winced. "They're calling for Katlin," she said.

"Who is?" Katlin asked.

"Oh! Van! He's outside!" The girl said this like it was beyond comprehension.

Katlin took a breath and let it out slowly. "I'll be right there."

The girl took one last look at the bloody sight, and scampered off.

"I'd better go," Katlin said, and then to Julius, "Can I trust you?"

"Don't be ridiculous. It's insulting."

"I'll take that as a yes."

"She's finished the assessment probe," Louden announced. "Julius, sterilize your hands and take over, please. Help her set up the vitals sensors." He then took Katlin by the elbow and led her out into the hallway.

Katlin shivered. She was terrified of what Louden was about to tell her. "He's going to die, isn't he?" she said, the words catching in her throat.

"Maybe," Louden said. "I'm not going to lie to you. The bullet punctured his large colon. The genie—with our help—can deal with the rest of the damage, but the colon needs surgical repair."

"The genie can't … do it, can she?"

"She could have ten years ago, but not now, she'd need her manipulation arms."

"Can't Julius get one of the arms working?"

She knew the answer, but there was no option too remote to explore with her father bleeding away his life.

"You know he can't, hon." It had been years since Louden had called her that. "The med-genie's parts are highly specialized. Julius used up all the spares long ago. And even if he could, there's no time."

Warm tears ran down her cheeks. "Can't we do it?" she said, crying now. "Can't we do the operation?"

He nodded. "I'm going to try. The med-genie will watch and instruct me every step of the way." He patted her shoulder and smiled. "We'll do the best we can. It might just work."

She nodded vigorously, unable to talk through her tears. She squeezed his hand hard, and hurried off towards Meyer's office, the nearest com-link access.

She assumed the Ops Head was hiding somewhere, and stopped short when he appeared around a corner. He paused only a moment before coming towards her. He seemed distracted, as though deep in thought. He barely glanced at her as he passed, asking simply, "Is he dead?"

She couldn't believe it. He was going to walk right by, not even waiting for an answer. Let him. She wouldn't know what to say anyway, other than to scream curses.

He stopped, though, and turned back to her. "Have you heard any word from outside?" he asked.

Katlin stared at him, speechless. He stood there waiting for an answer. "I can't talk to you," she blurted. Rage, starting low in her belly, was beginning to bubble. "You don't have a right to know."

He seemed confused for a moment, and then his eyes widened, as though he suddenly understood what she'd said. "Are you stupid?" he asked, genuinely wondering. A change washed over his face, and he blinked as if with new lucidity.

"Can't you see?" he asked, stepping up and thrusting his face towards her, forcing her to step back. "I'm the base leader now."

She was intimidated, but the rage firing her belly refused to be restrained. "You can't become the base leader by a coup d'état, you asshole!" she yelled hoarsely.

His eyes narrowed, calculating his prey. "Your father brought it on himself."

She was breathing heavily, wondering what it would be like to grab his throat and squeeze until he choked for mercy. "You don't feel any remorse whatsoever," she said. This wasn't just a provocative thrust. It was true. "You're insane, aren't you?" she asked, wonderingly. The idea suddenly rang stunningly true.

His eyes grew wider and wider, his jaw muscles worked, and he reached behind him. A moment later, his arm wrapped around her neck, and his gun pressed her temple. "That is inexcusable!" he yelled. "I will not abide insubordination!" She felt him twisting the gun, as though searching for the most lethal angle. She knew he was going to pull the trigger. Every fiber of her silently screamed that his insanity was capable of anything.

"Dirk! Put the gun down!"

It was Louden, calling from around the far corner.

Katlin's head jerked as Meyer swung his arm away and fired down the hall. The detonation seemed to crack her head open. Her right ear buzzed, as though vital wires had been yanked loose. Through the numbing haze, she heard shouting.

"Dirk! Listen to me! I queried the doc-genie. I know that you forced her to increase your dose. It's affecting you, pal. Put down the gun before it's too late."

A deep growl came from Meyer's chest. He pushed her away and fired again down the hall, then swung the gun back at her. "Move!" he screamed, then fired again at Louden.

She stumbled off. *That's three bullets*, she thought, her mind racing in high gear. *No, four. The first one shot Daddy. That leaves just two left.*

They came to a split, and she turned right, towards the locks without thinking. "This way!" Meyer screamed, waving the gun madly.

She gasped. Meyer's gun wasn't an old six-shooter like in the John Wayne movies. It had a cartridge, and she had no idea how many bullets it held.

He was leading her to his office, to the com-link. Inside, he waved for her to sit in his chair and handed her the headset. As she slipped it on, he said, "You do as I say, or you're dead." He held the gun to her head, and flipped the switch that activated the speaker.

"Katlin!" Van's voice said. "Is that you?"

"Yes," she said, glancing at Meyer's wild eyes. "It's me. Uh, what's your status?"

"Hey," he said, "the shuttle's trying to communicate with some kind of code. They can hear our com-link transmissions, but can't talk."

"Um, okay."

"They're flashing their lights. We think—Tyna thinks—that there's two kinds, long ones, and short ones."

"Do they come in groups?"

Van laughed. "They said 'yes.'"

"I thought they couldn't talk to you."

"They flash their lights for 'yes,' and just stay dark for 'no.' Ha! He flashed his light—he agrees with me."

"Dammit!" Meyer yelled. "Enough with the games! Ask them why they haven't taken out the invader."

"Is that Ops Head?" Van asked.

Meyer leaned in and Katlin had to tilt her head back. The gun followed her. "Yes!" he shouted, "and you are to fire on the intruder. That's an order!"

The com-link was silent. Katlin imagined Van and Tyna talking with their helmets pressed together.

"Van!" Meyer yelled. "Confirm your order."

A click indicated that Van had re-connected. "I'd like to talk to Zeedo."

Katlin looked at Meyer, and he shook his head threateningly. "He—" she started. "He's—he's hurt," she managed, struggling to contain a sob. "He can't come."

Meyer ripped the headset from her. She yelped and put her hand to her head to make sure her ear hadn't gone with it. "I'm the base leader now," Meyer said into the mouthpiece. "You have your order."

Silence.

"Do you understand, Van?"

"How badly is Zeedo hurt?" Van asked. "How did it happen?"

The vein in Meyer's temple throbbed. He still held the gun to her head. In his building rage, she could see him pulling the trigger reflexively. She slowly lifted her hand, intending to gently move the tip of the gun away, but he threw her a warning glare. "That is not important now!" he screamed into the microphone.

Burl's voice came on. "Hey, I have an idea. If we could set the intruders to work on the platform, Ops Head could then order them to go away with no dispute."

Katlin felt the spittle flying when Meyer screamed, "There is no dispute! I am base leader." He paused, breathing deep, labored breaths. A calmness came to his face that scared Katlin even more than the rage. "Burl," he said calmly. "You're a dead man. Your years of abuse are about to come full circle."

Silence.

"Um," Van finally said, "the ship's flashing. It seems urgent."

Meyer stared at the wall a moment, and then handed the headset to Katlin. To her relief, he also removed the gun from her head.

"Van," she said, "you there?"

"Yeah. Hey, Katlin." He sounded relieved. "Any ideas on the code?"

She nodded, even though they couldn't see her. It was good to be *doing* something. "You said that there seemed to be long and short flashes, and that they came in groups?"

"Uh, yeah. That sounds right."

"It's probably Morse code."

"Uh, okay. I've never heard of that—wow! Hold on. The ship is agreeing with you."

"Good. Each group of flashes is an individual letter. You say they can hear us?"

"Yes."

"Okay, normally you'd have to gauge the length of spaces—of darkness—to distinguish between letters and words, but since they can hear us, I suggest we just take the letters and words one at a time."

"They've flashed that they agree. Uh, you know this code? I mean, you know the whole alphabet?"

"My dad—Zeedo—made me memorize it." She'd never called him that before, but it felt right, like she was aligned against his new enemy, a madman. "I guess for just this sort of situation."

The decoding was tedious—letter by letter, then word by word, the message from the ship slowly unfolded. "They've gone dark," Van announced. "Maybe they're waiting for an answer?"

Katlin scanned what she had written. "Yeah. It looks like we have a question ... they want to know if we have the Chinese crew—"

Meyer had slapped his hand over her mouth. "Ask them if they're Iranian," he called into the microphone.

"Uh," Van said, "they can hear you directly, you know—looks like they're replying."

A minute later, Katlin had the response. "Here it is, 'Yes, of course.'"

"Wait," Van said, "there's more."

Katlin decoded and scribbled, and finally looked nervously at Meyer. "They're repeating the question about the Chinese crew."

Meyer tilted the microphone towards him, dragging Katlin along. "You are trespassing on American territory, and you need to leave immediately. Your presence is an act of war." After a moment, Meyer said, "Van, what are they doing?"

"Nothing. Wait, they're replying—you ready Kat?"

She decoded and wrote. "They say, 'How act of war?'"

Again, Meyer pulled the microphone to him. "You know damn well! Your exhaust can melt *rock*, for God's sake." He took a deep breath. "Van, what's happening—"

"A reply."

When Katlin looked at what she wrote, she sighed. "Same thing. They want to know if the Chinese crew is safe."

"Ops Head," Van said, "why don't we just tell them the situation? That the rover didn't make it all the way, but that we were able to save Mai Dung and Tuan."

Meyer stared at the speaker. His brow furrowed. "Van, did they just hear that?"

After a moment that Katlin guessed was carefully calculated, Van said, "Oops."

Katlin closed her eyes at what was about to explode. And it did. "God *dammit* it, you stupid idiot!" Meyer screamed, his temple again throbbing. "How in God's name could you be so goddamned *thick*?"

She kept her eyes closed, imagining what Burl was going to say—perhaps that Ops Head had managed to squeeze a lot of God into that. But for once he kept quiet. He must be taking Meyer's threat seriously.

"Message coming in," Van reported.

After the ship was done, Katlin read the result. "They say, 'We have a problem.'"

Meyer grabbed the microphone. "What kind of problem?"

After a minute, Van said, "They're dark, Ops Head. Sorry."

Meyer chewed on his lip. "Van, time's up. Fire on them."

Silence.

"Van, report."

"Sorry, Ops Head. The gun is jammed."

Katlin suppressed a smile.

"How the hell can it jam?" Meyer raged. "It's worked fine for a dozen years."

"I know, Ops Head. It's kind of ironic."

Meyer slapped the microphone back, and it hit Katlin painfully on the cheek. While he paced his small office, she tried to collect her thoughts. Van probably caught the gist that Meyer was lost in deep rage, but he didn't know that Meyer had shot her father, or that he was holding the gun on her now. More importantly, he didn't know the reason why.

"Hey, Van," she said, trying to sound casual.

Meyer stopped and stared at her.

"Yeah, Kat," came Van's voice.

"The ship's still dark?"

"Yeah."

Here goes. "Hey, once this is all over, there's a movie I think we should cue up."

He took a moment, probably puzzled by the non sequitur. "Yeah? Uh, what?"

"It's one you've never seen. Bradley Cooper. It's called Silver Linings Playbook. In the middle, he really shoots himself in the foot—"

"Cut the damn chatter!" Meyer ordered.

"Hey!" Van said, excited now. "Something's happening!"

"What?" Katlin said. Meyer stepped up close to the speaker. He held the pistol cradled in both hands.

"The ship is—oh, crimps!"

"What?" Katlin practically yelled. "What's happening?"

"The hatch on the ship. It opened."

Blaine C. Readler

Chapter 16

Van winked off his microphone and jammed Tyna's helmet against his. "What was that about?" he yelled.

The distant reply came back. "You mean the Bradley Cooper thing? I don't know. I guess she was asking you out on a date. I'd expect you'd be thrilled."

He rolled his eyes. "Be serious. We played that movie for the fifth time just a few weeks ago. She knew I was there."

"How do you know that?"

"We talked afterwards. I remember. She said Bradley Cooper was a great actor, and I said that exactly half the nexgens agreed, and coincidentally they were all females."

"Okay, so she forgot about that," Tyna said.

"Kat doesn't forget things."

"So, it's 'Kat' now, is it?"

"Come on. Be serious."

"I am. I think she just asked you out on a date."

Van didn't think that was it. She wouldn't date a nexgen, and even if she did, she certainly wouldn't ask over the public com-link. Besides, he was uncomfortable knowing that Tyna thought he was going to hook up with Katlin.

"Ops Head's getting antsy," Tyna reminded.

Meyer was calling for an update. He was even more irritable than usual, if that was possible. No matter how they had annoyed him in the past, Van couldn't remember him screaming over the com-link like that. He'd never threatened Burl with violence. Van guessed it was the stress of all these alien contacts, and being a Manager.

He winked on his microphone. "Ship, can you hear me?"

A light flashed.

"What's the next move?" Van asked.

The ship answered with a word in Morse Code, and Katlin translated it as 'Talk.'"

"You want me to come into the ship?"

Flash.

"I'll go too," Tyna said.

"Ship," Van said, "is there room for two of us?"

Darkness.

"Sorry," Van said, giving her a little nudge.

The com-link snapped and cracked, and Van winced, knowing that Meyer was going to shout directly into his microphone again.

"Van, you are not to go near that invader. Do you understand?"

Tyna looked at him questioningly. "I understand, Ops Head," Van said, "but the visitor is nowhere near the platform."

"Goddamn it! I told you! I'm the base leader now!"

"Sorry, sir, I'll need to hear that from Zeedo. I'm going to investigate the ship."

Van tried to tune out the threats and vivid details of punishment as he made his way towards the open hatch. Meyer finally ordered Burl to fire on the ship, regardless of that son-of-a-bitch Van's proximity, to which Burl offered his apologies, but his gun had now jammed as well. Suddenly an ear-splitting crash came across the com-link, and Meyer was silent. Van had reached the shuttle, just a looming silhouette in the starlight. The open hatch ten feet above him held even deeper darkness. Meyer was still absent.

"Ops Head?" Van finally said, but there was only silence. He repeated, but still no response.

"I think he smashed his terminal," Burl offered. "It's just a wild guess, and I could be wrong, but something tells me he might be angry with us."

Van grinned. He was glad Burl was at his back. The sweet-and-sour dish offered up by the mess-genie would be just bland dessert without the sour part.

Suddenly, the inside of the tiny airlock above him lit up, beckoning him. "Goodbye, Kansas," he said as he grasped the sides of the ladder built into one of the landing legs and pulled himself upward.

"Are you sure his air valve is open?" Burl asked quietly.

"Shh!" Tyna admonished in a whisper. "It's from The Wizard of Oz. You'd know that if you weren't busy scoffing through the whole movie."

Van reached the open hatch and slid inside. The cavity was barely larger than his body. "What now?" he asked.

The light inside the lock flashed off and back on.

He wasn't sure what that meant. "Um, do you want me to do something?"

Again the light flashed off and on.

"Kat?" he asked. "You there?"

Silence. Maybe Meyer had indeed smashed his com-link terminal. If so, it was a radical departure—a stunning reversal—from the normally stern, no-nonsense Ops Head.

The light flashed.

The ship was waiting for him. *What does it want?* He stood, staring out across light years of vacuum at the distant stars. *Vacuum.* "Oops," he said. "Uh, should I close the hatch door?"

The light flashed twice.

"I'll take that as an enthusiastic yes," he said, reaching out to grasp the handle and pull the door closed. It ended up two inches from the tip of his nose. "Do I latch it somehow?"

Flash.

He found that he could turn the handle. He did this by feel, since there wasn't enough room to look down. He turned it once, and then twice, and a green light came on in front of him. He waited, and soon heard the swelling hiss of inrushing air, which quickly subsided. *What now?*

He found out a moment later when the wall behind him suddenly flopped away, and he fell backwards into blinding bright light. Someone caught him, and pushed him upright. Blinking in the dazzling light, he turned to face a man who seemed to have stepped out from the movies.

Most of the nexgens, and the Managers as well, wore their hair fairly short, and shaved only when their beards began to interfere with the helmet controls, but this man looked like a doll. The black hair on his head was less than an inch long, and impossibly even, as though each individual hair had been measured to an exact, equal, length. He wore a beard, but it looked more like a felt covering than Van's wild sprouting. He wore a uniform—a crisp, clean *uniform*.

The man glanced at his hands distastefully, and accepted a cloth from another man, which he used to wipe them. He nodded at Van, and gestured towards his helmet. Van took it off, and had a reflexive impulse to slam it back into place. For a brief moment, completely illogically, he thought there was no air in the ship. It smelled like *nothing*.

The man who had caught him, on the other hand, looked suddenly aghast. He glanced at his companion, who raised his eyebrows and shrugged, and then rolled his eyes, and slyly put his hand to his mouth.

The first man, seeming to collect himself, bowed a little, hesitated, and then offered his hand, which Van shook. "I am Captain Namazi," he said in an accent similar to ones Van had heard in the movies, "and this is Lieutenant Paria. I assume you must be Van."

"Yes," Van replied, looking around at the inside of the shuttle. Everything was so clean and *new*. He noticed Paria surreptitiously hand his superior the cloth to wipe his hands again. Van glanced down at his own hands, and realized that people in movies really were as clean as they appeared. Embarrassed, he clasped his dirty hands behind his back.

Namazi's countenance turned serious. "Why did you fire on my ship?" he asked harshly.

The challenge caught Van off guard. The ship—the entity communicating via flashing lights—had seemed so cooperative, so helpful. They had indeed fired on them, though. "My friend—my co-worker—thought you were going to damage our air locks."

"On *purpose*?" Namazi asked, appalled.

Van shrugged sheepishly.

The shuttle captain studied him. "You take orders from … the

'Ops Head'?"

"Uh, only when we're working on the platform—that is, when we're mining product. That's the, uh, operations. That's where—"

"The 'Ops' title comes from," Namazi concluded, nodding. "There is contention between your Ops Head and someone named Zeedo? There is a struggle over leadership?"

Van took a breath and let it out. "The name 'Zeedo' is short for the initials CTO, which stands for … uh …" He'd forgotten.

"Chief Technical Officer?" Namazi offered.

"Yes! That's it. His name is Cummings, Arthur Cummings. And honestly, I don't know what's going on. I don't know why Meyer—that's Ops Head—thinks that he's now the base leader. They said that Zeedo—Mr. Cummings—is hurt somehow. I guess Meyer thinks he's next in line."

Namazi studied Van another minute. "This Meyer. He seems very … aggressive. He ordered you to continue firing on us, even though we had retreated and de-activated the main drive." He tilted his head a little. "Do you know something?"

The shuttle captain was adept at reading Van's face. "I was told that Meyer, uh, that he doesn't like you—he doesn't like Iranians."

Namazi's brows furrowed as he absorbed this.

"Um, actually, the word he used was 'detest.'"

Namazi held his hands out in surrender. "Why? I believe your base has had no contact, certainly no contact with Iranians, ever since the flare."

Van shrugged. "That's true. I don't know. Something from his past." He threw his host a quick glance. "On the other hand, we heard that you attacked the Chinese base."

Namazi stared with puzzlement. Then he laughed. "Attacked? Where in heaven's name did you get that idea?"

"From Mai Dung—one of the survivors in the Chinese rovers."

Namazi shook his head. "I can't begin to guess where that came from. There were arguments, certainly. Heated discussions, but that was business. Business is negotiation, and often negotiation is arguing." His face clouded. "I am not proud to admit that part of the negotiation involved food and supplies for their base. But in the end, both sides received what they needed."

Van believed him. "I think Mai Dung was afraid we'd send her and her son back. She was intent that we accept them as refugees."

Namazi considered a moment. "I can understand why she would want to get her son away." He glanced at Paria. "Conditions at the Chinese base are … let us say they are not ideal." He nodded. "Yes, I can understand why Mai Dung would lie. I probably shouldn't tell you this, but the Chinese leaders were willing to pay us to retrieve their rover." Namazi glanced again at Paria. "They told us that saving the four 'thieves' would have to be at our own expense. You should understand that we came specifically to make sure Mai Dung and the others were safe. We had no intention of bringing the rover back without them. In fact, we coerced the Chinese leaders into promising not to prosecute the father who had stolen food for his son."

Paria said something in their own language. Namazi smiled. "My lieutenant claims that the Chinese are not fit to do business with. I try to be a little more forgiving. Living so isolated on the far side of the Moon cannot be an easy life."

Van just looked at him.

Namazi smiled again. "Of course, this is the only life you know. I am not in a position to judge. But, tell me, what happened to the other members of the rover—I believe it was Mai Dung's husband and his brother."

Van described how they'd found the rover and hauled it back to the base, and that Mai Dung's husband and brother-in-law were already dead when they found them. Namazi in turn explained that they, the Greater Persia mission, consisted of four members—he was the mission commander, and two others remained in orbit with the larger transport ship. Of the four, he, Namazi, was the only one who spoke English. He had completed his graduate studies at Stanford.

He explained that the Chinese economy had faltered, as had most of the world's, after the flare, and their government had found it increasingly difficult to make the scheduled transport runs to the Moon. The government of Greater Persia had made a deal to establish their own transport runs to the Chinese lunar base for a period of three years. Part of the deal was that he and Paria were to oversee the distribution of supplies throughout the base, and this had been the main negotiating problem when they arrived.

Searching for the rover—following the tracks—had been slow, and consumed a considerable amount of propellant. He had to turn back, and he dropped the beacon where he'd left off.

"I found it," Van said, "and took it back to our base."

Namazi nodded. "You had me scratching my head. I was beginning to doubt our Persian engineers, and they are not happy when that happens. They are a prideful bunch."

"But, why couldn't you talk to us on our com-link?" Van asked.

He nodded again. "Ah, I'm afraid our engineers are indeed to blame for that one. They have, in my opinion, over-engineered our communications. Our transmissions are encoded to a degree that makes them unintelligible to your outdated equipment."

Namazi paused a moment and glanced at a display. "I am afraid we are about out of time. Before I turned back the first time, I thought I saw lights some distance away—"

"That was our operations platform," Van said. "We, uh, turned off all the lights when we saw you."

"That makes sense. In any case, I guessed that the lights meant that I was close to your base—I knew we had been heading in the general direction, just as the rover had been. I made a gamble this time, hoping to contact your base and acquire additional propellant."

"I doubt we have what you'd need." Van said, "Remember, we're outdated."

Namazi smiled. "Touché. I apologize for offending you. That was not my intent. But you see, our propellant is water."

Van blinked. "Did you say water?"

"Yes. Actually, any number of liquids can serve, but the engine has been designed specifically to use water. It is, after all, rather universal." His smile tilted to the sardonic. "On Earth, that is. It is most precious on the Moon. I had to pay a very dear price to obtain more for my second trip." He shook his head. "Even though it was to save their own crew. But now I must leave. I have barely enough to return, and even sitting here on the ground, I am using up the invaluable stock."

"But your drive isn't running," Van said.

Namazi looked at Paria, who was now watching the same display nervously. "Do you understand how an anti-matter drive works?" he asked.

"Not really," Van admitted. He didn't even know what anti-matter was.

"Well, as a rocket drive, the process is as simple as can be. The anti-matter is combined with normal matter in minute amounts, releasing enormous amounts of energy which heats a stream of water to extremely high temperatures, which exits the nozzle at such tremendous velocities, that even small quantities of water produce prodigious thrust."

Van had never heard the word "prodigious" before, but he guessed the meaning.

"That's the easy part," Namazi continued. "The difficult part is keeping the anti-matter from coming in contact with normal matter until it is needed. This is done with powerful magnetic fields, but it requires a large amount of energy to produce them. Can you guess where that energy comes from?"

Van hadn't expected to be tested, and was taken aback. He blurted the first thing that came to mind. "The anti-matter itself?"

"Exactly!" Namazi crowed. "Parallel to the main drive, are turbines that run on super-heated water, which is fueled by anti-matter. These turbines produce the electricity that maintain the magnetic fields." He paused and gazed at Van seriously. "Can you guess what would happen if we run out of propellant, or if the turbines should fail?"

"The magnetic fields would go away, and ... uh-oh."

"Uh-oh, precisely. Nothing would prevent the anti-matter from contacting the ship. As soon as a tiny bit came in contact, it would cause such a disruption, that the rest would contact microseconds later. And you know what that means."

"Boom," Van said.

"And what a boom. We carry enough anti-matter to equal several hydrogen bombs."

"Hmm," Van said, "I think I see. You have to keep the turbines running all the time, which means you need to use some amount of water continuously." He stopped and stared at Namazi.

"You're wondering how that can be?" the Persian captain asked. "How does one ever turn it off? One does not. Once the ship is loaded with anti-matter, it never shuts down completely."

Van hated to disagree with the visitor, but … "Everything fails eventually," he said. That was his world—failing machines.

Namazi nodded once, soberly. "Indeed. This is why anti-matter drives are not allowed on Earth. It is the one thing the entire international community can agree on." He eyed Van a moment. "You nearly obliterated your entire base by firing on my ship."

A tingling skittered up and down Van's arms as he thought about this. He shivered. "You could refuel from our water supply. How much would you need?"

Namazi shook his head. "We need about eighty liters to return, and we have just about that much. Any amount on top of that helps, but that's not the point, I think." He looked at Van knowingly. "Your Ops Head has made it very clear that we are not welcome—he considers us invaders who, by our mere presence, have committed an act of war. His last command was for your colleague to 'take out' my ship, regardless of your safety."

Van sighed. "Meyer has always been a grump, but this, I just don't understand. Even if he holds some grudge against your country—"

"I believe the term was that he detests us."

"Right." Van lifted his shoulders in surrender. He could apologize, but he didn't have the authority to officially offer that.

Paria said something urgent, and gestured at the display. Namazi nodded. "We must leave. One last point—I infer that you and your colleagues resist to some extent the authority of Meyer.

Van felt himself blushing. "Well, you see, he doesn't have—shouldn't have—authority away from the platform—"

"Never mind that. It was obvious in the way you pretended to accidentally communicate to me the status of the rover occupants, and then lied about your guns jamming—"

"Well, wait a second—"

"Don't get me wrong. I am grateful. The fact is that you resist his authority, but you avoid direct disobedience. You find ways to undermine it by cooperative subterfuge."

Van stared at him. It was true, but it was hard to have it thrown in his face.

"Please understand," Namazi continued, "I agree that Meyer does not seem like a man who deserves loyalty. I am not faulting you. My point is simply that I presume that the inferred message from your female colleague had some significance."

Van shook his head. "I don't know what you're talking about."

"I mean the reference about the movie. It was completely out of context. She seems smart. I assumed she was trying to communicate something. I could be wrong. You would know better than I."

Paria spoke again, more urgently, and when Namazi glanced at the display, he nodded. "Van," he said holding out his hand, "thank you for your help. I hope that we have a chance to meet again someday under less troubled circumstances."

Van took his hand and shook it, and then found himself shoved back into the airlock. Paria spoke again, and Namazi looked at a different display. "One of your colleagues has emerged from your base," he reported. Paria said something and laughed. Namazi chuckled. "Yes, this one's pressure suit is clean," he said as he reached to close the inner air lock door. The last thing Van heard him say before the door latched shut was, "And blue."

Chapter 17

Katlin slid down the wall next to the air lock until her butt rested on the floor. Hugging her knees, she let her forehead fall onto them. She was exhausted. She'd never imagined how taxing it was to deal with a madman holding a gun. It was the overshoot of adrenaline, she knew, but it felt like she'd just gotten off the gym bike.

She looked up at the sound of pounding feet. Julius turned the corner, and Louden followed some distance behind. "Are you okay?" Julius asked, concerned.

"Yeah," she said, accepting his helping hand to stand up. "How's my father?"

"I did the best I could," Louden said, huffing to a stop. "He's in the med-genie's hands now."

"Where's Meyer?" Julius asked, and she gestured towards the lock. "Christ! Did he take the gun?"

"Oh, yeah," she replied. "Good riddance, I say—good riddance to them both."

"Jesus," Julius muttered. "The son-of-a-bitch completely ruined the com-link terminal. I wish I'd caught him."

"Can't you pick up the link from the com shack?"

"No. The audio feed was routed through his office terminal."

"You wouldn't want to talk to him," Katlin assured. "Believe me, he's off the deep end. Ask Louden. Meyer would have killed him if he could."

"No," Julius said. "You don't understand. I have to warn him about the ship—the anti-matter drive."

"I thought you didn't believe it used anti-matter."

"I analyzed the data," he said in a tone that told her not to push the point.

"Well, I told him to be careful," she said. "If he caused the ship to crash, it could explode. I could have told him his hair was on fire with the same result."

"No," Julius insisted, "no, you don't understand. It's worse than that. A whole lot worse. An anti-matter drive is essentially a nuclear bomb with a hair trigger."

"You really think it uses anti-matter?"

"Unless they've overturned all the physics I know. It's the only source of enough energy to explain what Van described."

"It's just a pistol," she said, taking one last stab at peace of mind. "The bullets are no bigger than beans."

Julius shook his head with confident dread. "An anti-matter drive is like a house of cards—disrupting almost any piece will bring the whole thing down. Except in this case it doesn't come down. Pieces of the ship—and us—could be blown into orbit."

"We're buried, with solid rock between us," she reminded him.

"You still don't understand the situation," is all he said.

She let go of her last shred of peace of mind.

Ж Ж Ж

Van turned to watch when an orange light illuminated the ground around him. He felt Tyna's hand on his arm, and they watched together as the shuttle rose and tilted, the translucent violet pencil reaching out behind it, nearly horizontal. The ship accelerated away, back over the top of the crater wall. This close, the super-heated exhaust seemed deeply beautiful, a ghost born on an Earth that had continued to evolve without them.

Tyna spun him around and wrapped her arms around him. It was awkward in the pressure suits, and he wasn't sure what to make of it. After a moment, she reached up and pressed his helmet against hers. "I was worried about you!" she called in a tiny voice.

"Why?"

"You disappeared into the ship, and then went silent. I thought they were going to—I don't know, kidnap you or something."

"Silent? What are you talking about—" And then he noticed it. He'd somehow turned off his com-link while taking off his helmet. "Sorry! It was an accident."

"Don't turn on your link yet."

"What's up? How's your air?"

"Um, let's see … oh, I'm down to about ten minutes. That's not what I wanted to talk about. Meyer came out."

"They saw a Manager. I was hoping it was Zeedo."

"He's hurt, remember?"

"Yeah, that's why I was hoping it was him."

"Meyer's gone berserk."

"Still ranting about the Iranians?"

"Oh, yeah."

"Well, they're gone now. Maybe he'll cool down."

"Maybe … before we reconnect, though—"

"What is it, Tyna?"

"Something's not right."

"I'll say."

"No. I mean with Meyer. I've never seen him this way."

"Yeah. I told the shuttle captain the same thing. Maybe it's stress."

"Remember when the crusher shorted and we lost over half the base power just a couple of days into the night cycle?"

"Yeah, I see what you mean. That could have been a total disaster, and he kept his cool right through it."

"Something's wrong with him."

"Like what?"

"I don't know. But Katlin didn't seem herself, either."

Van had noticed that, but he wasn't comfortable talking with Tyna about Katlin. "What are you thinking?"

"I don't know, but don't you think it was odd that Katlin would bring up that movie? I mean, just at that time?"

"You thought she was asking me on a date."

"I was kidding."

Van didn't think she was kidding at the time. She probably just had time to mull it over. "The captain of the shuttle brought up the movie as well. He thinks she was trying to communicate something."

"Yes. I think so too. But what?"

Van considered it, tapping his thigh with his gloved hand. "What was the movie about? Cooper plays a guy who enters a dance competition."

"Hmm, that wasn't the main theme of the movie, and I don't see how dancing relates to what's going on."

"Uh, there's gambling. Cooper's father—"

"Van, you're such a guy."

"What do you mean?"

"Van, the movie was about mental illness."

"Are you saying that Meyer is mentally ill?"

"That seems obvious, depending on how you define it. But there's something else. Cooper's character stops taking his psycho drugs. This causes him to revert back to belligerent behavior."

Van had only a vague memory of this. "You're saying that Meyer has stopped taking some kind of psycho drugs?"

"Maybe not that specific. Maybe Katlin was just trying to tell us that there's something causing Meyer to be—off."

"Could be," he said. "I heard rumors Meyer's been taking some pain medicine."

"She said that Cooper's character really shot himself in the foot."

"Was she talking about him going off his psycho medicine?"

"Yes. But maybe she *was* being more specific here."

"Of course! Meyer has a gun!"

"He *does*?"

"You were outside. He almost used it on me. He would have if—"

"If what?"

"Never mind."

"If *what*?"

"If Katlin hadn't come along."

"I see," she said. "We'd better tune in and see what's going on."

She might have been a little miffed. There was no time to explain, though. And he wouldn't know what he was explaining anyway.

Van winked on the com-link, and was immediately assaulted with a blast of Meyer's cursing. The general gist was, first, they were all idiots for letting the shuttle get away, and second, where the hell was Van, anyway?

"I'm here, Ops Head," Van reported.

"Where the fuck is 'here'?"

In the dim light of Tyna's faceplate, Van saw her wince. This was a word that they rarely heard, and it invariably meant that a Manager was furious enough to weather a rebuke from Zeedo. "West of the base, a couple of hundred yards. Near the slag dump."

This was the first time in twelve years that Meyer had come outside, and he probably wouldn't know the lay of the land. "I'm on my way," Van said. "Stay near the locks."

"You'll pay for letting the sons-of-bitches get away," Meyer snarled. "Those scum."

He should have let Meyer rant, but felt compelled to defend the genteel man he'd met. "He was actually very helpful, Ops Head," Van said, as he and Tyna started towards the locks.

"Helpful? Because he didn't burn you where you stood?"

"He trusted us, even after we shot at him."

"Who's 'he'?"

"Captain Namazi, commander of the Persian mission here. They have a contract with the Chinese government to service their base—"

"How do you know this?"

"Uh, he told me."

"When?"

"When I was in their ship."

The connection went silent, and Van thought he might have accidentally winked off his com-link again.

"You were in their ship," Meyer said quietly, almost calmly. "You fraternized with the enemy?" His voice rose in both volume and bile until he was shouting again. "You slimy little toad! You traitor! I will have you chained to a wall!"

Van was speechless. Tyna grabbed his arm, a show of support, and maybe a warning. "A traitor to what?" he finally managed.

"To the United States!" Meyer screamed. "To everything we hold sacred!"

Van heard Burl mutter something softly.

"What did you say?" Meyer snapped.

"I said," Burl replied clearly, "that would be a mountain of platinum. You can't seem to make up your mind whether you want the scum to leave or stay—"

A low rumble started. Van wasn't sure where it came from, but soon realized it was Meyer. The guttural growl formed into words. "I warned you, Burl, you worthless piece of shit. You're a dead man. You hear me? A dead man. Where are you?"

"Well, you see, Ops Head," Burl said with exaggerated calm, "outside, where all the actual work is done, we locate each other by our headlamps. I can see *you* perfectly."

Van could indeed see Burl's light a couple of hundred yards away. Kim stood next to him, a point of light just slightly shorter. Meyer's beam swung to the left, and locked on the two. His light then started towards them, bouncing with each step.

Tyna gripped Van's arm. "Ops Head," Van said. "Don't do it." He knew those were empty words. "Sir," he said, "let's stay focused on the mission. The Iranians have left." *Talk to his sense of duty,* Van thought. "We should get the shift back online. We're falling way behind this cycle's target."

"Van's right, Ops Head," Burl said with mock seriousness. "That pile of sacred platinum doesn't grow by itself."

Van groaned. "Crimps, Burl, shut up. Just this once."

Meyer's silence was far more frightening than the raving. There was just the labored breathing of the older man, a haunting overture of determined violence.

Tyna's grip tightened. "Oh, crimps—Burl, Meyer has a gun."

The only sound was Meyer's menacing exhalations.

"Burl. Did you hear me?" Van asked.

"Yeah," Burl said. "Yeah, I heard you."

The mock calmness was gone. For once, his friend was serious.

Tyna's grip screamed panic. "Ops Head," Van said, "don't make the biggest mistake of your life."

No response but the man's uninterrupted huffing.

"Ops Head," Van said, "listen to me. I know about your drug problem."

Still just the huffing and puffing.

Damn. "Ops Head, your obsessive hatred of Iranians is insanity. You know that."

Nothing.

Crimps! "Meyer," he said, "the nexgens call you 'Dickhead' behind your back."

That did it. The bouncing, predatory light stopped, turned, and flashed bright for a moment as the beam swept across him. "You're next, Van," Meyer said ominously. "Say your goodbyes."

"Van," Tyna whispered, urgently.

"Burl," Van said, "maybe you two should run."

"Yeah," Burl agreed. "Kim, go!"

"Not without you!" she cried.

"Go!" Burl yelled. "Run!"

Meyer's light was closing in, about a hundred feet from Burl. Van saw Kim's light heading in the opposite direction. There was a slight rise in the crater floor before it descended to the main, flat plain. Kim's light gained altitude as she came to the crest.

"Ops Head!" Burl called. "I have the poker gun pointed right at you. Stop, or I'll shoot."

Van saw Meyer's light stop, but a moment later, a flash appeared just below his headlamp. It lasted a fraction of a second. Another one followed, and Kim cried out.

"Meyer!" Burl cried. "You—oh my God! Van! He shot her! Meyer shot Kim!"

The killer light started bouncing forward again.

"You murderer!" Burl shouted. "You brought this on yourself, you bastard."

Meyer's deadly evil flash spat again. Burl gave a pitiful groan and simultaneously a flicker of light leapt upwards. The poker slug meant for Meyer shot into the lunar sky as Burl fell backwards.

"Oh, God!" Tyna whimpered. "Van, are they …?"

He put his arm around her, and she wrapped both hers around him. "It's okay," he assured. "Zeedo promised me we'd all be archived."

"It's—it's *not* okay," she said, crying now.

Van looked and saw that Meyer's bouncing light had turned towards them. "You had your chance, Van," he said.

"Come on," he said to Tyna, "we have to go."

"Run, Van," Meyer said, "I'll get you eventually. I have more air than you."

"Fuck you!" Tyna shouted through tears.

"Okay, Tyna," Meyer said levelly, "you, too."

Van winked off his microphone and motioned for Tyna to do the same. Jamming his helmet against hers, he shouted, "We can run faster! We'll circle around to the locks!"

"Okay!" she shouted back.

"How much air have you got?"

She looked down. "Enough. Let's go."

"Tyna, how much?"

"A few minutes. I'll be okay."

Van closed his eyes. *Shit!* "Listen. I'm going to lead him away. Turn off your lamp. When you see him following me, make for the lock."

She grabbed his shoulders. "No! You're not sacrificing yourself for me!"

"You're out of air! Don't be stupid!"

"I'm not leaving you! Forget it!"

Meyer was getting closer. It was too late to make a direct beeline for the locks. They had no choice. They'd have to retreat before circling around.

"Okay! Come on!" he said, starting away.

"Van!" Tyna said over the com-link.

He stopped and she ran into him. "We can turn off our lamps."

Meyer would have heard that, but he'd know anyway. She was right. They knew the lay of the land—enough to feel their way in the starlight, anyway. He flipped off his light, and she went dark a second later. They stood surrounded by a galaxy of piercingly sharp points of stars—and one bouncing light that approached, ever closer.

ж ж ж

"Really, Katlin," Louden said. "Give me just a few minutes."

Katlin shook her head. "No time. When was the last time you were in your suit?"

"I don't see how that's relevant—"

"Where *is* your suit? Point to it."

He glanced around, then looked at her, defeated.

She gave him a hug as best she could in the stiff suit, and stepped back. "When I was little, I used to call you Uncle Louden, but you've been more like a second father."

He smiled. "I should be so lucky."

Darkness clouded her thoughts—a surrogate father might be all she had left.

"He'll be alright," Louden said, reading her.

She returned his smile wanly. "I wish we could know that," she said, stepping into the airlock and putting on her helmet.

"Give 'em hell," he said as the door closed.

Katlin waited for the little chamber to evacuate. Julius knew how to use his suit, but hadn't offered to come along. He might be frightened, but it could also be that he simply thought he was more useful cobbling together another com-link terminal.

The outer door slid open silently, revealing utter blackness. She stepped out, letting the door close behind her, cutting off the lock's light. Now the heavens blazed forth, and she stood frozen in awe, as she had each time of the few times she'd ventured outdoors. She shook her head, breaking the spell—she hadn't come out to admire God's creation. Scanning the landscape, her eyes caught a light in the near distance, off to the left. It didn't move. Staring, she realized that there was another light a little farther on. She didn't see the Iranian shuttle, only an endless expanse of vague gray lunar rock under the ghostly starlight. Perhaps it was behind a hill. The last she'd heard before Meyer smashed the com-link terminal was that Van was going off to investigate. That had been barely twenty minutes ago. "Van?" she said tentatively. Nothing. "Van?" she said louder. Still nothing. "Tyna…Burl, Kim?"

Nobody responded to her query, and then she noticed. "Nice one, Kat," she muttered, and winked on her com-link. All she heard was heavy breathing, as though she was hearing someone stalking a footstep behind her. She decided to keep silent until she understood the situation.

Flipping on her headlamp, she loped off towards the motionless lights, the only indication she had. She took care not to trip.

Then Meyer cursed. It was just a quick, hoarse whisper, spoken to himself, but she recognized the harsh voice.

She was expecting to find someone standing at the closest light, so she was confused a moment when she realized that the light was essentially on the ground. She gasped when her headlamp found Burl lying there.

Meyer's heavy breathing paused a moment as he listened, then carried on.

Katlin froze in horror. She wasn't sure at first what she saw. It looked as though a pot of boiling spaghetti sauce had been poured in Burl's lap. Viscous red goo bubbled and steamed as she watched. It was his blood.

Chapter 18

Burl lifted his hand, waving Katlin down.

She gasped again in surprise, making a little yelp. Meyer paused again. "Ah, Tyna," he said darkly. "You're struggling. Good."

His heavy breathing resumed.

Kneeling clumsily in the uncooperative pressure suit, Katlin let him carry on with the misunderstanding. Burl waved her closer with both his hands. When their helmets were practically touching, he grasped hers and pulled it against his. She heard him shout, "Off!"

Again Meyer paused for just a moment.

Katlin didn't know what Burl was talking about. Did he want her to get off of him? If so, why had he waved her down?

He was mouthing silent words, dramatically, like he was delivering a soundless Shakespeare soliloquy.

She finally got it, and winked off her com-link. She knew about the nexgens' crude form of one-on-one communication. Meyer always hated the idea that they were talking behind his back, but there was nothing he could do about it.

"Kim!" Burl shouted.

Again Katlin was perplexed, thinking he was confusing her for the younger nexgen. She shook her head.

"She's up there!" he yelled, pointing.

"Ah!" she said, finally understanding. This was the other light she'd seen. "I'll check on her!"

Burl nodded, and fell back, exhausted.

Katlin knew from twenty feet away that Kim was dead—bubbling red goop lay spread across her chest. She had to make sure, though, and it was the hardest thing she'd done in all her seventeen years. Approaching slowly, she circled around to the side. A sob caught in her throat. She forced herself to look through the faceplate, and cried out, closing her eyes against it and turning away. She wouldn't have known it was Kim. Her face was swollen grotesquely, with obscenely bulging eyes.

Katlin prayed she would someday lose the image.

She returned to Burl, knelt, and pushed her faceplate against his. "Where are you shot?" she shouted.

"How's Kim!" he yelled.

"You first!"

He gave his head quick little shakes. She could see that he was struggling against intense pain. "Kim!"

"She can wait! Where are you shot?"

"She's dead?"

Katlin sighed. "Yes! Damn it! Where—are—you—shot?"

He nodded, the same little nervous shakes. "My thigh. I think the bone's broken."

Kim's bloated face hovered in the shadows, waiting to visit her nightmares. "Why haven't you decompressed?"

"My suit has sealed off that leg!"

"I didn't know they could do that!"

"Me neither! It's not a perfect seal!" He glanced sideways. "I'm down to two PSI!"

She noticed now that he was breathing one deep lungful after another. The tight seal was probably also acting as a tourniquet. "Here we go!" she said, pulling away so that she could slide her arms under him, but he was waving again frantically.

She jammed her helmet back against his. "Meyer!" he shouted. "He's gone after Van and Tyna!"

She sighed again. "Nothing I can do about that now. We need to get you inside! Where's the ship?"

"It left!"

She grunted as she lifted him. He only weighed twenty-five pounds in lunar gravity, but her muscles had acclimated to her easy life long ago. She struggled with conflicting feelings about the ship. On one hand, its exit simplified the situation, removing one menace. It took with it, however, Earth. The fact that it was Iranian—a different country, culture, and language—seemed a trivial detail. It was *Earth.*

Katlin smiled wryly. A crew member from the ship could have lifted Burl with one hand.

As she plodded back to the air lock, thick, gooey blood fluttering in the stream of air exiting the bullet hole in Burl's suit. She was racing against time. Her arms grew tired, and she was afraid she was going to drop him. She lay him down, and pressed her helmet against his. "I have to drag you! Sorry!"

He grabbed her helmet tight. "You have to get Kim inside!" he yelled.

He's lost too much blood. "I told you! Kim is dead!"

"I know that! The vacuum! It's doing damage!"

"So what? Burl, she's *dead!*" Then it came to her. "You're worried about her archiving!"

He nodded, those nervous little shakes.

She took a breath. "Forget that! I have to get you in!"

His grip on her helmet was like a vise. "No! Kim first!"

"Burl! Forget it!"

She gazed at his frightened, determined face inches from her own. *Enough is enough.* "There is no archiving!" she shouted.

The fear on his face twisted in puzzlement.

"My father made it up! There is *no such thing* as archiving!"

She had never formed the complete thought, but now that she'd mouthed the words, she knew absolutely that it was true. "I don't know why he did it—maybe so that we'd feel safer. What I am sure of is that he made it up!"

Burl stared at her.

"I'm sorry! Really sorry! But we *have* to get you inside!"

His hands dropped away from her helmet, and she grasped them in her own and began dragging him, pulling him along on his back as he gazed up at the star-studded blackness of the universe.

Meyer's heavy breathing had been a constant in the background, and now he suddenly spoke. "Son-of-a-bitch! Oh, no, you don't!"

Katlin glanced around. Off to the right, she saw a light, a

headlamp, bounding towards her—no, probably running towards the air lock still a hundred feet beyond her. The light stopped, and a flash of light just below it splashed for just an instant. Unlike the point-source of the headlamps, this one was more of an elongated smear, probably the propellant exhaust of a gun—Meyer's pistol. The flash had reached out sideways to her. There, another headlamp was bounding towards the lock. No, there were actually two headlamps. The second a little lower than the first, and bouncing about almost randomly. She couldn't imagine why this was, but it was clear that it must be Van and Tyna.

"Christ!" Meyer muttered. "You still alive, Burl?"

Katlin looked at Meyer. Again, the momentary flash of the gun, but this time it didn't smear—just a little ball that blinked on and off. At the same instant, she felt a subtle thud through her feet. She looked down, and saw a small, elongated crater in the dust just inches away. Meyer was shooting at her.

ж ж ж

Van winked on his com-link. No need to keep quiet now. "You there, Tyna?" he asked. She was limp in his arms. He didn't expect her to answer, and was surprised and relieved when she mumbled something. It didn't matter what, any response meant she hadn't completely asphyxiated yet.

Meyer had stopped, giving Van a few precious seconds to make headway towards the lock. His pursuer had muttered something and shot, but it was in a different direction, towards … "Burl!" Van exclaimed, seeing a headlamp. "You're alive!"

"Not for long," Meyer sneered.

"It's me!" came a female voice.

"Katlin?" Van and Meyer said together.

"Meyer," she said, "stop shooting. Burl's wounded, but alive. It's not too late."

She didn't mention Kim—Meyer must have killed her. Katlin's unexpected appearance was giving Meyer pause, and Van continued for the lock. He was used to hauling loads with a partner, and it was clumsy and slow carrying Tyna. But, with Katlin's distraction, he might just make it.

"Meyer, listen to me," Katlin went on. "Louden broke into the med-genie log. We know you didn't wean yourself from the synthetic opiate you were taking for pain. When you forced her to make a substitution after you used up an ingredient, she warned you that it could affect your amygdale. Do you hear me, Meyer? It's messing with your mind."

Van saw an elongated momentary smudge of light, Meyer's gun firing, and heard a grunt from Katlin. Her headlamp disappeared.

"Katlin!" Van called. "Katlin, you okay?"

Meyer, said, "She was no better than her father. Scientists," he spat, as though they were in the same league as child-raping soldiers.

Despite a lifetime of practice, Van was breathing heavily, using unnecessary oxygen. His heart pounded as his mind raced. Burl was wounded—how could that be? Surrounded by vacuum, you were either completely untouched, or dead. There was no in-between. He tried not to think of Katlin. Mourning would have to wait. He had just minutes to get Tyna inside, if it wasn't too late already.

"Oh, no, you don't," Meyer said. His headlamp bounced forward, much quicker than Van expected. The Manager seemed to be finding his legs inside the suit. It was a race to the lock that Van was going to lose. Even if he beat Meyer there, he would still need precious seconds to close the door. And Meyer was nuts. He might shoot right through the door. And then both Van and Tyna were as dead as if he'd shot them in the head. It would be suicide for Meyer as well, but the man seemed beyond reason.

"Burl!" Van yelled. "Go for his legs."

"Nice try," Meyer said, not even slowing down.

Whatever part of his brain was malfunctioning, it wasn't the cold, calculating part.

Meyer's headlamp angled inexorably ahead. Fifty feet from the lock, Van stopped. Meyer's light was in front of him, blinding him. Van could have cried. *So close. Why doesn't he shoot?* From the movies, he knew that guns held only so many bullets. Maybe he was being careful with the last one.

Meyer's headlamp went out. "Turn it off," Meyer ordered.

Van saw no advantage in leaving it on, and reached up and flipped it off. In the utter lunar darkness, Meyer's face floated twenty feet away, lit by the reflected light of the faceplate display.

His own face would be illuminated the same.

"I want to watch you die," Meyer said, walking towards him.

Van knew his life was ending in a matter of seconds. Suddenly, the burden he'd been carrying seemed more valuable than anything in the entire universe. "Okay," he said. "You win. Just let me put Tyna in the lock. She's done nothing to you."

Meyer shook his head. "Nice try. You just don't give up, do you?"

"No—I'm not trying to fool you. Look, *you* can put her inside. *Please!* Don't kill her!"

"No," he said, shaking his head again. "She's already dead. You've been carrying her for—what?—five minutes? It was a noble effort, though. You would have made it without her. You nexgens stick together like a pack of rats."

"Please, Ops Head, just let me get her—"

"Put her down."

"Please—"

"Put her down!" he yelled, waving the pistol.

Van hesitated, and then lay Tyna's limp body on the cold lunar ground.

"Nexgens," Meyer snarled. "Nothing but trouble. I worked my butt off for sixteen years with Cummings playing the almighty intellectual, and nexgens dragging their feet whenever possible."

If Burl were alive, he'd set him straight about who had worked their butts off. He had the sense that Meyer was content for the moment to have an audience. Playing the part could buy him a few more seconds. "It hasn't been easy," he agreed.

Meyer glared at him. For a moment, Van thought that Meyer had seen through his acting. His face relaxed, however, and he said, "Things have changed now, though. The tables have turned, and it's payback time. Time to reap the reward."

Van held his gaze, trying to appear sympathetic. If Meyer did find his way back to Earth, he'd spend the rest of his life in jail. *That's it.* "It'll all be for nothing if you don't put the gun away," he said. "All that work—all your efforts will go *un*-rewarded."

"Not at all. In fact, I'm going to kill you, and still have my cake and eat it too."

He really is crazy. "You can't possibly get away with this. Not if you want to go back to Earth."

Meyer's stone face broke into the slightest grin. "You can't conceive how much that pile of platinum is worth. There was a time when it was based on rarity, but now it has intrinsic manufacturing value—*high* value. You don't understand that on Earth, enough money can buy anything. Lives have monetary value, and I have enough to buy all of you."

The Manager stared at Van. "You've always been intrigued with Earth. It's your secret wish to go there. Isn't it?"

"Uh, sure," Van said. It was true.

Meyer's wicked grin returned. "The fact that you'll never breathe the sweet, pure air of Mother Earth is deeply satisfying," he said, raising the pistol.

Blaine C. Readler

Chapter 19

Katlin returned from blackness more complete than power failures inside the base. Obviously, she'd been unconscious, but why still the total darkness? Her eyes were open. She blinked to make sure.

She was lying face down. *Right*. Meyer had shot at her, and she'd dived to the ground. Then her mind had exploded in dazzling light. She pushed herself up, and as she lifted her head, the stars above came into view. She must have banged her head into her faceplate. She reached up, and cursed herself that she'd forgotten about the suit. *Lucky I didn't crack the helmet*. Sitting up, she turned her head back and forth, watching the stars, making sure there weren't any cracks. She toggled the switch on her headlamp. The light must have broken in the fall.

Meyer was talking on the com-link. Something about money and Earth.

Burl! She'd forgotten about him. She looked around frantically. His light was out too. Had Meyer come over and shot him again? Had she been out that long?

Something caught her eye. Suddenly, seemingly out of nowhere, it appeared from over the crater wall. For the briefest moment, she thought it was a meteor. She remembered her father holding her hand in their yard in Illinois, watching a meteor shower as he explained that they were the remnants of comets.

Her fogged brain settled—meteors burned only on Earth, where the atmosphere tore viciously at their orbital speed. This impossible meteor was soon joined by another, and then yet another. In any case, their tails pointed *down*, not *up*, and they held a fixed position with each other.

In an instant, it came to her that she was looking at a spaceship. This had to be the Iranian shuttle. What else could it be?

The sight was awesome, miraculous, even. She knew, of course, about spaceships—she'd come to the Moon on one. But to *see* one now, to have it hovering above her as though perched high on invisible legs was spectacular—godlike.

The last she'd heard before Meyer smashed the com-link terminal was that Van was going to investigate the ship. Her first thought was that it had come back to attack, but if so, where was the anti-matter exhaust? Van had described it as clearly visible from far away. She saw nothing of the sort. The pilot must be using just maneuvering rockets.

Van was hollering madly over the com-link, hooting and yelping. He seemed … happy—ecstatic. Meyer, on the other hand, was cursing like the mythical sailor. A headlamp came on. It was Van, calling to somebody named Namazi. The ship tilted and glided towards them, sinking as it cleared the crater wall.

Another headlamp came on—Meyer's. She saw him doing something with the gun in his hands. A moment later a smear of light reached out towards the shuttle. Julius's warnings screamed in her mind.

"Meyer!" she yelled. "Stop! You'll blow up the whole base!"

He ignored her, reaching out to fire again at the ship as it approached ever closer. It was as though he didn't hear her, and she guessed this was probably the case. The com-link transmitter of the fragile, twenty-year-old suit had likely failed during her fall.

Meyer's headlamp shone on the gun he held. He aimed at the approaching ship, but nothing happened. He was out of bullets. At the same instant, one of the shuttle's small rockets sputtered and went dark. Unbalanced now, it tilted over and surged off, away from the lock doors. The pilot spun the ship on its vertical axis and managed to right it, slowing the uncontrolled sideways dash, but then a second maneuvering rocket sputtered, burning its last bit of fuel.

Katlin held her breath. She knew what came next when the shuttle crashed to the Moon's surface. She wouldn't see it. The anti-matter would obliterate them all so quickly, her body would be torn to atoms before she knew what happened.

It didn't fall. The last of the little rockets went dark, and the ship remained hovering, perched atop a thin, translucent, violet pencil. It was just as Van had described, except much more beautiful than she'd imagined. The pilot had obviously waited until he was safely away to engage. After a moment, the ship sank, the pencil shrank to just a stub, tilted, and then disappeared.

The Moon was once again a dark expanse covered by an umbrella of stars.

Except for the heavy breathing of Meyer. The soundtrack to a final struggle.

ж ж ж

Van grunted as he lifted the dead weight of Tyna's body. He should have started earlier, but he'd been sure that Captain Namazi would get the best of Meyer. If only he'd known how low the ship was on maneuvering fuel.

He took off for the open lock. *Crimps!* He remembered that he still had his headlamp on, and he reached up and flipped it off. That was a mistake. He should have stopped. Carrying Tyna was clumsy enough, and he tripped on a rock, and fell. He let Tyna fall ahead of him so he didn't land on her. Cursing himself, he rolled over and reached for her. Off to the side, he saw Meyer running for the lock. The madman stopped for a moment and took something from his leg pocket, then ran on.

Van hefted Tyna again and took off, lifting his feet higher to avoid falling. He cursed himself again for turning off his headlamp. Meyer's gun was out of bullets. It didn't matter if he saw him. The danger now was that the bastard would make the lock first and cycle it closed.

But Meyer had turned off his headlamp as well. All that remained was the small green light above the lock door, beckoning him, promising life-giving oxygen. Closer, closer. He was going to make it. Maybe Tyna wasn't dead. He might still save her.

The next instant, he was blinded by a light shining directly in his eyes. He decided to just plow on through, past Meyer, but hands pushed against him, and he stumbled sideways, struggling to hang on to his precious burden. Meyer looked down, fumbling with his hands, slipping something into the handle of the pistol. Van had seen enough movies to know that the murderer had brought an extra clip full of bullets.

The pistol lifted as Meyer's light blinded him again. He couldn't see it, but he knew the barrel tip was pointed at his chest.

"You son-of-a-bitch traitor," Meyer growled. "You thought you had it all planned out, didn't you? Your Iranian comrades were going to storm in and save the day."

"No," Van said. He had no hope of convincing Meyer, but he had to try. "I had no idea they were coming back."

"Bullshit. It doesn't matter. This just makes it that much easier."

"Listen, Ops Head. One last time. The lock's right there. Just let me put Tyna inside and cycle. Please."

"Sorry."

From behind the blinding light came a wild cackle. Van recognized it as Meyer, but it was so out of character and bizarre, it gave him goose bumps.

"This is like eating ice cream," Meyer said. "Why didn't I do this a long time ago?"

Van knew that Meyer's finger was poised on the trigger. He knew that the finger was going to pull the trigger. It was an absolute certainty. It was simply a matter of when, maybe ten seconds from now, maybe the very next instant.

"Goodbye Van. I'd say it was nice knowing you, but that would be a lie—"

Van blinked. The blinding light was gone. In front of him was just the calm green light above the lock. *What in crimps?*

He reached up and flipped on his headlamp. Meyer was gone. He just disappeared.

Something caught his eye off to the left. He turned his head, and his lamp played across an image that took a moment to coalesce into a recognizable pattern. It was Meyer. He was sitting on the ground, leaning back against a vertical section of the crater wall. His arms were spread wide, as though he'd finally come to his senses and was welcoming everybody back to the fold.

It was a macabre illusion, like Captain Ahab's mindless death-wave as the great whale carries him away entangled in rope. Meyer was dead. A vicious gash ran sideways across his chest, and from it bubbled his blood.

Van blinked again. Intuition told him to turn in the other direction. There he found Katlin's clean blue pressure suit. The slim, form of the young woman stood, legs spread for balance, holding Burl's poker in both hands. She let it drop, and lifted her right hand until it rested against the top of her faceplate.

Van smiled and returned the salute.

Blaine C. Readler

Chapter 20

The faint whoosh of air quickly built to a gale as Katlin watched the OK light, waiting for it to turn green. It seemed to take forever. She was the last to cycle through the lock. She'd helped Van get Tyna and Burl inside, and it would have been a squeeze for her, so she'd let them go. It wasn't clear whether anybody other than Van would tumble out alive on the other side. There'd been no indications of life from Tyna in over five minutes, and the last conscious act from Burl was when he turned off his headlamp as she lay in the lunar dirt recovering from her self-inflicted concussion. She was still dizzy, and a mean, throbbing headache was forming somewhere above the part of her brain she thought with.

When the inner lock door finally slid open, the staging area was empty. Dirty burnt-sienna pressure suits hung from their hooks like so many lost souls waiting out eternity. She dropped her helmet and took off at a run for the infirmary. Nexgens peeked from around corners and door frames, eyes wide with wonder at the sight of a Manager in a clean blue pressure suit. She tried to prepare herself. If Burl was dead, she'd probably spend the rest of her life wondering if she could have done something differently.

She turned the last corner and found Van sitting on a bench outside the infirmary, tapping away at his thigh. Next to him sat Tyna. *Alive!* She was pale, and she leaned back against the wall, eyes closed—drained. She turned her head when she heard Katlin's footsteps. She smiled. It was a weak attempt, but sincere. Then she turned her head back and closed her eyes again.

Katlin knelt beside them and placed her gloved hands on Tyna's knees. "How're you doing, kiddo?"

Without opening her eyes, Tyna said, "I'm older than you."

Katlin grinned and looked at Van.

"You're surprised she's alive," he said.

"Thrilled. But, yeah, surprised."

"She metered her air."

Katlin's face must have shown her ignorance.

"You should use your suit now and then," he said. "She reduced her feed pressure to just one PSI—enough to keep her alive, but it would have eventually damaged her brain. Not that it would be obvious."

Tyna opened her eyes, swiveled them in his direction, and then closed them again.

"I'll pay for that," he said.

"Hopefully a fair sum," Katlin said. Her smile faded and she felt her stomach knot. "How's …?"

"Burl? Louden says he'll probably live, but the med-genie's not sure about his leg—whether she can … uh, save it. I think Louden's doing some sort of surgery."

Katlin realized that she'd been holding her breath, and she took a deep, grateful lungful. It would be horrible if he lost his leg, but she could live with that—*he* could at least live with that.

But, if Burl was on the table, then … "What about my father?"

Van blinked. It was probably the first time he'd ever heard her refer to him as her father. "They've taken him to his room, I think."

She searched him for meaning. "Because he's …"

Van blinked again. "Alive! Yeah, sorry. Louden thinks he's going to be okay."

Katlin glanced at the door to the infirmary. It could be who-knew-how-long for more news about Burl. "I'll be back," she said, rising stiffly in the unyielding suit and heading off for the Lab. She glanced back. Tyna sat with her head back, dozing. Van sat watching her, protective, his hand tapping away some private rhythm on his thigh.

Her father was in bed, apparently asleep. Katlin turned to walk quietly away, when he called weakly to her. She returned to his bed and took the hand he offered. "Oh, Daddy," she said, and broke down crying. Relief that he was alive—piled on top of saturated adrenaline—overwhelmed her, and soon she was bawling, holding his hand to her face as she soaked it in her tears. After a minute, she took a deep breath and sucked back snot. "I'm such a girl!" she said.

He smiled and squeezed her hand. "But you're my girl." His smile softened. "At least, that's what I've always liked to believe. The truth is that you've always been your own girl, and now you're your own woman."

He winced, and carefully repositioned himself. Holding his hand was causing him discomfort, and she gently placed it back on the bed.

"Rumor has it that the Iranian ship returned," he said, forcing a smile.

He doesn't know. "Daddy, I have some … bad news."

His brow furrowed, and he waited.

She took a deep breath and let it out. "Daddy, Kim and … Meyer are both dead."

His face awoke with alarm, and he moved to sit up, but fell back, moaning.

Not yet. Later. "It wasn't the Iranians, if that's what you're thinking. Daddy, Meyer went completely insane."

Her father's face held a moment, and then relaxed in unhappy acceptance. "Louden told me about the flawed synthetic opiates he was forcing the med-genie to make. Meyer must have put a lot of effort into finagling and hiding it."

"Addiction knows no master," she said.

"That's right … who said that?"

She shrugged. "I did. It was very selfish of him—I mean to use up all the ingredients to make opiates. What if somebody else needs them now?"

Her father just nodded sadly.

"Daddy, you should know—the Iranians, if anything, they saved us."

He glanced at her. "From Meyer?"

She nodded. She wanted to leave him in peace. She loved him, and would do anything for him, and it was so very hard to go on. But she had no choice. "Daddy, I would really like to save this for later, but with Kim … gone, it can't wait."

He watched her curiously. She was surprised he didn't seem to know what was coming. "Daddy … the archiving—" His face clouded, and she had to force herself to go on. "It's … not true, is it?"

He turned his head and stared at the ceiling. "It had to come out eventually. Maybe it's time."

"It's not true, then?"

He turned and looked at her. "Of course not. It's ridiculously fantastical if you think about it."

That was the problem—like the nexgens, she'd always taken it for granted and had never really thought about the impossible difficulties.

"Why, Daddy? Was it to … control the nexgens?"

This seemed to cause him visible pain. He turned back to the un-judging ceiling and his eyes glistened with tears. "It was so long ago. We had dozens of little children, all rendered orphans in one instant. They were traumatized. We were at our wits end about how to calm them. They were too young to understand. I was afraid that they'd be crippled—mentally crippled—for life."

"It made them feel safe," she suggested.

He nodded. "Many of the children—particularly the older ones—were terrified that whatever killed their parents would get them as well. We tried to explain that they were perfectly safe inside the base, but they were beyond listening to reason—"

"We were just little kids, Daddy," she reminded. Her memories had faded with time. What remained were remembrances of urgency, and heated arguments, and a general feeling of danger.

"Yes," he said. "You were. Your mother would have known exactly what to do." He looked at her, and his eyes begged for forgiveness. "We did the best we could."

"I know that, Daddy," she said, placing her hand on his arm. "And in the end, you saved our lives."

His brow furrowed in doubt.

"Daddy, you kept us all alive against terrible odds for twelve years."

He turned back and sighed, wincing with pain. "But to your earlier point. The idea of archiving was indeed created to control the nexgens, but that wasn't my idea."

The answer was obvious. "Meyer."

He nodded. "The program—the rules about points and punishment—evolved when Meyer slowly brought production back on line as the nexgens became old enough. I probably should have stopped it, but it seemed so obvious that production needed to be re-established."

"Because of Earth's investment," she said, then wishing she hadn't.

He shook his head. "No, for stability."

"Because the nexgens needed it as much as Earth did," she said, repeating their conversation of days earlier.

Over the last days, she'd come to understand something, something that had always been there in front of her face. Now, Meyer was dead … "They've been abused, Daddy. They're worked hard, and are given no opportunity for … what? Cultural advancement, for membership in the culture they sprang from. Their history of America—of Earth—is derived from movies."

He looked at her, and then turned back to the ceiling.

"I don't blame you," she said. "It was all Meyer's doing."

"I didn't stop him," he said to the ceiling. "I have to live with that."

"Meyer hated that you were the base leader," she said.

He nodded once, agreeing.

"He took it out on the nexgens. He knew that the platinum production was what Earth really valued, and he made sure he demonstrated himself as the most capable leader of that most important part. And by capable, that meant maximizing platinum output."

Her father took a deep breath, winced, and let it out. He turned to look at her. "Peaches, you take after your mother. She's smarter than me."

"You mean, 'than I.'"

He grinned and closed his eyes. "If she'd been here, they could have had religion."

Katlin didn't know what to make of that. "I don't understand, Daddy. Because she's … an angel?"

"That she is. I mean, she could have managed it."

"Religion needs to be managed?"

He looked at her. "Of course. All those young kids, feeding on each other's fantasies—who knows where it would have led? They'd have painted themselves and danced around the mess room naked."

"*Lord of the Flies*," she said.

"Exactly."

Katlin had thought that William Golding had meant the book as a metaphor, but her father might be right. She'd have to give it some thought.

He closed his eyes again. "I think I need to sleep now." But then he opened them again and looked at her in alarm. "My Lord. What am I thinking? You said that both Meyer and Kim are dead. Oh, my. I blame my incompetence on the drugs the med-genie must have given me. We'll need to—"

Katlin gently gripped his arm. "Daddy, stop. You are seriously wounded, and need to recover. I'll take care of things. Just rest now."

He nodded. "I guess the time has come."

"Time for what, Daddy?"

"That you start taking over the base."

His eyes were closed and he didn't see her surprised reaction. Earth had arrived, there was an Iranian shuttle sitting just outside. Nothing was going to be the same. The future was a wide open spectrum of possibilities.

She didn't say any of this, hadn't told him that it was she who had killed Meyer. She just patted his arm and got up to leave.

"Your birth date," he said under closed eyelids.

"What, daddy? What about my birthday?"

"Your birth *date*. That's the combination to the archiving room."

She paused. "Okay," she said simply and left, quietly closing the door behind her.

Katlin started back to the infirmary, but stopped at the first intersection. She considered for a moment, and then turned left.

She came to the door marked "Human Archiving," and stood, staring at it. This door genie had been dead as long as she could remember. Her father had probably made Julius deactivate it. There was so much to see to, but she couldn't resist. She punched her birth date into the little backup keypad, and the door clicked open. Hesitating just a moment, she walked inside. Lights came on, and she stopped short. The room was not large, no bigger than a regular apartment, and lined on every wall with metal shelves. Attached to the front of the shelves were names, and she immediately recognized them. They were the same surnames as those of the nexgens. On the shelves themselves were piled a vast variety of objects—pictures and books, clothes and small boxes, but, most intriguingly, personal electronics. She picked one up, what must have been a com-tablet. She'd never seen an actual one, but had read about them, and seen them many times in the movies. She'd had no idea they'd been brought to the Moon.

"They belonged to their parents," Louden said.

She gasped and spun to find him in the doorway.

"But, I guess that's obvious," he said, coming inside. "Your father finally told you the truth?"

"More like I dragged it out of him," she replied. "You knew?"

"Of course. Julius, your father, Meyer, and I—we had the unhappy task of collecting it all."

"But … why?"

"Why bring it all here and lock it away? At first, it was just to keep it all safe. We fully expected Earth to come any day, and we felt a duty to make sure it was passed on to relatives back home— back on Earth."

"At first," she repeated. "After years and years, when it was obvious Earth wasn't going to return soon, why not give it to the children, to the nexgens?"

He shrugged. "I asked the same thing. It was …"

"Meyer," she guessed.

He nodded. "His argument was that it would be confusing to them, would cause deep yearnings that were impossible to fulfill. He said that he wanted to spare them the melancholy."

She snorted. "What he really wanted was to avoid dissatisfaction among the minions." She remembered Van's embarrassment at not knowing the name of the first human to land on the Moon. "He didn't want them to know too much." She gestured at the electronics. "These probably contain whole encyclopedias, entire libraries of literature. Education is the bane of dictators."

Louden mulled that. "Who said that?"

"What?"

"Education is the bane of dictators."

She shrugged. "I did."

She walked along the shelves, taking in the fantastic array of belongings, probably more variety and personal value than all the rest of the base combined. A thought occurred to her, and she turned and stared at the rotund scientist.

Louden blushed. "You're wondering why I—the rest of us— didn't oppose Meyer?"

She felt herself joining in the blushing. "Yes. Why didn't you?"

He sighed. "Have you ever heard the story about the frog in the pan?"

"I know what a frog is, and I know what a pan is, but I've never imagined them together."

"The story goes that frogs have simple nervous systems. They are wired to react in direct response to changes in their environment—a fly whizzing by, for example. The idea is that if the environment changes slowly enough, they don't detect it, and thus don't react. So, supposedly, you can put a frog into a pan of water, and if you heat the water slowly enough, the frog will eventually be boiled to death, and never even know it's happening."

"It could have easily hopped out, but missed the obvious signs that danger was building," she said. "Do you think that it's true? That a frog would do that?"

"I don't know. But I have proof that a man could."

She nodded, sorry she'd forced him into a confession.

He eyed her. "Has your father told you what happened on the day of the Blast?"

She shook her head. "He's never talked about it. I've asked, but he changes the subject."

"Sounds like him. We had a warning, of course. The initial assessment from Earth was that the dense core—the most dangerous part—of the super coronal mass was going to miss the

Moon. Your father wasn't taking any chances, and he ordered a lock-down. He was busy coordinating shielding the sensors, and assumed that Meyer was calling in the crew—the nexgens' parents. Instead, Meyer told them to finish up the current run, and then begin locking down the equipment according to procedure. He failed to communicate the potential danger, and they took their time. When your father finally got word that the core was indeed going to graze the Moon, there was barely ten minutes of notice. Even then, Meyer could have gotten everybody inside, but he insisted that the crew finish the lockdown procedure. They argued. Your father got on the com-link and ordered the crew inside, and Meyer immediately countermanded it, claiming production authority."

Katlin stared at Louden, and he stared back.

"Meyer let the nexgens' parents die while protecting his turf?" she concluded.

Louden shrugged. "In his defense, he didn't understand the true magnitude of the danger."

"You're defending him? He murdered them."

He shook his head. "No. There's no real excuse for what he did. I wouldn't call it murder, though. More like involuntary manslaughter."

"Tell that to the nexgens."

He blushed again.

"Sorry," she said. "It's obvious, though, that my father has been carrying the guilt ever since, and he has no reason."

"No, he doesn't," Louden agreed.

"I don't think Meyer felt any guilt at all."

"If he did, he hid it quite well."

Meyer and Kim are waiting. "I have to see to the casualties. And, oh Lord, there's an Iranian shuttle still sitting out there. Wait! How's Burl?"

Louden lifted his shoulders. "He's in the med-genie's hands— or sensors and med feeds—now. She's not sure yet whether he'll lose the leg."

As Katlin was leaving, she stopped at the door. "We'll have to get Julius to disable this," she said, pointing to the lock keypad.

Louden nodded. "It's about time."

Katlin turned a corner and stopped short. Nearly all the nexgens were lined up on both sides of the corridor, at the end of which lay the air lock bay. She asked the first one, a lanky fourteen year-old, what was going on. "Kim's coming in," he whispered.

At that moment, the air lock opened and two suited nexgens repositioned their holds on the dead girl. They glanced around at the gathering, and without further ado, headed down the hall towards Katlin. As the informal procession passed, the first nexgen snapped a salute. Each in turn followed suit as their fallen companion passed.

Where did they learn that? She moved aside to let them pass. *The movies, of course.* She raised her hand in a farewell salute, tears rolling down her cheeks.

The ad hoc honor guard began to break up, but everybody stopped and stared as the air lock door opened again. A bizarre alien creature stepped out. It looked distinctly human, but as she gawked, Katlin couldn't fathom what sat atop the shoulders. It wasn't a head. It was vaguely head-shaped, but there was no face, no ears, no hair—just an oblong dome rising from the base of what should have been a neck. It occurred to her that the creature had come in from a vacuum. If it was human, it should have been wearing a helmet.

The oblong protrusion twisted back and forth with the eerie semblance of a featureless face scanning the area. As it turned, she saw a compact equipment assembly astride its back, and she immediately recognized it as a vacuum pack—oxy and support electronics. She was just beginning to accept that the alien was a person wearing some sort of outrageously streamlined pressure suit, when it used two hands to manipulate controls at its belt, and its body melted. The melting lasted just a second, as the internal pressure collapsed, allowing the loose material of the suit to lie against the body proper of the person inside. They lifted their arms, fiddled with something on the back of their neck, and pulled the now-limp covering forward, revealing the actual face of an actual person.

It was a man. A man with impossibly precisely trimmed black

hair and beard.

She'd never imagined that a man could be so handsome.

Blaine C. Readler

Chapter 21

Van had left his two most senior nexgens with directions to prepare Kim for the recycler, and was heading back to the air lock when another breathless nexgen met him with the news that someone had come through—from the ship outside. Van sprinted to the lock bay and found Namazi talking to Katlin, with a couple dozen nexgens hovering at the perimeter, curious, but cautious of this stranger, this flesh-and-blood person who'd stepped right out of a movie.

"Captain!" Van called as he made his way through the crowd.

Namazi's face lit up when he saw him, and he extended his hand. Van shook it and said, "I owe you my life. What made you come back?"

"You," Namazi replied. "Your plight. I can explain in detail later, but right now it is I who needs your help."

Van glanced at Katlin, who was gazing at Namazi, mesmerized. She was reacting like the other nexgens—astounded at laying eyes on the first new person of their lives.

"Anything," Van replied. "What can we do?"

Namazi's face turned sober. "I would wish that you *could* do anything, for it seems that this is what it will take. Your attacker—Mr. Meyer—got very lucky with one of his gunshots—lucky for him. His first bullet embedded in the impact shield—"

"Impact shield?" Van asked.

Namazi glanced around, as though reminding himself that those surrounding him were frozen in a time long past. "The outer covering of the ship consists of polyweb—an extremely light foam made from carbon nanotubes—that absorbs the energy of impacting micrometeoroids. This can easily stop a bullet, and it did for Mr. Meyer's first one. His second bullet, however, came—shall we say—right up my derriere."

"The main drive's exhaust," Van said.

"Exactly. This is the one area of the ship that can't, of course, be protected. His bullet found its way to one of the gimbal bearings of the containment field generator—I don't have time to explain in detail, but let me just say that when the ship experiences a force vector—as it does when sitting on the Moon's surface—the failing gimbal bearing requires that the ship be oriented in a vertical position."

"Otherwise …?" Van asked.

Namazi nodded as though agreeing with him. "Otherwise, the stress on the bearing will cause it to fail, and, well, we know what happens then." He glanced around and sighed, realizing they didn't know. "The containment field fails."

He looked at them solemnly.

The crowd of nexgens gazed on, perplexed.

"Boom," Van said.

Namazi took a breath and let it out. "Yes. Big boom."

"The shuttle's not vertical," Katlin said, alarmed. "I saw the exhaust tilt just before it went dark."

"Yes," Namazi said, his face relaxing its somber concern, even smiling when he talked to her. "The ship was not designed to land on the main drive alone. It's tricky, and one of the landing legs collapsed."

"Why don't you just … leave?" Van asked.

"I would if I could. Departing on the main drive alone would be even trickier, and if I didn't strike the ground on takeoff, the horizontal stresses imparted as the ship struggled to turn upward could well cause the bearing to fail instantly."

"In both cases," Van said, "boom."

"Yes, boom."

"What if you could refuel the maneuvering rockets?"

"I would have a better chance, yes. I doubt you have a reserve of hypergolic fuel, though."

"Not unless it goes by another name," Van said.

"Darn," Katlin said. "No, we have none." To Van, she explained, "Hypergolic fuels consists of two parts that automatically ignite when mixed."

Van had the impression that this was more for the captain than him. "We're stuck, then. We don't have fuel for you, and you can't take off. What if we got the ship upright?"

"That's why I'm here. It would buy us time, and I might just be able to take off on just the main drive from that position. We would need some sort of mechanical lifting or leveraging device."

"Your ship has a flat tire, and you need a giant jack," Katlin said.

Van threw her an impatient look. This wasn't a time for joking—unless one had ulterior goals. "We have those. The platform—the derrick over our mining area—has a variety. Powerful ones."

"How long before you could move one to the ship?" Namazi asked.

Van considered. "A few hours—maybe two."

Namazi shook his head. "The bearing won't hold that long."

"How long do we have?"

He looked unhappy at the answer. "I can't predict with accuracy, but anything over an hour would be essentially borrowed time."

Katlin's smile faded and her face turned white. "The rover," she said. "We could get to the Chinese base—"

She didn't finish, and her white face turned red. Van was glad she had abandoned the idea of selecting just a few survivors.

Something pulled at Van's arm. It was Glenda. "We can do it," she said, leaning in to say it quietly. She was intimidated by the stranger.

"That's what we're discussing," Van said. "Captain Namazi is saying that we don't have enough time—"

"No, we can lift the corner of the ship," Glenda said, glancing at Namazi, fearful that he'd disapprove.

"You mean without a jack. Just our hands?"

She nodded enthusiastically.

Van was about to explain that they had to stick to serious alternatives, when he noticed Tyna nodding in agreement.

"How much does your ship weigh?" Van asked.

Namazi looked from Glenda to him, skeptically. "Ten thousand kilos," he replied, "but that's Earth weight."

"Twenty-two thousand pounds, Earth," Katlin translated. "That's about thirty-seven hundred pounds, lunar. Impossible."

Glenda leaned in again, "But we'd only be lifting one corner."

Van nodded. "I understand. Thanks. We'd be lifting about half of that—say a ton." He sighed.

"We can do it," Tyna whispered, not for Namazi or Katlin, but for him. Tyna's bloodshot eyes still reflected her ordeal, but she was recovering.

"No," Katlin said. "We're wasting time. The only viable solution is to remove a jack from the platform. You'll just have to work faster."

Glenda crossed her arms over her chest. "Let's show them," she said quietly, her eyes shining with determination.

"I said no," Katlin said. "The first step is to decide which platform jack to use."

"We can at least consider it," Van objected.

"Do you understand 'no'? Now leave it."

Van stared at her. This wasn't the Katlin he knew. "What if I don't leave it?"

"You *have* to obey me," Katlin insisted.

Van took two breaths while she glared at him. "Why?" he asked.

Katlin's brows drew together. "Because … because …"

"Because you're Zeedo's daughter?"

She glanced at Namazi. "Because I'm right," she said to Van.

He took her by the arm and led her off. He expected her to resist, but she came along without comment. When they'd turned the corner, she said, "Van, we don't have time for this squabbling."

"Are you going to give me some points? Have you inherited the key to the archiving?"

At this, her eyes went round, as though she was having a heart attack. She stared past him, and then focused on his face. Her eyes glistened with tears. She suddenly lifted her hands and buried her face in them.

"Uh, Katlin?" he said.

She didn't respond. He saw her shoulders shaking ever so slightly. She was crying.

"Hey," he said gently. "What's wrong?"

She lifted her face and took a deep breath, then wiped her sleeve across her eyes. "I'm so sorry. I don't know what came over me—no, I do know, and I hate it."

When they got back, she said to Tyna and Glenda, "I'm sorry. We have to all work together. I understand that."

"Okay," Tyna said, back on track. "Van, should we call everybody to the hanger, or do we all just suit up and head over?"

"Wait," Katlin said. "Shouldn't we decide on a jack before going out?"

Tyna, confused, glanced at Van.

"No," Van said, "we're going to try the manual method first."

Katlin looked stricken. "But, that's *crazy*! You can't just lift a spaceship!"

Van grinned. "Only half of one, remember?" He placed his hand on her shoulder. "Kat, you're outnumbered."

He thought that she was going to yell, or even slap him. Her face tightened, and she said, "Well, even if they *can* lift it, they can't just hold it. We're going to need something to prop it up."

Van smiled and released the breath he'd been holding. "Good point. Why don't you and Glenda take whatever nexgens are already suited, and go to the platform to find something that can serve as a prop. Tyna, we'll round up the rest to get suited."

Katlin nodded, seeming relieved. Glenda looked at her new partner skeptically.

As they broke and began to scatter, Namazi grabbed Van's elbow. He waited until the others were out of hearing. "Are you confident about this?" he asked.

"No." Van replied. "But I am confident that removing a jack from the platform and setting it up at your ship will take more than two hours."

Namazi stared at him a moment and then nodded. "Very well. Let me know what I can do to help."

After looking around to make sure everybody had left, Van whispered, "Keep Katlin out of our way. She'll listen to you."

Namazi pulled back, surprised. "Why me?"

Van grinned. "I think she's soft for you."

The captain straightened with dignity, but then leaned in. "You think so?"

ж ж ж

Katlin turned to find Glenda and another nexgen about to be crushed by a beam. The stark lights of the platform revealed a third nexgen pushing it over to topple onto them. "No!" she cried, but immediately bit her tongue. Luckily, her warning was lost among the chatter of Van and his lifting crew hundreds of yards away at the Iranian shuttle. Katlin saw that there was a cable attached to the top of the beam, which eased it down onto the waiting cart as gently as Mai Dung would lay her sleeping son onto a couch.

Katlin had been biting her tongue ever since coming outside. She was superfluous. That had become obvious as soon as the four of them arrived at the platform. Glenda and the other two nexgens communicated by contacting helmets, leaving the com-link for Van's much larger group. They'd tried to include her, but it was slowing them down, since she knew nothing about the platform, and so she backed off. She had spent the last twenty minutes trying to find some way to be useful, and failing.

Katlin still burned with embarrassment about her behavior towards Van, still puzzled at what she had done. She tried to chalk it off to the swirl of events.

But that Namazi. He was so … intriguing.

The nexgens had the beam, the last of three, secured on the cart, and Katlin eyed a tempting sight—a handle lying in the dirt unmanned. She jumped at it, and the three nexgens shrugged to each other and moved to the back to push so that Katlin could pull.

Near the shuttle, the play of dozens of headlamps looked like a swarm of fireflies, something Katlin had read about. Once a part of the hive of activity, it was an exercise in avoiding being bowled over by suited bodies positioning six-foot bars beneath and within the crippled landing strut. Van's crew had grabbed the most accessible material, which happened to be from the stockpile of processed platinum. These glistening, lustrous bars would provide a purchase for many hands to supplement those grasping the strut itself.

"Come on, you guys," Van said, pulling one bar out and handing them another. "That one's too thin. It'll bend—Oh!" he exclaimed, turning to find their cart. "Good work, Kat. Okay—I think we're ready!"

"Wait," Katlin said, "I didn't do anything. It was Glenda and . . ."

Nobody was listening to her, and she was just cluttering the channel. She turned to shrug an apology to her co-workers, but they were busy lifting the heavy beam and placing it next to the other two. One of the nexgens had rigged an ingenious ad hoc hinge mechanism at the end of each of the beams so that, when positioned under the lifted strut—assuming they *could* lift it—the beams would form a stable tripod.

"Ten-hut!" Van called, and, like magic, every nexgen stopped and listened. "Positions!"

A couple of minutes of seeming chaos followed, rendered surrealistic by the disciplined utter silence, as the crowd of nexgens jostled and maneuvered to find a handhold. Once everyone was settled, Van said, "Lift at my mark. And remember, it's all or nothing. If we're not successful on the first try, somebody's likely to get crushed." He stepped up into a position he'd reserved.

Katlin knew that if she tried to join in, she'd just get in the way, so she reluctantly stepped back, ever the outsider. She felt a bump at her back, and turned to find Namazi standing there—she assumed it was him, since his nipple-shaped head covering was opaque. He reached up, grabbed her helmet, and pulled her to him. She thought he was trying to give her a kiss before she remembered that this is how people spoke to each other in a vacuum. She heard a soft thud as her helmet was smashed against his.

"You should move back," he said. His voice was much clearer than Burl's had been—his pliable material afforded more contact surface. "If the shuttle should fall over, you'll be squashed."

"If it falls over, we'll all be blown apart into individual atoms!"

"That is so," he said. "In truth, I just wanted to talk to you."

She felt a tingling. Talking to Namazi was like stepping into an Earth movie. He was Henry Cavill, Ben Affleck, and Chris

Hemsworth all rolled into one. Searching for a word to describe him, all she could come up with was "suave." If only she wasn't trapped between his clasped hands, hoarsely yelling responses through her helmet.

Her dilemma was solved when Van's voice shouted, "Lift!"

Namazi let her go, and they turned to watch. Thirty-eight dirty arms extending from nineteen filthy suits—all there was room for under the strut—straining to lift a lunar ton with muscles developed in weak lunar gravity. At first, that's all there was, the straining grunts and huffs of teenagers struggling with all their might. "Lift, damn it!" Van called again, and the spider web of collapsed ship struts and protruding platinum bars moved an inch, and then two.

Go! Katlin urged under her breath, *go!*

The audible sounds of mighty straining swelled, and the ship tilted visibly upwards. Now a full foot, and some of the nexgens shuffled further underneath to keep their hold.

Suddenly, four nexgens fell away as their platinum handhold slipped from its precariously balanced position. The others groaned in despair at the additional effort they had to apply. The top of the ship wavered, threatening to tilt back over, crushing those that had moved underneath the landing struts.

Katlin leapt forward. The four ejected nexgens had picked themselves up, and were positioning the bar back into its previous spot. "No!" Katlin said, squeezing her way through the straining crowd. "Not there—here," she said, moving the bar so that it jammed between two angled pieces. Now as they applied pressure, the angled slot would grip the platinum bar ever tighter. There was just enough room for her, so she remained, pushing upwards.

Straining until her elbows shook with the effort, Katlin felt her arms slowly straighten as the ship tilted upward. She was directly under the landing assembly. If the nexgens lost their grip now, she'd be crushed to pulp. Only one of twenty, she pushed as though she alone held the ship in place. They all did. It was the only way it worked, each of them exerting to the limits of their ability.

"Got it!" one of the nexgens called. "The tripod's in place!"

"Don't let it go yet!" Van called, his voice contorted with effort. "Ease it down *slowly*!"

Katlin continued pushing with all she had, and the ship came down inexorably onto her as others eased their effort. She had a moment of panic at the monstrous weight bearing down, but the progress suddenly stopped as the crushed landing leg settled on the tripod. *Uh, oh.* She realized that they wouldn't know if the tripod was going to hold until they'd all relaxed, at which point it would be too late to push it back up.

At that very instant, her palms felt a shock, and the metal above settled down farther. A collective gasp filled her ears, but the ship halted its fall after just a few inches. "The tripod hinge has bent flat," the nexgen reported, "but I think it'll hold now."

"Okay," Van called. "Everybody out at the count of three. One … two …"

Katlin looked around. Only she and Van were left under the ship. "Three?" she suggested.

Van sighed and stepped out from underneath with her. They surveyed their work. Katlin's heart sank when she saw that the ship, although significantly more upright, still visibly listed to starboard.

Namazi joined them and mashed his head against Van's helmet. After a moment, Van announced that the Iranian captain said that this would be sufficient—superb, in fact.

"Hey!" Van yelled.

The crew had picked up the platinum rods they'd used to lift, but one nexgen was still struggling with the bar that Katlin had placed. It had jammed itself good, and the teenager was yanking at it. "If you want to commit suicide," Van said, "I'll help you find ways that don't take us all along."

The nexgen looked at him, shrugged, and joined his colleagues.

Katlin stood by herself. Van, Tyna, and Namazi stood watching the crippled ship. Sometimes you just have to fess up and admit you were wrong. "I told you it was impossible," she said into the com-link.

Everybody—Namazi, Van, Tyna, and all the other nexgens—turned and looked at her silently. Her earpiece sputtered with little bursts of static, the song of the stars. Like everything else in the base, her radio circuitry was starting to fail.

"It was a joke," she said.

Through his faceplate, she saw Van smile. He waved her over. Wrapping his arms around both her and Tyna's shoulders, he led them all back to the base.

Chapter 22

Van took off his helmet and watched as Namazi's suit deflated and he pulled away his flexible head covering. A suit like that would really speed up transiting in and out, but Van knew that he'd miss his old workhorse, despite all its failings. Actually, he admitted, the failings were accelerating, and would probably kill him someday.

"Do you think twelve gallons will be enough?" Van asked. Namazi had decided to go directly back to the transport ship in orbit rather than return to the Chinese base.

"Plenty," Namazi said. "It will take about a hundred liters to return to orbit, and the ship had seventy-five when I crash-landed. If we trust Katlin that twelve gallons of water is equivalent to forty-five liters, then I should have twenty liters to spare."

"If you trust Tuan to translate Chinese," Katlin said, walking towards them down the hall, "then you should trust my metric-to-English conversions."

Namazi broke into a broad smile at the sight of her. He gave a courteous little bow and said, "My trust in you is complete. Beauty shines with many facets, and integrity is but one."

The Katlin that Van had know most of his life would have called him on the schmooze, but she just blushed and looked at her feet.

"It's not called English measurements anymore," he added.

"No?" she said. "What do they call it? American

measurements?"

"Indeed they do, where the 'they' is the rest of the world."

"I know you're probably anxious to leave," Katlin said, "but my father would like a quick word before you do."

"Anxious is not the right word. Regretful, maybe."

Van rolled his eyes, but neither of them saw. They only had eyes for each other.

As they walked towards the Lab, Van asked, "Why did you come back?"

"I wasn't sure what I could do to help," Namazi replied, "but I remembered your Ops Head was intimidated by my anti-matter drive. I came in on the maneuvering rockets alone, of course, but I was counting on him not being sure, since I believed that he had never actually seen my ship in flight."

"But how did you know? That we were in trouble?"

"Your suit communications."

"The com-link? But you wouldn't have picked it up once you were out of sight."

"Ah, Lieutenant Paria arranged to bridge us through via the satellite."

"You can *do* that? Pick up our suits—way up there?"

"Only because we're in the Moon's shadow. Otherwise the Earth noise would drown you out."

They came to Zeedo's apartment. The door was open, and the base leader opened his eyes when he heard them. "Come in," he said, waving them through the door.

It was a tight fit as they crowded around the bed. Zeedo held his hand out and Namazi shook it firmly. "Welcome to Daedalus crater base," Zeedo said. "I apologize for not having a proper reception ready. There's not even room for a chair."

"I wouldn't have time to sit if there was. I congratulate you, sir, on keeping your base alive for nearly twenty years."

"Only twelve of that was marooned on our own."

"Only twelve, Mr. Cummings, is like saying your crew 'only' lifted half my ship off the surface of the Moon. Unfortunately, however, time is indeed of the essence. I imagine that you'd like to make arrangements? Some service I can render once I return to Earth?"

Zeedo seem troubled. "That is the question, for sure. The problem is I don't know what to ask for—I don't know who you'd contact. Do you know if AMC still exists?"

"They not only exist, they comprise a substantial portion of the American economy, along with Mexico, Indonesia, and many others. The corporation has changed its name several times, and now calls itself simply UP, which stands for Universal Products, but many believe that it secretly means Uninterrupted Profits."

"I see …" Zeedo said, considering this.

Namazi watched him, like a nephew presented with a long-lost uncle. "I remember the Great Flare," he said. "I was in school at the time."

"Great Flare?" Van said, and then made the connection. "The Blast?"

Namazi nodded. "That's probably a better description. It nearly destroyed human civilization. Power grids came down—melted—all across the United States and Europe in the dead of winter. Thousands froze to death the first night, and many thousands followed in the next days. With no electrical infrastructure, everything came to a halt—no communications, no way to pump gasoline, whether at a gas station, or tanker depot. Within a week, all transport came to a standstill. Every family, huddled together in their freezing homes, were left to their own devices. There was never an accurate count of how many starved to death."

"And yet America survived?" Katlin asked, her voice trembling.

"Barely, and at great cost. Asia was left relatively unscathed. Greater Persia, my country—once known as Iran—was at the edge, and only slightly damaged. But the world had become one great economic engine. The financial system was completely wrecked, and global trade froze. Many thought it was the end, that human civilization could not recover."

"But it did," Van said as a reassurance for Katlin.

"It did," Namazi agreed. "The centralized, authoritarian government of China may be lacking in individual freedoms, but in times of crisis like this, it has great advantages. Also, the Australians—a people of great resilience—stepped up admirably. Within a few years, the east had lifted the west back onto their feet. At a cost, of course. Billions of dollars still flow across the Pacific and Mediterranean each year in loan repayments."

"It's easy to see how we would be forgotten," Katlin said.

"Not forgotten," Namazi said, "but ignored for awhile. Once the western countries got back on their feet, your plight was resurrected. The US tried to force AMC to fund a rescue mission, or at least attempt an assessment, but the company's board pled insolvency. Miraculously, only a year later, the company, now operating under a different corporate umbrella, posted impressive profits."

"Sarcasm?" Van asked.

Namazi smiled. "France tried to broker a deal between the US and China to send a mission, but US politicians squabbled over the cost, and never approved it. There was so much else to attend to, and considering that it had been three years and nobody really expected anyone on the Moon base to have survived, you were left to fade into the history books along with Percy Fawcett and Amelia Earhart."

"So," Zeedo said, still troubled, "where does that leave us? Begging for rescue?"

Namazi grinned. "I think that you are going to be very grateful that you've so diligently continued your mining operation over the years. You see, platinum is, if anything, even more valuable now than twenty years ago."

Zeedo was blushing. It was mad-Meyer, after all, who had been mostly responsible for the effort.

"Once UP corporation learns of your accumulated stockpile," Namazi continued, "I expect they'll purchase a Persian transport ship outright, and be knocking at your front door within a month."

For the first time, Van saw Zeedo visibly relax. Their leader lay back and closed his eyes. After a moment, he opened them again. "So, that's it, then," Zeedo said. "All we need from you is to inform UP of the situation."

"Perhaps," Namazi said, rubbing his chin. He glanced around at Katlin, and then at Van, and Tyna who stood listening from the hallway. "But there are extenuating circumstances, as they say."

"Such as?" Zeedo said, brows again furrowed.

Namazi waved his hand, dismissing his concern. "All in your favor. You see, soon after the Great Flare, even before the crippled

US congress agreed to China's recovery package, they warned the Chinese government away from your base. They were fearful that China would take advantage of the west's weakened situation to make land grabs. Once America was back on their feet, after you had faded to legend, the United States once again began eyeing the Moon and asteroids for possible mineral exploitation. With the Moon all to themselves—or so everybody thought—China had begun to assume de facto title. In response, America spearheaded a UN-sanctioned definition—through ICLM—of what constitutes an independent colony."

"Ha!" Katlin exclaimed. "An independent Chinese colony would uncouple China's mineral rights."

Namazi grinned. "Intelligence as well as beauty."

Van thought Namazi quite the charmer, but he saw Tyna rolling her eyes.

"At this stage," Namazi went on, "China had far too much global influence to lose her rights to her Moon base, and, in an effort to save face with their voting base, the American politicians settled for a watered-down definition rather than admitting complete defeat."

Zeedo had been watching him carefully. "I presume this has some relevance to us?"

Namazi nodded. "Quite possibly. You see, one of the few remaining provisions of defining an independent colony—one that China could prove did not apply to them—was that of abandonment."

The room went silent.

"We were abandoned," Van finally said.

"Indubitably," Namazi said. "America is on record as forsaking France's efforts to broker a rescue mission. Further, with the painfully slow economic recovery, the American mood became very anti-immigrant, and laws were passed to provide priority rights for native-born individuals."

Again, silence reigned.

"The US government would be hard-pressed to argue in opposition to their own laws," Namazi prodded.

After a few seconds, Katlin said, amazed, "The base belongs to the nexgens!"

"It could be so argued," Namazi agreed.

They turned their gaze to Zeedo. A grin spread across his weary face. "Don't look at me. They're more than welcome to it."

Chapter 23

"Do you *want* to lose your leg?" Van said.

"Is that what Katlin calls a rhetorical question?" Burl asked from his bed. "I don't think you actually expect me to answer that."

Van glanced at Tyna, but her face only offered sympathy for his effort to convince Burl. The med-genie had saturated him with antibiotics and ad-hoc synthesized pain drugs, and Van was impressed that his friend could think this clearly—if refusing one of the two slots on Namazi's shuttle constituted clear thinking.

"Zeedo didn't hesitate to accept a ride back to Earth for treatment," Van argued.

"I'm glad for him. He actually has a chance of making it."

The med-genie had indeed recommended surgery for Zeedo to improve the hasty repair Louden had performed under her direction.

"Well, so do you!" Van urged.

"Bullshit," Burl said, "to borrow Meyer's favorite expression. She thinks I'm going to lose it either way."

He was referring to the med-genie, and they were waiting for Louden to arrive with a detailed report. "That was just a preliminary assessment," Van urged. "I'm sure she'll recommend it. We should get you ready to go."

"You're sure. Well, Doctor Van, maybe you'd like to take a stab at fixing me with the scalpel. Hey, I made a joke. Get it? Make a stab?"

Van turned to Tyna and said quietly, "Looks like the drugs *are* affecting him."

"They are not," Burl said. "I'm inherently funny. Hey, do you think the Chinese will want their rover back?"

"You're babbling," Van said. "The drugs are affecting you."

"Look, buster," Burl growled, grabbing Van's leg in a vice grip. "If the drugs were affecting me like you say, then why am I in so much pain? Maybe I keep talking to take my mind off it. Ever think of that?"

"Okay, okay," Van said, pulling Burl's hand away with effort. "I asked Namazi about that. He just suggested that we look up the history of international salvage rules."

Burl nodded. Van wasn't sure his friend had actually absorbed that. "I heard Julius complaining about something in the com shack," Burl said. "What's that all about?"

"Lieutenant Paria brought along their spare spread-spectrum receiver when he came with his suit. He's showing Julius how to hook it up. We should be able to establish a link with Earth. Isn't that great?"

"Yeah, great," Burl said with zero enthusiasm. "Why's he bringing his suit? Is he staying with us?"

"No! It's just temporary. They're using his suit to carry Zeedo—and you—to the ship. It's easier than ours."

"Speaking of which—" Tyna said.

Van turned to find Louden at the door. "Wow!" the scientist said. "Those Iranian suits are fantastic! We had Arthur suited and out the door in no time." His face turned serious when he looked at Burl. "The news from the med-genie isn't great," he said.

Burl's mouth tightened, and he stared at the far wall.

"If you stay here," Louden continued, "you lose the leg."

"And if he goes to Earth?" Van asked.

Louden sighed. "On the assumption that the trip takes two days—that's the best Namazi can offer, and it's going to cost him dearly in propellant—she gives you a better chance."

Burl turned his stare on him. "Obviously my chances are better if I leave. When staying is zero chance, then the only thing worse is dying."

Louden blinked and just stood there.

"I'll *die* if I leave?" Burl exclaimed.

"No!" Louden finally said. "I mean, she says there's an five percent probability that you'd die in transit. But she gives you a *sixty*-five percent probability of saving your leg."

"Well," Burl said, turning back to his study of the wall. "That settles it."

"You're going?" Van said hopefully.

Burl threw him a glare. "What? You're trying to get rid of me?" He turned again back to the wall. "Of course I'm not going."

Tyna said something that Van didn't catch. They all turned to her. "I said that he's afraid to leave."

"Yeah," Burl said sarcastically. "I *am* afraid of dying."

"That's not what you're really afraid of," she insisted softly. "You're afraid of leaving home."

Burl glared at her, started to say something, and turned back to the wall.

"Ho, boy," Louden said. The kindly man looked completely dejected.

"What's wrong?" Van asked.

Louden sighed. "The med-genie said that if he doesn't leave for treatment, then we need to … take off the leg as soon as possible." He sighed again.

"That means you, doesn't it?" Van said.

He nodded ruefully, then looked over at Van. "Unless you want to give it a shot?"

Van shuddered at the thought.

"I expected not," Louden said.

Namazi cleared his throat from the hallway. Van hadn't noticed that he'd arrived. "I came to get Burl," the shuttle captain said, "but it seems the situation has changed?"

"Looks like it," Van agreed. "Seems that you'll have only one passenger."

Namazi rubbed his chin. "I do have room for two."

"That means less cargo," Burl reminded.

Namazi grinned. "I've already been paid."

Van looked at him, surprised.

"The platinum bar," the captain reminded.

"The one that Katlin got stuck?" Van asked.

"In the process of saving my ship, yes," he said. "That single bar more than makes up for the lost Chinese cargo, and then some."

Van put his hand on Louden's shoulder. "How about it? Home on the first ship? Best of all, you'll dodge taking off Burl's, uh, performing the operation."

The beefy man shook his head. "I can wait. The good captain assures us that if AMC, or UP, or whatever the bastards call themselves now, doesn't arrange transports for purchase of our— excuse me, of *your*—platinum, then he will personally borrow the funds to make the voyage himself."

Namazi shrugged. "It's not a selfless proposal. I am confident there would be great profits in the venture."

"In any case," Louden said, "I have a lot to make up for."

Van glanced at Tyna. "What do you mean?"

The scientist turned somber. "I was a willing participant in the, um, pretense."

"The archiving lie?" Tyna said. Her brashness surprised Van.

Louden winced. "Yes, the lie. Also, there's the matter of ... education."

"I don't understand," Van confessed.

"Katlin knows," Louden said. "She more or less forced a confession from her father. I expect that Julius and I will spend the next few months getting you on your feet, helping you learn to navigate the educational material, and the fundamentals of running the base. Your platinum will buy replacements for all the aging equipment, but that will take time." Louden suddenly looked pensive.

"What is it?" Van asked.

Louden shook his head, seeming amazed. "I automatically assumed you're all going to stay."

Van looked at Tyna, and they both burst out laughing. "You're wondering if we might want to leave? To go to Earth? No. Don't worry about that."

"Maybe for, like, a vacation," Tyna said hesitantly, then thought better of it. "For you, Van. I don't think I'd like it."

Van nodded. "Yeah. A vacation to Earth. Maybe someday. Not

now, though. Not when Louden's going to educate us."

"And Julius," Louden reminded.

Van sighed. "And grumpy Julius," he agreed.

Tyna's brow was scrunched.

"What's up?" Van asked.

"What about Mai Dung and Tuan?" she asked.

"What about them?"

"Maybe they'd like to go back to Earth."

Van turned to Namazi. "Would you have room for them both? Mai Dung is tiny. She and her son together hardly weigh more than me—certainly less than Louden."

Tyna gave him an elbow in the side for that.

The captain nodded reluctantly. "Yes, I guess so."

"Is that a problem?"

"No," Namazi said, "No, the woman and her son would be fine."

He seemed disappointed somehow, though.

"She doesn't want to go."

It was Katlin. She had also arrived without them noticing.

"I asked her," she explained. "I don't know what happened back on Earth, but she says she likes it here. She says that she can work very hard. She has experience mining."

"And it seems certain that contact with the Chinese base will be ongoing," Namazi said. "A fluent translator would be invaluable."

"We had a translator," Burl reminded from his bed. "It burned out. We could just buy another—"

Tyna coughed loudly, interrupting him. She gave him a hard look.

"Sorry," Burl said. "It's the drugs talking."

Van sneaked a peek at Namazi. The man seemed visibly relieved at Katlin's news. It suddenly came to him. *Should I?* he wondered. Oh, hell. "How about Katlin?" he said.

They all looked at him.

"What about me?" she asked.

"Why don't you take the extra slot? Your father would do well to have you along."

Namazi's eyes practically jumped from his face. He sobered immediately, and simply looked questioningly at her.

Katlin looked around at everybody. "Me?"

"Why not?" Namazi said. He shrugged, a little too forced, it seemed to Van. "After all, somebody should take the slot."

She seemed confused, stunned at the possibility. "I ... I couldn't."

"Why not?" Namazi asked mildly.

"I ... I don't know. I hadn't given it a thought. I'm not ready!"

The captain glanced at his wrist band, and his face jerked with shock. "Oh, my! I have let the time slip away." He turned to Katlin. "I am sorry, but I must leave in fifteen minutes. I have to meet up with the orbiting transport. With the failing gimbal, I can't afford to miss the next pass."

Katlin stared at him, as though she'd gone catatonic. She blinked, and looked around at them all again. "Okay!" she shouted. "Fifteen minutes? Oh God—hey, how much can I take?"

Namazi's grin broke into a broad smile. "Um, let's see ..." He shook his head, as though clearing it. "Let's just say whatever you can carry." He seemed to have second thoughts. "But keep it light."

Katlin nodded energetically. "Okay, light it is," she said and sped off, but skidded to a stop, turned, and ran back.

She gazed at Tyna a second, and then gathered her into her arms for a close hug. She let her go, and turned to Van. Looking deep into his eyes until he thought he was drowning, she grabbed him by both sides of his head and gave him a kiss on the forehead. She stepped back and looked at them both. "I would have been honored—deeply honored—to have been a member of the new base, part of the nexgen crew, if you would have had me, that is." Before they could respond, she laughed and sped off.

"I must take my leave," Namazi said, shaking Louden and then Van's hands. He took Tyna's hand and held it a moment, what Van took to be an Iranian custom.

Tyna grinned. "We'll be able to buy things—from Earth— won't we?" she asked.

Namazi nodded slowly. "What would you buy if you could?"

Her expression turned bashful. "A dress?" she wondered.

Van snorted.

"What?" she said, turning angrily to him.

"You?" he said. "A dress?"

She blushed and pulled her hand from Namazi.

Van wanted to kick himself, to take it back. He imagined Tyna in a dress, and decided he'd work on taking it back. It might take a while.

Namazi bowed slightly to her. "A dress it is. It will be with me on my return." He sighed and nodded. "But now I must run—literally."

And with that, he trotted away.

Van turned to Tyna, but she had already stalked off.

ж ж ж

The line was moving slowly. Once word spread that the Greater Persia Lunar Transport Shuttle was about to launch back into orbit, every last nexgen wanted to get outside. Van could have invoked his seniority priority, but that felt like cheating, since he had no good administrative reason to be out there before them.

And, also, it would mean leaving Tyna behind. Seemingly by chance (although he hoped not) she had ended up next to him in line to see Namazi off. She had spent the whole time talking to another nexgen, and, try as he might, he hadn't been able to insert himself into the conversation.

It was finally their turn, and he and Tyna and three other nexgens squashed themselves into the lock. They were used to squeezing the maximum amount through, and each made sure their helmets were on before jamming inside, otherwise he or she would find themselves breathing vacuum before they had room to finish the job.

As they waited for the lock to cycle, Van heard short, curt bursts of communication on the com-link, shorthand interaction for the various nexgens already outside to arrange themselves. Tyna was silent, possibly being respectful of the limited bandwidth. Julius had said that he knew what they needed in order to restore multiple channels. That would be really nice, Van thought. They'd have to add that near the top of the to-buy list.

The outer door opened, and they spilled out into the lunar night. The shuttle was immediately obvious, as two spotlights shone down along the sleek, clean sides. Van had warned his crew about keeping their distance, and he suspected that the captain was using the lights as marker beacons.

Van's suspicion was bolstered when the lights flashed on and off a few times, a clear warning. The last batch of nexgens cycled out of the lock just as the ship's spot lights were doused. Utter darkness hid the ship, but a few seconds later the familiar violet pencil jabbed downward, throwing a shower of sparkling, incandescent lunar dust into a billowing skirt around the shuttle. The com-link breathed with a collective gasp. The pencil lengthened, reaching upwards towards the canopy of stars. On top of the pencil, Van knew, rode the invisible ship, carrying away two people he'd known all his life.

He thought about Zeedo—always just "sir." Now with Meyer dead, it was clear that the two men had always been at odds, one consumed with maximizing production, the other simply trying to keep them all alive until Earth returned.

And, Katlin. He'd known her since he was eight years old, yet he felt as though he'd only just met her. In a way he had. Zeedo had always kept her within the fold of the Lab, not to avoid contact with nexgens, but to keep her from the oppressive thumb of Meyer. He wondered if he'd ever see her again. Earth was far away—a thousand times farther than the Chinese base. Maybe when they established the link with the Chinese satellite. In the movies, people were always exchanging messages.

For a reason he couldn't fathom, the thought of Katlin—always in clothes different from theirs—invoked the image of Tyna in a dress. His heart skipped a beat at the same instant that the shuttle suddenly burst into view. One instant there was just the otherworldly violet ghost, and the next, the blinding image of the ship erupting in stark, dazzling light. For one terrifying instant Van thought that the anti-matter drive had exploded, but, of course, he wouldn't have even known if it had happened.

It's the sun! He'd lost track of time, but it was due, ready to rise over the eastern horizon.

The fleeting panic of an exploding anti-matter drive was replaced by Van's abiding fear of the sun. The fireball's lethal radiation had killed their parents. The Managers reinforced the anxiety by avoiding being outside altogether if possible.

Katlin had explained that the Blast—the Great Flare—that had killed his parents was a freak event, a once-in-a-thousand years probability. He trusted Katlin, now more than ever, but her logic was battling raw emotion. She had been right about the ships orbit and the com satellite. She *knew* things, things that they were going to learn, now that the true meaning of the archive had been revealed.

If they were going to own the base, to be the first lunar generation of colonists, then they would have to learn to trust the knowledge and science at hand. She had assured them that the sun wouldn't kill them. Dread still froze his bones, but he decided that he was going to act on his trust.

Thoughts of Katlin morphed into another image of Tyna in a dress. *Damn!* He couldn't escape it. He felt a tenderness for her that—

He jumped at a blow to his side. It was Tyna. She'd whacked him with the back of her hand. She was pointing off to the right, up the crater wall. He saw it. Far up, two brilliant points of light, the sun catching the tips of the highest peaks. As he watched, a third slowly winked on.

Van knew there was no great urgency. It took more than a day for the lunar sun to move as far as it did in one hour on Earth. They could go inside, shower, eat, and be asleep before its stark rays struck the crater floor.

He wasn't going to succumb to fear. If they were going to thrive as the new masters of this airless world, then they had better learn to *live* in it, to live in *all* of it.

He tapped Tyna's shoulder and pointed up the crater wall, to where a path climbed in uneven switchbacks up its side. She held her palms up in question, and he gestured for her to come along, and took off. After a minute, he turned, but she still stood there, looking at him. As the flat crater floor began to angle upward, the jumbled indications that their feet had churned in the dust over the years tapered away. They'd had little reason to go here. Now, only the path he was following—over the crater wall to their toxic disposal site—showed where the Moon's surface had been disturbed after untold changeless millennia.

When he came to the first switchback turn, he saw a bouncing point of light making its way across the crater floor. He waited until she reached him, and then he turned and continued on. No words were necessary.

Up and up they went, stopping every few minutes to catch their breath. Each time, Tyna stood nearby waiting, offering no hint of her mood. When he finally topped the last switchback leg, one of the sunlit tips lay just above him. He could have stretched on tip-toes to touch it, but he continued on.

The path now followed a steady, slight incline for another hundred feet before finally leveling out onto a narrow, flat spine, the top of the crater wall. Van walked along this last stretch, relaxed now that the climb was behind him. Suddenly, he was unusually warm, and the right rim of his faceplate glowed with an angry glare. Simultaneously, he heard a sharp intake of air over the com-link. He turned and was blinded by a light his eyes had never before seen.

The overwhelming flash lasted just a second—his faceplate had obviously reacted, filtering most of the energy. Now a bright, white ball was floating before him—the sun!

"Van," Tyna said.

He turned to her, but everything around him was utter darkness. Even vastly reduced, the sun's light erased everything in shadow, and Van had walked out from behind the shadow of a vertical projection fifty miles away on the far crater wall.

Tyna stepped from out of the absolute blackness. She quickly transformed before his eyes. Her faceplate, normally a glinting dark, turned bright metallic. Her entire pressure suit became silvery, shining in the sun like the angel in the first book taken from the archive room. Van held up his arm, and saw that his suit had done the same, reflecting away the sun's radiant energy. The suits were designed for working both night and day.

Tyna gave him a little shove, pushing him along. She nodded back towards the night from which they had emerged. He didn't understand, and was about to ask her, when another person appeared, transforming into an angel. The nexgen froze, staring down at her magically altered body, and then moved along as another, and then another emerging angel appeared, each stopping a moment to marvel at the transformation.

All the nexgens had followed them up the crater wall.

As Van and Tyna stood back, making room for the enthralled

parade, he slipped his arm around her silvery waist. She took his arm and grasped his hand, intertwining her fingers in his, and they both turned to watch their people step out into a new day.

About the Author

Blaine C. Readler is an electronics engineer, inventor of the FakeTV, and surprisingly, a writer. He lives in San Diego, where the weather allows him to walk around outside year-round thinking about stories.

He encourages you to visit him:
http://www.readler.com/

www.ingramcontent.com/pod-product-compliance
Lightning Source LLC
Chambersburg PA
CBHW060315260626
47160CB00007B/2613